Christie Barlow is the author of thirteen bestselling romantic comedies including the iconic Love Heart Lane series, *A Home at Honeysuckle Farm*, and *The Cosy Canal Boat Dream*. She lives in a ramshackle cottage in a quaint village in the heart of Staffordshire with her four children and two dogs.

Her writing career came as a lovely surprise when she decided to write a book to teach her children a valuable life lesson and show them that they are capable of achieving their dreams. Christie's dream was to become a writer and the book she wrote to prove a point went on to become a #1 bestseller in the UK, USA, Canada, and Australia.

When Christie isn't writing she enjoys playing the piano, is a keen gardener, and loves to paint and upcycle furniture.

Christie loves to hear from her readers and you can get in touch via Twitter, Facebook, and Instagram.

facebook.com/ChristieJBarlow
twitter.com/ChristieJBarlow
bookbub.com/authors/christie-barlow
instagram.com/christie_barlow

Also by Christie Barlow

The Love Heart Lane Series

Love Heart Lane

Foxglove Farm

Clover Cottage

Starcross Manor

The Lake House

Primrose Park

Heartcross Castle

The New Doctor at Peony Practice

New Beginnings at the Old Bakehouse

Standalones

The Cosy Canal Boat Dream

A Home at Honeysuckle Farm

THE HIDDEN SECRETS OF BUMBLEBEE COTTAGE

CHRISTIE BARLOW

One More Chapter
a division of HarperCollins*Publishers* Ltd
1 London Bridge Street
London SE1 9GF
www.harpercollins.co.uk
HarperCollins*Publishers*
Macken House, 39/40 Mayor Street Upper,
Dublin 1, D01 C9W8

This paperback edition 2023
1
First published in Great Britain in ebook format
by HarperCollins*Publishers* 2022
Copyright © Christie Barlow 2022
Christie Barlow asserts the moral right to
be identified as the author of this work
A catalogue record of this book is available from the British Library

ISBN: 978-0-00-841317-0

Printed and bound in the UK using 100% Renewable Electricity
by CPI Group (UK) Ltd

For Emily, who makes me proud every day.
Love Mum x

Loveheart La

Primrose Park

The Lake House

CLOVER COTTAGE ESTATE

The Old Bakehouse

The Bo

Bumblebee Cottage

Starcross Manor

Scott's Veterinary Practice

THE GREEN

HIGH STREET

Primary School

Post Office

Peony Practice

Ha
Vi
S

Callie's apartment

Solicitors Office

Dolores' apartment

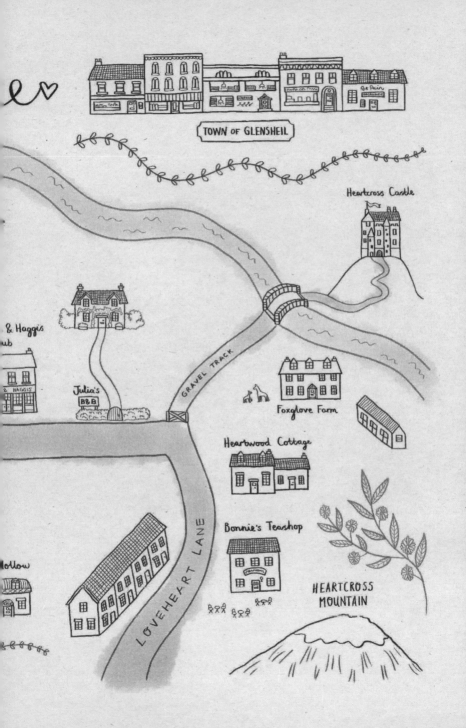

Chapter One

Jinny sat nervously waiting in her father's office. She'd rehearsed the conversation over and over in her head for the last twenty-four hours, but now that she was sitting in front of his desk, her mind was completely blank and she had no clue what she was going to say or how this conversation was going to pan out. Finally, hearing the lift doors open, she braced herself and reminded herself to breathe. Jinny knew she was about to disappoint her father on a brand-new level but she was prepared to suffer the consequences. It was now or never.

Taking a deep breath, she watched her father shuffling papers in his hands as he walked into the room. It was business as usual with hardly any pleasantries.

'What are you doing here? You should be out, chasing that story,' he muttered, barely looking in her direction.

Ralph Birdwhistle had worked his way up through the ranks of *The Daily News* from the age of eighteen and it had been his life ever since. It was no surprise then that he'd expected his daughter, Jinny, to join the family business straight out of school. But after working for her father's newspaper empire for the last ten years, things needed to change. Her father had dreams that one day she would step into his shoes and take over the newspaper when he retired but this was an ambition she had never shared and she was finally ready to make that clear to him.

Jinny didn't reply. She sat in silence and watched her father log on to his computer then check his emails. He flapped his hand in her direction. 'Make sure the photos are clear. We can run this story in Sunday's print if you pull your finger out. This will sell a fair few copies.'

Jinny was still sitting there, her heart thumping. In all of her working life at the newspaper she had been reliable, if a little conservative, and got on with every task she had been given. knowing there were worse jobs and possibly worse employers. She had never refused a direct order and knew her father would not be expecting what she was about to say.

'Camp out in the car if you have to,' he continued. 'I want photographs of her walking into the supermarket. She has to eat sometime and the rumour on the street is that's exactly what she's been doing – potentially the *only* thing.'

Jinny couldn't stop her eyebrows from rising.

This latest assignment was the straw that had broken the camel's back. Her father had never had any qualms about delving into people's private lives and the upset it could cause them, their loved ones and their careers, but now it had to stop. Jinny couldn't handle being a part of it anymore.

Over time, her father's lack of warmth, compassion and basic people skills had begun to grate on her. The only thing he was interested in was selling stories to the masses and, of course, making money. She had never received praise for the extra unpaid hours she put in, just more criticism. She racked her brains. When was the last time he had shown her any compassion or warmth? Jinny couldn't even remember the last time he had told her that he loved her.

'Park as close as you can to the supermarket doors and don't move until you get that photo,' he repeated, giving her the once-over. 'Well, what's keeping you? Time is money.'

Feeling fearless for once, Jinny looked him directly in the eye. 'It's unethical.'

Immediately, Ralph stopped typing on the keyboard and looked down at her through the spectacles that were balancing on the bridge of his nose. His icy glare indicated he couldn't quite believe what he was hearing. 'Say that again.'

Jinny knew there was going to be a backlash as soon as those words left her mouth, but she had wanted to say this for a long time. She'd always avoided any sort of confrontation, and right at this second she was as far out of her comfort zone as she'd ever been, but she needed to stand up for what was right.

'I said, it's unethical,' she repeated, hoping her voice didn't sound as shaky as she felt. 'This person stepped away from the limelight a long time ago and no longer wants to live under public scrutiny. I'm not doing it.' Jinny could tell by the look on her father's face that he wasn't quite believing what he was hearing.

'You have no choice. It's your job,' he said harshly.

'I do have a choice and I'm choosing not to report on this story. This woman is someone's daughter, mother and wife and she's entitled to privacy. Just because she was once a pop star and living in the public eye doesn't mean the press can still hound her now that she's retired. Who cares if she doesn't have the body of a twenty-something anymore? This woman is sixty and there is no need to compare how she looks now to then. She's grown old gracefully, without resorting to cosmetic surgery, and all that photo is going to do is shame her and make her feel like she's not worthy just because she's put on a few pounds. That's not fair.'

'It sells papers and that is our job.'

'But at what cost?' Jinny held her father's gaze.

Ralph leaned forward on the desk, his hands clasped in front of him. He was staring at Jinny in a way that unsettled her. 'Are you telling me you are refusing to cover this story?'

She swallowed. 'Yes, I am.'

'Do you want to reconsider that?'

Jinny shifted uncomfortably in her seat. 'I don't think I do. I don't want to do this anymore. In fact, I'm done here.'

'Done?' Her father's voice rose. 'And you think there are jobs out there that will give you the same financial stability?'

Jinny remained silent. There was nothing more to say. She wanted out of this career. Pushing her chair backwards, she stood up.

Ralph didn't take his eyes off her as she turned and walked towards the door. 'If you walk out of here, that's it. There's no coming back.'

Jinny hovered at the door before glancing back over her shoulder. 'That's fine by me.'

Ralph began to rant. 'You have wanted for nothing. You've been handed a luxury flat, a top-of-the-range car, a career… Let's see how you get on without any of those things and no income coming in.'

'I'll get another job.'

'Not one that gives you everything you have now.'

'Maybe I don't want that. Maybe I never wanted that.'

Looking like he was about to spontaneously combust, Ralph stood up. Without another word he held out his hand. Jinny rummaged inside her bag and grasped her car keys before bypassing his hand and placing them calmly on his desk. 'If it's okay with you, I'll clear out the stuff from my apartment by the weekend,' she stated, heading towards the door.

'You see how far you get making your own way in life,' he scoffed. 'Your mother would be so disappointed in you.'

Jinny stopped at the mention of her mother. Affronted, she swung back round towards him. 'No, my mother would be disappointed in *you* because there's one thing I have that you don't: morals.'

The strange strangled sound that came from her father's

throat in response was her cue to leave. Her heart was beating nineteen to the dozen as she quickly walked out of his office without so much as a fleeting glance backwards towards that life. As soon as the lift doors closed, Jinny pressed the button for her office floor and let out a huge sigh of relief.

This was going to be the last time she walked through the newspaper office, which as usual was a hive of activity. It took a matter of minutes to clear her desk and with her head held high, Jinny left behind the loud sounds of her ex-colleagues' chatter, phones ringing, printers shuttling out paper and the tap of fingers against keyboards.

She stepped out the front doors onto the busy street. Heading for the Tube station, Jinny felt like a huge weight had been lifted off her shoulders. With mixed feelings of excitement and trepidation, she juggled the cardboard box in her arms while navigating the steps to the Underground. Feeling liberated, she realised this was the first time she was ever going to be financially independent. Her brand-new life started right here, right now, and she was going to grasp it with both hands.

Chapter Two

Within seconds, Jinny had jumped on the Tube at London Bridge and with one hand held on tightly to the aluminium pole in the middle of the carriage as the Underground stations whizzed by. She knew she was tiring of life in the big smoke when she watched the crowds of people around her jostling for their own little space as more commuters stepped onto the train. Thankfully, within five minutes she was back in the fresh air and pushing her legs down a side street in the direction of her favourite wine bar. As soon as she opened the door, Jinny was greeted by the smiles of the regulars and the sight of her favourite barman, Jay, leaning against the pumps with his usual air of confidence.

He looked straight at her. 'Who died?'

'My career,' Jinny replied, sliding the cardboard box onto the top of the bar.

Jay peered inside. 'What do we have here?'

'The contents of my desk,' she replied, pointing to the bottle of Hendrick's gin behind the bar. 'Make it a double.'

'It's only lunchtime.' Jay cocked an eyebrow but reached for a glass anyway.

'It's been a long morning.'

Jay poured her a double and slid it over the bar. 'What's up with your job?' he asked curiously.

'I haven't got one. I've finally walked.' Jinny had confided in Jay numerous times about how unethical she'd found her job. She knew she had been guilty of perpetuating negative tabloid culture over the years but that had to stop. She wanted to better herself and the only way to do that was to finally have the courage to take on the wrath of her father.

'And I thought I'd go for the hat-trick…'

'Huh?'

'I also now have no car and no apartment.'

Wide-eyed, Jay folded his arms and leaned on the bar. Jinny now had his full attention.

'Are you serious?' he asked.

'Deadly serious. But it's my choice. My father infuriates me and I don't want to turn into him. Reporting on people's misfortunes just to make him some money. I told him enough is enough and boom! As expected, he demanded my car and home back.'

'He's really kicked you out of your apartment?'

'Yep. Then I found myself on the Tube and when your good

friend is the manager of a wine bar it's a no-brainer. Drink first, then plan the rest of your life.' Jinny exhaled. It was a little daunting to think she wasn't going to have a regular income coming in but she didn't regret her decision. She wanted to find a job that filled her with happiness and contentment.

'He really didn't react well,' mused Jay. 'What you need is a holiday to recharge your batteries.'

'That would be ideal but as I have no money now…'

'You can swap houses with someone like in that film. What was it called?'

'*The Holiday*,' replied Jinny, amused.

'That's the one.' He pointed at her. '*The Holiday*. You swap houses with someone, go away, fall in love and never come back.'

'Don't tempt me! But what you've forgotten is that I don't actually have a house to swap.' Jinny took the glass Jay had just refilled for her and swigged back the gin.

'Fair point. You are a bit scuppered, but then there are other options. Kill two birds with one stone. You need a job that comes with accommodation. There are websites for that sort of thing.' He nodded knowingly.

'Ooh, I like that idea a lot.'

'Do you want to stay in London? Or go a little further afield?' asked Jay, grabbing his laptop from underneath the counter and placing it on the bar. 'You could do anything; the world is your oyster. Fruit-picking on a farm in Devon, Alpaca farming in Peru…'

She smiled. 'My father would freak if I moved to Peru.'

'You wouldn't really move to Peru, would you?' Jay asked curiously.

'Maybe not Peru.' Jinny pointed to the laptop. 'Do you mind?'

'Go ahead. I'll serve these customers but don't you go signing up for anything without running it by me first. I know how impulsive you can be.'

Jinny grinned. 'I promise.' She took another sip of her drink before focusing back on the laptop. 'I think I fancy Scotland. I mean, men in kilts, what's not to like?' She gave Jay a wink and he shook his head before turning to the new arrivals.

While Jay served the customers, Jinny began tapping away. 'Scotland is just under six hundred miles away. That'll do! At least my father can't just turn up out of the blue.'

'Have you ever even been to Scotland?' asked Jay, handing over the customer's change before focusing his attention back onto Jinny.

'No, never,' she replied, still looking at the screen. 'But it looks beautiful with its spectacular scenery and fairy-tale castles,' she added, feeling all dreamy. Bringing her hands up to her heart, she added, 'It beats congestion and angry commuters on the Tube.'

'I've not been either but I believe Heartcross is the place to live if you're going to head up north.'

Jinny looked up. 'Heartcross? Why does that ring a bell?'

'You should know all about Heartcross, what with being a journalist and all that. Remember a few years ago? The village was catapulted into the news because there were those extreme weather conditions and a bridge collapsed, leaving all the villagers stranded. There was only one way in and one way out of the village. Since then it's become a magnet for tourists. In fact, it's like a mini St Tropez, famous for the River Heart, and there's the noteworthy chef on the TV who airs his cooking show from Heartcross Castle...'

'Andrew Glossop,' Jinny supplied. 'I've watched his shows.'

'And there's also Flynn Carter, the multi-millionaire who owns the extravagant hotel, Starcross Manor, and the celebrity restaurant, The Lake House. Oh! And my friend Felicity lives there,' he added, washing the dirty glasses in the sink behind the bar.

'You know someone who lives there? How does that even happen? It's miles away.'

'Before this place, I used to work in a pub called the Chatty Banker. It's off one of the side streets just near Leicester Square Tube station. I had a colleague called Polly, and Felicity was one of her friends. Actually, Polly has also upped sticks and left and now lives in the village too. Apparently, once you visit Heartcross you never want to leave.'

'Blooming 'eck, small world.'

Jinny googled the village of Heartcross, reading aloud from the top search result. '"Heartcross village is a tranquil place off the beaten track, surrounded by majestic mountains, heather-wreathed glens and beautiful waterfalls

– a place untouched by time. The famous Bonnie's Teashop—"'

'That's the place Felicity owns,' interrupted Jay.

'Really?' Jinny looked up to see Jay nodding, then continued. '"Bonnie's Teashop, snuggled away next to the trim necklace of whitewashed houses on Love Heart Lane, is the first place to visit." It sounds idyllic. And look at these images!' Jinny swizzled the laptop towards Jay. 'There's a village pub called The Grouse and Haggis, a local store, The Old Boat House, Primrose Park, and Foxglove Farm, where they breed alpacas! I won't have to go to Peru!' trilled Jinny. 'A castle and mountains too. This place looks and sounds amazing. I can see myself now, ambling along the lane for breakfast, or taking a stroll up the mountain pass and indulging in walks in the park. This could be just what I need to recharge and rethink what exactly I'm going to do next with my life.'

'There's the hotel or a place called Julia's B&B. You could book into there. A two-week trip would do you good,' enthused Jay.

'Look, there's kayaking on the river, a summer fair, an annual boat race…'

'Haven't you got all that here? Covent Garden, boat races and it may have escaped your notice but there's a huge river that goes by the name of the River Thames,' he teased.

Jinny rolled her eyes. 'But this is different. The mountain air is fresh and there's no Tube filled with hundreds of commuters. I want a slower pace of life and a job that's just nice.'

'Define "just nice".'

Jinny shrugged. 'Just nice is… working in a bookshop, or at a gallery, or in a clothes boutique or a craft shop that sells knickknacks. I don't know, just the opposite of what I do now.'

Jinny typed 'jobs in Heartcross' into the search bar and hit return. A number of administrative posts came up including some at Starcross Manor, a vacancy in the council office and a position in the Town Hall.

'There's nothing that's grabbing me,' Jinny admitted, feeling a little deflated. 'I don't want an office job. I want something…'

'You don't know what you want,' teased Jay.

'I'll know it when I see it.' Jinny started searching houses to rent near Heartcross instead. Then she began to flap her hand frantically towards Jay while she was still staring at the screen.

He raised an eyebrow. 'Are you having a stroke? Do I need to call an ambulance?'

Jinny wasn't listening. She was too busy skimming the words on the screen. 'Jay, this is fate.'

'What's fate?'

Jinny began to read aloud. '"Bumblebee Cottage is situated in the heart of the Scottish Highlands. It offers not only a beautiful home but also a fantastic business opportunity for the right candidate."'

'Tell me more!' encouraged Jay.

'It says it's a chutney and honey production business called "Bees' Knees". I have to ring for more details and "ask for Molly or Cam".'

'Is there a closing date?'

'Yes. Today!' exclaimed Jinny.

'There you go. It's decision time. To ring or not to ring?'

Thoughtful for a moment, Jinny sucked her bottom lip. 'Ring! It can't do any harm.'

Jinny was reaching for her phone while Jay looked over the details. He tapped the screen. 'It says here, "must like bees". When have you ever liked bees? You won't even sit out in the garden in the summer.'

Nothing was going to dampen Jinny's mood. 'I'm not going to let a small thing like that put me off.'

'Or the fact you have no clue about making chutney or honey,' teased Jay.

'I can try!'

Jay watched in amusement as Jinny scribbled the phone number on the back of a beer mat and pinched an order pad and pen from the side of the bar before taking herself off into the corner of the room. After a bad start to the day, Jinny was feeling excited as she dialled the number and waited. Within three rings the call was answered.

'Good afternoon, The Old Bakehouse, Molly speaking, how may I help you?'

'Hello, I've just seen your advert on the internet for the rental and business opportunity at Bumblebee Cottage. If I'm not too late, please could I have some more details?'

'Yes, of course,' replied Molly. 'The cottage is for rent costing £650 per month plus the bills. The business makes twice as much as that at the present time and my partner and I take a ten per cent cut of the profits as we own the land and company trademark. There's room for future expansion of the business but initially the position is for six months with a view to becoming permanent for the right person.'

'This sounds like just what I'm looking for. Please could I have some more information on the actual business?' asked Jinny, feeling excited.

'Bees' Knees was founded by my partner's late grandmother, Dixie Bird, in partnership with her husband, George, who looked after the bees and ran the honey side of things. The chutneys and honey are made on the premises at the cottage and the business supplies all the local delis in the area and the neighbouring town as well as the local residents. We also grow the main ingredients on the land at Bumblebee Cottage too.'

'This sounds amazing. Am I still in time to apply for the position?' Jinny asked, crossing her fingers that it wasn't too late.

'You certainly are. Would you be able to come to Heartcross for an interview?'

Jinny happily agreed and gave Jay the thumbs-up as she scribbled down the details of the meeting. After saying goodbye she hung up the phone and hurried back towards the bar.

'Well?' asked Jay.

Jinny was fit to burst. 'This is meant to bee! See what I did there?'

Jay rolled his eyebrows. 'Never mind bee puns, tell me everything.'

Jinny filled Jay in on the details of her call. 'And also, Molly and her partner Cam live next door to the cottage at The Old Bakehouse. Doesn't that sound divine too?'

After listening to Jinny, Jay typed 'Dixie Bird' into Google. 'There you go. This tells you all about the business and it seems Bees' Knees has won awards in the past for their delicious chutneys and honey.'

Jinny took a moment to read. 'According to this, Dixie and George were a huge part of the community and championed other local businesses too.' She looked up at Jay. 'This is what I want. I want to be part of a community that's like family and looks out for each other. And there's not one bad review anywhere about Bees' Knees, just praise. There's something I can't say about my father's business.' The more she read, the more she wanted this opportunity. 'Could you imagine if I was successful and got the job? This is my chance to prove to myself that I can stand on my own two feet, be independent and be successful in a business that's a million miles away from being a journalist. And this is definitely what I class as a nice job!' she enthused. 'There's a list of all their products, which I will learn inside and out. All I've got to do is pass the interview.'

'And when is this interview?'

A huge grin spread right across Jinny's face. 'Three days from now, which gives me plenty of time to research Dixie's company and quickly learn the basics of chutney making!' Jinny held up her glass. 'Cheers!'

Jay shook his head in disbelief. 'Do you remember when I said, "Run it past me first before you go doing anything on impulse"?'

'I'm running it past you now!'

Even a sceptic like Jay had to admit that this was the perfect opportunity for Jinny. This morning she was downtrodden and now the world was her oyster. All she had to do was work hard to learn everything she could about the business over the next few days and do whatever it took to get the job.

Jay grinned. 'You are such an inspiration but when they take one look at you...'

'And what's that meant to mean?' asked Jinny, pretending to be hurt.

He leaned across the bar and looked her up and down. Jinny was perched on the stool, her size-eight figure draped in the usual well-tailored designer suit. Her pale pink blouse matched the colour of her nails and her six-inch heels looked beautiful but painful to walk in. 'No offence, but you don't look like the chutney-making type.'

'That I can change. I'll show you!'

'Good for you! I have everything crossed that you get the job.'

Jinny drained the last mouthful of her drink and jumped off the stool. She flung her arms around the cardboard box.

'Where are you going now?'

'To start packing and researching.'

'Are you absolutely sure about this? Why don't you sleep on it?'

'No, I'm absolutely sure.' She put the box down and clapped her hands together. 'What's keeping me here? Except for you, of course!'

'And what if it doesn't work out? What's the plan then?'

'There is no plan "*bee*", *bee*-cause I won't fail. This is fate!'

Jay lifted up the hatch and walked towards Jinny with his arms open wide, swathing her in the biggest hug. She hugged Jay back like her life depended on it.

'I can't believe this. It's all happening too quickly. One minute you're a journalist chasing celebrity stories and the next a chutney maker in Scotland. You are so impulsive.'

'I hope they like me!' Jinny kissed him firmly on the cheek.

'You're really going to do this, aren't you?'

'I am!'

Jay took his hands in hers. 'You have a safe trip and message me or Facetime me the second you arrive. I want to see exactly where you are and how you are.'

'I will,' Jinny promised. '#JinnysNewLife starts right now!'

Standing on her own two feet without her father to rely on if things got tough was going to be one of the hardest things she'd ever done, but Jinny was confident she could do this. 'Eek!' she squealed, slinging her bag over her shoulder and looking down at her shoes. 'What if they don't like me?' she asked, suddenly feeling a little hesitant.

'Just *bee* yourself!' Jay bellowed, waving as Jinny rolled her eyes. A second later the wine bar door closed behind her as Jinny enthusiastically hot-footed it back towards the Tube.

'Jinny, your box,' Jay shouted after her.

But Jinny was long gone. Jay took a quick look inside.

'I don't suppose you'll be needing any of this stuff,' he said, placing it under the bar.

Chapter Three

Three days and 580 miles later, armed with a holdall and a rucksack, Jinny stepped off the bus at the bottom of Love Heart Lane and took in the magnificent view. The whitewashed terraced houses looked even better than she'd expected; the Google images she'd viewed hadn't done them justice. They were standing in a row to the side of the narrow lane, hanging baskets with tumbling blooms adorning the duck-egg blue front doors alongside window boxes full of colour. Bonnie's Teashop could be seen at the top of the lane and to the left of her was a wooden signpost that read, 'Foxglove Farm', with comical-looking alpacas grazing in the field beyond. A majestic mountain towered over the scene, standing tall against the beautiful cerulean sky where sporadic clouds sailed slowly past in the light breeze. Jinny pinched herself. The village already seemed utterly perfect.

'So, this is Heartcross,' she murmured, taking a breather and perching on a nearby bench while taking a swig of water from her bottle. She tilted her face up to the sun and briefly closed her eyes. The trip had been long and exhausting with the train carriage packed to the rafters for most of the journey. It was only on the last leg that Jinny had been able to sit back and begin to relax as most of the commuters had departed at Glasgow Central. She'd switched off her phone for the whole journey, choosing instead to get lost in her own thoughts and in a notepad of Dixie's recipes that she was memorising, readying for her interview. For the last two days, Jinny had researched the history of Dixie's business from the date it was founded, to the very first chutney ever produced, to the current offerings. Jinny knew the first step was to be successful at the interview, then she had six months to prove her worth. Yesterday, she'd had a go at making a simple chutney recipe and had been pleased with her attempt. But knowing the chutney needed to mature for a minimum of eight weeks before the flavour could be sampled at its best, she would have to wait and see how it turned out.

The peaceful moment was soon interrupted when Jinny switched on her mobile phone and it beeped in quick succession. It seemed she was in demand. There were six missed calls from her father and umpteen texts. Yesterday, Jinny had taken the time to visit him. After sharing her interview news he'd scoffed at the idea of her taking on a chutney-making business. When Jinny had refused to let his opinion dampen her spirit, the visit had ended in a heated exchange of words leaving Jinny asking him to give her space until everything had calmed down. Judging by the missed calls, he was disregarding her request.

All she wanted to do was concentrate on the interview and give it her all so to appease him she quickly pinged her father a text, keeping it simple.

I've arrived safely. I'll ring you soon.

Taking the last mouthful of water, she tossed her empty bottle in the bin nearby and smiled as she looked down at her clothes. Jay had been right. Her usual attire was not going to suit the chutney-making world so Jinny had swapped her designer suit for a pair of denim dungarees painted with colourful flowers, which she'd found at a vintage shop in Covent Garden. Her hair was tied up with a floral headscarf, and on her feet she wore a pair of short Wellington boots, which she was now thinking were a big mistake as her feet were sweltering in the heat. But that didn't matter. She looked the part and was going to embrace country living with everything she had.

Taking a quick selfie, she posed next to the Love Heart Lane sign and sent the image to Jay.

#*JinnysNewLife*, she captioned the photograph.

Arrived safe! And there's not a power suit or a pair of heels in sight!

Immediately, her phone beeped with Jay's response. She grinned.

What the hell have you gone dressed as?

Jinny replied:

A country bumpkin!

She smiled as she slid the phone back into her bag. Jinny was ready for everything Heartcross was going to throw at her.

'Let's go and meet the villagers,' she said out loud, as she went in search of a cup of tea and breakfast.

Hauling her rucksack up onto her back and pulling her holdall over the uneven ground, Jinny admired Heartwood Cottage, which neighboured the teashop. It was picture-perfect with the wooden heart hanging on the front door and purple wisteria clambering over the weathered oak porch.

The sun was beating down and Jinny knew it would be a scorcher by mid-afternoon. She checked the time. Her interview was just before lunch, which gave her a couple of hours to relax and re-read her notes. Provisionally, she had booked a night in Julia's B&B, which was situated in the village, but Jinny had everything crossed that if she was successful at the interview she would soon be moving into Bumblebee Cottage.

It didn't take long to reach the top of the lane and with

the delicious aroma filtering from the teashop, Jinny felt the rumble of her stomach. She hadn't eaten since late yesterday afternoon and her plan was to eat a hearty breakfast, drink a pot of tea and use the bathroom of the teashop to freshen up for her interview. With a trendy chalkboard with specials written on it standing on the pavement and yellow and white striped awning already shielding the front of the teashop from the morning sun, this place looked like a slice of delightful happiness as she pushed open the small wooden gate and ambled up the path. There were groups of hikers huddled around tables devouring mouth-watering full Scottish breakfasts, which Jinny immediately decided she was going to order.

After abandoning her holdall just outside the door and placing her rucksack on the table, Jinny placed her hands on her hips and took in the magnificent view of the mountain in front of her, which was simply breathtaking. It felt like she had been transported into a different world. Something nudged against her leg making her jump. She looked down, startled to see a pair of mournful eyes peering back at her from under the table. She bent down and stroked the shaggiest dog she'd ever set eyes on. There was something about dogs that always put Jinny in a good mood and this one was adorable.

'How blooming gorgeous are you?' she said ruffling the hair on top of its head.

Suddenly sensing someone was behind her, Jinny spun round and was captivated by a pair of hazel eyes, tousled hair and a sheepish grin. Her mouth dropped open and she knew she was catching flies but couldn't help it. The man had the most perfect olive skin that Jinny had ever set eyes on, and a beard, which she'd always found super sexy.

'Thanks very much for the complement,' he joked, giving her the warmest of smiles.

She couldn't quite place his accent but as his words sunk in her eyes diverted back to the dog.

'No, I mean your dog…' she said.

'Oh, I didn't think I was that bad,' he protested, with a spark of humour and a glint in his eye followed by a smile that was to die for.

Knowing she'd never believed in love at first sight until possibly right this second, she felt a slight crimson blush heat her cheeks along with a flutter in the depths of her stomach. For the past ten years she'd been surrounded by men in her job and not a one had been as handsome as the man standing in front of her now.

'I'm not quite sure how to answer that,' she replied, feeling her heart thump a little faster. 'I suppose you're not too bad…' she added, now grinning, not quite believing that she'd arrived in Heartcross a few minutes ago and here she was already flirting with a stranger.

'Glad to hear it.' His eyes sparkled. 'And his curls always get the girls,' he replied, ruffling the top of the dog's head then looking back towards her.

'I'm not surprised,' added Jinny. 'He's adorable.'

'I agree, especially when he's asleep. But don't be fooled, underneath all that shagginess he can be a grumpy old man, especially if he doesn't get his sausage roll for breakfast.

Believe me, he sulks.' At the sheer mention of the words 'sausage roll', the dog immediately sat up straight, his front paws dancing and his eyes fixated on the sausage roll that the beautiful stranger was now taking out of a white paper bag he'd had hidden behind his back. With literally one gulp, it was gone. 'It's a waste. He doesn't even taste it.'

Jinny couldn't help but think the dog was smiling underneath all that hair.

'I'm Jinny, by the way.' She thrust her hand forward, immediately thinking it was a little too formal.

'Gabe,' he replied, looking at her hand in amusement before shaking it. 'Resident or tourist?'

'Resident… hopefully. I'm here for an interview. I've come all the way from London,' Jinny replied, crossing her fingers. 'I have two hours until I get to display my knowledge and convince the interviewer I know how to make chutney.' Jinny knew she was babbling but she was suddenly feeling nervous and the words were tumbling out of her mouth.

'And you don't?'

'Between you and me, I'm a complete novice,' she whispered. 'But I need this job. It would save my life.'

Gabe raised his eyebrows, looking amused. 'Gosh, well, I hope you're successful.'

'Thank you,' she replied, watching him untie the dog.

'Maybe we'll see you around, and hopefully you'll have some good news to tell us.'

'I'd like that. Same time tomorrow?' she joked. 'Sausage rolls are on me.'

As soon as those words left her mouth, she wanted the ground to swallow her up. Who the hell invites someone to grab a sausage roll together?

Gabe grinned, his hazel eyes glistening as he locked on to hers. 'I'll look forward to that.'

Feeling like a babbling fool, she watched him walk down the path towards the gate. He glanced back over his shoulder to add, 'And the adorable one is called Claude.'

'Good to meet you, Claude,' she shouted, feeling a burst of adrenalin electrifying her heart, which was racing at a pace she hadn't experienced in a long while.

As she watched them walk down the lane, Gabe extended Claude's lead and the dog suddenly let out a loud woof at an alpaca with comical hair that was grazing through the laurel hedging, and pulled a stumbling Gabe up the kerb towards it.

Jinny gave a soft laugh while Gabe looked back towards her and rolled his eyes. Once he managed to get Claude under control, they soon disappeared out of sight at the bottom of Love Heart Lane.

'Well, that was a lovely start to the day,' murmured Jinny, still smiling. Then she nearly jumped out of her skin as a voice trilled behind her.

'Good morning! How are you? Would you like a table?'

Jinny turned and was met by the most welcoming smile. Felicity was her name according to her name badge. 'Felicity. You're Felicity!' enthused Jinny, extending her hand. 'How lovely to meet you. We have a mutual acquaintance. I mean, a friend of a friend from London. I'm not explaining myself properly, am I? I've just arrived and I think this mountain air is making me a little giddy.'

Felicity was still smiling. 'You've come all the way from London?'

'My best friend, Jay, used to work in The Chatty Banker with Polly, your friend who I believe also lives here now.'

Felicity's face was one of surprise. 'You know Jay? This is surreal. And yes! Polly lives here in the village. She's been here for a few years. And how is Jay?'

'Oh, you know, he's still Jay. Comical, full of confidence and pours the best double gins in the whole of London.'

'That he does! Are you eating with us? I'll get you a menu and we can chat some more.'

'Yes, please. I'm starving!'

'Then you've come to the right place. Would you like to sit inside or out?'

'I've been cooped up on trains and buses so I think I'd love to sit here and watch the world go by,' replied Jinny, pointing to the vacant table that overlooked the lane. 'But could I possibly use your bathroom first? It's been a long journey.'

'London to Heartcross, I know that journey well. The bathroom is that way.' Felicity directed Jinny inside the tearoom. Taking in her surroundings as she moved through the room, Jinny couldn't help thinking the vintage teashop was Instagram perfect with its china teapots and cups and floral bunting draping the walls. The aroma inside was divine – coffee, toasted bread and cooked breakfast mixed into one. She passed the glass counter filled with glazed doughnuts drizzled with frosting and sprinkles, paper-wrapped muffins and a selection of savouries. There was a door open to the kitchen and Jinny could see another lady cooking up the breakfasts.

Ten minutes later, settled at the table, Jinny was tucking into a full Scottish when Felicity placed a pot of tea next to her then perched on a nearby chair. 'So, what brings you to Heartcross? Holiday?' she asked. 'The weather is going to be scorching for the next couple of weeks.'

'An interview and hopefully a new life.'

'This sounds exciting. What's the job?' asked Felicity, intrigued.

'Chief chutney-maker at Bees' Knees.' Jinny bent down and rummaged in her bag. She pulled out the print-out of the ad that Molly and Cam had posted and handed it to Felicity, who broke into a huge beam.

'Bumblebee Cottage! Dixie's business! You'll love living there,' enthused Felicity.

'I've got to get the job first. I've been brushing up on my chutney-making skills and researching the history of the business.'

'You have everything covered then. It's one of the best cottages in the village and such a lovely job too. Is that your normal line of work?'

'Far from it, but I have everything crossed. And I don't think I've introduced myself. I'm Jinny Smith.' Jinny had decided to use her mother's maiden name while in Heartcross. This was her fresh start and she didn't want anyone judging her on the antics of her father. His reputation amongst the general public was controversial at the best of times and hardly a week went by without Jinny reading unfavourable comments about him or the newspaper.

'And is there a plan if you don't get the job?' asked Felicity.

'Nope. I'm just hoping that I interview well because judging by what I've seen so far, this village looks like a beautiful place to live.'

'Oh it is, but there's something you need to know about this village,' Felicity said, grinning. 'And the sooner you know it, the better.'

Jinny raised an eyebrow. 'Which is…?' she asked curiously.

'Once you arrive in Heartcross you never want to leave. So, welcome! Even if you don't get the job, you're here to stay!' She threw her arms open wide.

Jinny laughed. 'That sounds good to me. Jay said you own this place. It's gorgeous.'

'I am indeed the proud owner of this quaint little teashop.'

'Co-owner,' said a voice directly behind them.

'Co-owner,' Felicity corrected herself as she and Jinny turned to look at the new arrival. 'And the other co-owner is my mother, Rona. Mum, meet Jinny. We have a mutual friend in London.'

Rona wiped her hands on a tea towel then smoothed down her pinny before extending her hand. 'Pleased to meet you, Jinny. You've come all the way from London?'

'I have.'

'Jinny's here for an interview up at Bumblebee Cottage,' added Felicity.

'It's the perfect cottage and job. Whoever is successful will be lucky. I thought about applying myself,' joked Rona.

'You would never leave this place,' chipped in Felicity. 'This teashop is your life.'

'That it is but I know Molly and Cam will be thankful to have help in the business. It's been tough ever since Dixie passed away. She was a huge part of this community for a lifetime. Dixie and her late husband George were the founders of Bees' Knees while George's brother Ted was an award-winning baker, living next door. He too has passed away but Cam, her grandson, took over the bakery and hopefully you'll be chosen to keep Bees' Knees on the map.'

'I hope so too,' replied Jinny.

'And right next door to The Old Bakehouse is Layers Treats, the chocolate shop,' added Rona with a smile. 'I will tell you now, moving to Heartcross is not going to be good for your waistline, believe me,' she joked, patting her stomach.

'I'm liking the sound of it already!' Jinny smiled. Everything sounded so wonderful. This opportunity already meant the world to her and she was praying she had done enough preparation for the interview.

'Is chutney-making your usual line of work?' asked Rona. 'What did you do before?'

'An office job,' replied Jinny not giving any more away. 'Boring, mundane and quite dull. I'm going to be honest, I've not worked in the food industry but I'm a hard worker, a good organiser and always deliver on time. I hope they give me a chance.'

'We have everything crossed for you. This little community is just the best and you are most welcome to join it, because as the saying goes, once you arrive in Heartcross you never want to leave,' said Rona.

'I can believe it,' replied Jinny.

'There's a BBQ planned at The Grouse and Haggis next week, the pub on the high street – you can't miss it. It'll be the perfect way to meet the regulars. Why don't you come along?'

'I will if I'm still here, thanks,' Jinny replied, thinking that would be the ideal opportunity to chat and meet with the locals. There was one local in particular that had popped straight into her mind: Gabe.

'Right, come on, Felicity, we have tables to clear and pots to wash,' ordered Rona, walking back off to the kitchen. 'Good luck with your interview.'

Felicity leaned in towards Jinny. 'She can be so bossy at times.'

'I heard that!' replied Rona.

Jinny and Felicity laughed.

As Jinny devoured her breakfast, the interview began to play heavily on her mind. She knew she needed to keep calm. There was a lot riding on it and thankfully there were still a couple of hours to look over and practise some interview questions that she had printed off the web before she arrived. After pouring the last of the tea from the pot, Jinny looked out across the lane, and noticed Gabe for the second time today. Claude was walking to heel by his side and they were heading back past the teashop towards the top of Love Heart Lane. Once again, she was staring, but couldn't help it. His thick, dark hair was wild on top and at a guess he was mid-thirties. She ran an approving eye over his outfit: a white T-shirt, navy cargo shorts, boat shoes and numerous woven leather bands around his wrist.

He caught her eye as he passed the teashop and smiled, leaving Jinny feeling the same flutter in the pit of her stomach again. They stared at each other in contemplative silence before he swung his leg over the stile and disappeared up the mountain pass with Claude now off-lead and running ahead, ferreting in the hedgerow without a care in the world.

'He's very handsome, isn't he?' remarked Felicity, who was clearing the plates from a nearby table.

'Busted! You caught me looking. Is he local?' asked Jinny, intrigued to know more.

'As local as they come,' replied Felicity. 'There's one thing I can be certain of: you're going to be seeing a lot more of him.'

'Why do you say that?'

'I just have a feeling,' replied Felicity with a mischievous look on her face before heading off towards the kitchen.

'Oh, and if you need to freshen up before the interview, feel free to use the facilities.'

'Thank you! That's so kind!' shouted Jinny after her, before glancing back towards the mountain. She hoped Felicity's prediction was going to be right.

Chapter Four

With a full stomach, Jinny walked along the high street and took in the sights. She was heading towards the green where Felicity had directed her to a bench under the shaded area of the trees, which would be perfect to look over the chutney recipes. First, she spotted the local pub, The Grouse and Haggis. Opposite that was a little village shop that was quaintly old-fashioned, with postcards stacked outside in the spinning carousel. A metal ice-cream swung in the light, warm breeze and fishing nets were lined up behind the fresh fruit laid out in wooden crates on the table. Children were running up the road, waving their nets then disappearing down a side street, which was signposted 'The River'. There were dog walkers, and she spotted a man sitting on a bench reading a newspaper, which she noticed was *The Daily News*. For a brief moment, she thought about her father. She didn't like there to be any bad feeling between them but knowing he was expecting her to go crawling back with her tail between her legs spurred her on even more to stand on her own two feet. Once she knew the results of her interview – hopefully positive – she would give him another ring.

Ambling along merrily, Jinny greeted everyone that crossed her path. She was at the end of the high street and once she turned the corner, she gave a tiny gasp. Bumblebee Cottage was directly in front of her. The thatched cottage was stunning. It was set back from the road and the low stone wall that edged the property was packed with tiny blue flowers that hung over the edges, adding to the beauty of the place. Next door, The Old Bakehouse was equally stunning. There were people wandering out of the bakery armed with fresh loaves and Jinny hoped she would be waking up to the aroma of freshly baked bread very soon. She wheeled her holdall across the green towards the bench where she perched cross-legged and began to look over her notes. There was an hour to go before her interview – her first, she realised, having spent all her working life on her father's staff – and she began to wonder about her competition. In the last twenty minutes Jinny had noticed two potential candidates leave The Old Bakehouse and now the nerves were beginning to kick in. She knew she had a well of skills and though they might not be the practical skills this particular job needed, Jinny was not going to let that deter her.

'Nerves are a good sign,' she said, trying to convince herself as she walked towards the bakery where the interview would be taking place. 'They mean you really want it.'

Stepping inside, The Old Bakehouse was exactly how she had imagined it would be from the outside. The shelves were packed with freshly baked loaves in wicker baskets and the glass counter in front of her was piled with all things sugary.

'Can I help you?' The girl behind the counter smiled.

'I'm here for an interview,' replied Jinny. 'It's Jinny Smith.'

'Hi, I'm Bree, manager of the chocolate shop next door.'

'Now that is a dream job – manager of a chocolate shop! I'm up for being chief taster of any new products,' Jinny joked.

'You and most of the village,' said Bree, laughing. 'It is a dream job, stress free and just everything about it is nice. A bit like Bees' Knees. Have you come far?'

'London,' replied Jinny, taking Bree completely by surprise.

'Wow, that is a long way. Welcome to Heartcross! I'm guessing the village is a little different to London,' she exclaimed, checking through a list of names attached to a clipboard, which caused a little slump in Jinny's mood. There had to be at least fifteen other candidates on the list and now Jinny was beginning to think she didn't have a cat in hell's chance. Surely some – most? – of those candidates had more experience than her.

'A little less busy,' replied Jinny, giving a nervous smile.

'I'll let them know you're here.'

Jinny watched as Bree disappeared out of the door at the back of the bakery. Then, thankfully, her inner voice took over and gave her a much-needed pep talk.

Don't be defeated. Believe in yourself. You are as good as anyone else.

She looked around at the shelves and an old dresser that housed glass jam jars bound with gingham covers secured with string and ribbons. She'd never seen so many flavoured chutneys in one place. Then she spotted the Bees' Knees honey. There was a small display sharing the backstory of the company. How the hives at Bumblebee Cottage provided all the honey and they sourced all the fruit for the chutney from orchards there too. Jinny turned around at the sound of footsteps. Bree popped her head around the door with a smile. 'This way.'

Jinny nodded and propped up her holdall by the counter before following Bree through the bakery kitchens.

'Good luck,' Bree whispered as she pointed to the door in front of them.

Jinny nodded her thanks before stepping into the room with a nervous smile on her face. Her heart was pounding nineteen to the dozen as she was met by the extended hand and warm smile of the woman who must be Molly, putting her immediately at ease.

'Hi Jinny, welcome to Heartcross. I'm Molly – we spoke on the phone.' She shook Jinny's hand. 'How was your journey?'

'It was long but worth it as soon as I stepped into this beautiful village.'

'I have to agree with you there. It's stunning, isn't it? I wouldn't want to be anywhere else.' Molly indicated for Jinny to take a seat. 'We're just waiting for my colleague.' Molly looked towards the door at the back of the room. 'Here he is now.'

Jinny glanced towards the door and her mouth slowly fell open as a familiar pair of hazel eyes locked on to hers. Gabe. His smile had such intensity that it set her hormones on fire.

'This is Gabe,' continued Molly, oblivious to the fact that Jinny and Gabe were staring at each other.

Jinny pulled herself together. 'We met this morning, at Bonnie's teashop,' she shared, wishing the ground would swallow her up as she replayed this morning's conversation between them over in her head. Why on earth had she divulged to Gabe that she had no experience in the chutney-making business whatsoever?!

'Were you treating Claude to his morning sausage roll?' asked Molly, turning towards Gabe.

Gabe was still smiling. 'I was, and Jinny was telling me this morning that' – Jinny thought her heart was about to pound out of her chest as she prayed he wouldn't share the contents of their conversation – 'that she has come all the way from London.'

Jinny exhaled slowly. 'I have.'

'I'm intrigued,' added Molly. 'How did you stumble across us here in Heartcross?'

'By accident. My friend was actually the one who mentioned Heartcross. Would you believe he knows

Felicity, from when she lived in London? That's why my first stop this morning was the teashop, so I could grab breakfast and introduce myself to her,' Jinny babbled, getting into her stride as they all sat.

'Small world! Anyone who's a friend of Flick's is a friend of ours and that makes you kind of family in our little community,' enthused Molly, writing something down on the piece of paper in front of her.

Jinny smiled. 'And after a little research I realised this was the village that had featured so heavily in the news when the bridge collapsed in the winter storm a couple of years back.'

'Yes, this little village seems to crave the limelight,' Molly agreed. 'Let me tell you a little bit about us. I'm a partner in the veterinary practice in the village and my partner, Cam, is the owner and baker at The Old Bakehouse. And Gabe...' Molly gestured towards him, indicating he should take the verbal baton.

'I'm the beekeeper at Bumblebee Cottage. I tend to the hives, make the honey and have kept things ticking over since Dixie—'

'The owner and founder,' interrupted Jinny.

Gabe looked amused as he nodded and carried on talking. 'Since Dixie passed away. I'll be at the cottage most days, taking the right candidate through every step of the business from the accounting, distributing, ensuring the food is growing on the land, making the chutney, et cetera, et cetera. I must say, you absolutely look the part of a chutney-maker. You said you're from London but you must be a country girl at heart,' observed Gabe, giving a sideward glance towards Molly who nodded.

'You definitely look the part,' agreed Molly.

The outfit she was wearing hadn't let her down. 'Definitely a country girl at heart,' Jinny announced a little too confidently knowing this wasn't the time to share that she was scared of bees – and any other flying insect for that matter. For the last few years, she had lived in an apartment at the top of an executive apartment block with all the mod cons and her only dealings of any sort with nature or fruit were when it was skewered through a cocktail stick in her gin glass. Jinny had never set foot in an orchard and had no clue about growing fruit or harvesting honey but she wasn't going to let that put her off. She wanted this job.

'Do you like bees?' asked Gabe, watching her closely. 'They're an integral part of the business.'

Just at that moment, there was a very loud buzzing and something caught Jinny's eye hovering at the side of her. She jumped out of her skin and began frantically waving her arms in the air. The amused look on Gabe's face didn't go unnoticed as he stood up and wandered towards her, swinging what looked like an electronic table tennis bat in the air. There was a loud crackle and the fly fell towards the floor.

Jinny had brought her hands up to her thumping heart. 'Sorry, sorry, it just took me a little by surprise. It's just the nerves getting the better of me. I've never actually had an interview before.' She reminded herself to breathe calmly. The last thing Molly and Gabe needed to know was that she wasn't a particular fan of anything that flies unless it was a first-class plane ticket.

'And how many hives are there at Bumblebee Cottage?' she asked, now panicking that the look of fear was actually showing on her face and desperate to divert their attention.

With a slight smile Gabe leaned towards her. 'Too many to count,' he replied with a wicked glint in his eye. Jinny shuddered at the very thought.

'But your main role will be carrying on Dixie's legacy and making the chutney,' chipped in Molly. 'Tell us a little bit about your background.'

This was the moment that Jinny had been dreading. She had no experience whatsoever in the food industry and suddenly felt a little tearful.

Molly noticed that she was teary-eyed and quickly handed her a tissue. 'Is everything okay? We aren't so terrible at interviewing, are we?' she asked in a soft, warm voice.

Jinny shook her head. 'No. I'm sorry, I'm not usually like this.' She took a breath. 'Can I be truly honest with you both? I've never done anything like this before. I know other candidates will have more experience than I do and have likely been working in the food industry for ages but I have lots of skills that can be transferred and it would be an honour to keep Dixie's legacy growing.' Jinny reached for the glass of water that had been placed in front of her and took a sip. 'I loved Dixie's story.' Jinny placed her hands on her heart. 'It was so romantic. I read online how the business began with a romantic trip to the South of

France and the number of local awards the business has won is astounding. Everything I've read about Dixie and George is inspirational and it would be an honour for me to be part of the continuing journey for Bees' Knees. I know this isn't my usual line of work but I promise you I will work hard.'

Molly gave a sideward look towards Gabe. 'I can appreciate that sometimes you're stuck in a rut and want a complete change of direction in a career. Would you believe a few years ago, Cam – my partner – was running his own dental practice and now he's an award-winning baker? I know from personal experience that people can step outside their comfort zone and succeed.'

Molly's words gave Jinny a little bit of hope and she knew that if she was given this chance, she wouldn't let Molly down.

'Can I ask why is it you want to move so far from home? We can appreciate a change in career but you're miles from anything you know. What if you get homesick and want to leave? We would have to start this process again and we really need someone who is committed from the start,' Gabe said.

'There's nothing keeping me in London.' Jinny thought the best way was to be honest. 'Without going into too much detail, my relationship with my father is a difficult one and my mother has passed away.'

'I'm sorry to hear that,' said Gabe with such warmth. 'That must be difficult for you.'

'I'm not going anywhere and if I'm lucky enough to be

successful I will grasp this opportunity with both hands and prove myself in this position.'

Jinny noticed that Molly gave Gabe an approving nod and she hoped that meant she was in with a chance.

'We were going to ask you to make chutney as part of the interview process but as chutney needs to mature before tasting, we thought we would have a bit of fun instead,' said Gabe, standing up and walking over to a tray that contained small lumps of cheese, crackers and three unlabelled jars of chutney. He placed the tray down in front of Jinny and spread the jars of chutney out in front of her. 'Here we've got three unlabelled jars of chutney. Have a little try of each, tell us what flavours you can taste and what name you would give it.' Gabe grinned as he pushed the tray towards Jinny.

'And there's no pressure,' added Molly.

Jinny was up for the challenge. She placed a small amount of cheese on top of the cracker and a spoonful of chutney on top.

As she took a bite and savoured the taste, she picked up the jar and took in the aroma. 'This would be perfect on a waffle too. I'm tasting apple and cinnamon and this chutney would be perfect for the dark winter nights and cold early mornings. I can picture log fires, decorated Christmas trees and family sitting around the kitchen table. Yes, it's definitely giving me a winter and Christmas vibe.'

'Very good,' confirmed Gabe. 'And what would you call the chutney?'

'I would call it the "Naughty and Nice Chutney"

because it could be on both Santa's naughty and nice lists. Naughty on hot waffles for that indulgent breakfast with maybe a spoonful of fresh whipped cream and nice in the evening with cheese and crackers.'

'I like that. "Naughty and Nice Chutney",' remarked Gabe, with a mischievous glint in his eye. 'I wonder what list we will all be on this year?' A smile hitched on his face and for a second Jinny wondered if he was flirting with her a little.

'I'm loving that,' added Molly. 'You've nailed the flavours and the image that Dixie conjured up. Try this one.' Molly pointed to the next jar.

'All these crackers, my waistline will be expanding,' joked Jinny, tucking into the next chutney.

'I think you'll be okay,' replied Gabe, still sounding playful and causing Jinny to look in his direction. Her heart gave a little flip, taking her by surprise.

'Mmm, this is different. Very tasty.' Jinny took another bite and thought for a second. 'This one could be enjoyed in any way.'

'What do you mean?' asked Molly.

'I'm thinking this chutney could be easily enjoyed with a tasty curry or added to a sandwich or cheese spread.'

Molly nodded. 'Exactly.'

'I'm tasting spices – orange, rhubarb, onion, ginger and… is that mustard seeds?'

'You've nailed the flavours,' said Molly. 'You're unbelievable.'

'To me this chutney represents summertime so I would name it exactly that... "Summertime Chutney".'

'Jinny, I don't know what to say. That's a perfect name and again you're bang-on. Dixie wanted this chutney to be enjoyed with several dishes but especially curry.'

'It tastes wonderful and I do love a good curry,' shared Jinny, enjoying the challenge. She could see by the looks on Molly and Gabe's faces that they were impressed.

'Last one.' Gabe gestured to the final jar.

It only took Jinny a couple of seconds to recognise the flavour. 'Plum Chutney.'

'Made with the plums from the orchard at Bumblebee Cottage,' added Molly.

'Perfect for any time of the year. It tastes divine and I'd call it "Cottage Garden Chutney",' suggested Jinny. 'They're all such wonderful flavours. Dixie created a really amazing business here and it would be an honour to champion all her hard work and keep her legacy growing.'

Molly smiled as she wrote something down on a piece of paper and pushed it in front of Gabe who cast his eyes over it. He scribbled a response and pushed it back towards Molly.

Under the table Jinny had her fingers crossed, feeling that the interview had gone well, even after the shock of seeing Gabe on the other side of the interview table.

'Where are you staying tonight?' asked Molly.

'I've booked into Julia's B&B for a few days. I explained about my interview here, and that I didn't know how long it would take to know the outcome.'

'We don't think you'll be needing any nights at the B&B. We both think you are the best candidate to take over Dixie's business. If you would like to accept, we would love to offer you the job and get the ball rolling.'

Jinny was fit to burst. 'Oh my gosh!' She brought her hands up to her mouth. 'I would *love* to accept,' she enthused. 'Is this for real?'

'It's for real,' confirmed Molly with a huge smile that mirrored Jinny's. 'Let me talk you through what happens next,' she continued. 'This is a six-month trial and then we review how it's working for both of us. The cottage is for rent only with the business opportunity so if you decide you no longer want the position within that time frame then the agreement states you must move out. But would you like to come and take a look around the cottage first before you make up your mind?'

Jinny shook her head. 'I don't need to. I know the cottage is going to be perfect.' She was brimming with excitement. 'And I'm confident I will learn the ropes quickly with Gabe talking me through everything.' Jinny couldn't take the smile off her face. She had a home and a business for the next six months and was going to do everything in her power to make sure that she secured the contract on a permanent basis.

'If you're sure? Have a read over the contract terms and conditions,' Molly said, pushing an official-looking document across the table to Jinny, 'And if there's anything you don't understand, Gabe will be able to help. In the meantime, I'll just go and get you the keys to the cottage. Congratulations!' Molly got up and left the room.

Gabe passed her a pen and once again, Jinny felt a flip in her stomach as his fingers lightly brushed against hers. She began to look over the terms and conditions but couldn't concentrate as she sensed Gabe studying her. She glanced towards him. He didn't break eye contact.

'I have to say, after your confession this morning that you didn't know a thing about chutneys I wasn't expecting much, but you've certainly pulled it out of the bag. I'm quite impressed.'

'Thank you, but I didn't just blag it. I did do a lot of research,' she confessed.

'And that paid off.'

Molly breezed back into the room jiggling a set of keys. 'Here you go! Time to explore your new home. Tomorrow, your day will start at nine a.m. and over the coming weeks, Gabe will take you through every step of the business until you both feel you can handle it on your own.'

'Sounds perfect,' replied Jinny, secretly thrilled at the prospect of spending copious amount of time with Gabe.

'Nine a.m. sharp,' replied Gabe. 'We'll start on the chutney side of the business followed by beekeeping training. There's also the order book, invoices and distribution of the chutney to review.'

'Do I have to distribute the product myself?' asked Jinny, realising she had no mode of transport.

'You do,' replied Gabe.

Jinny shook her head, worried her new dream life was all about to fall apart. 'I don't have a car. I came by train.'

'Are you thinking what I'm thinking?' asked Gabe looking towards Molly.

'I think I am and I think it would suit Jinny.'

'It'll certainly get her from A to Bee, if you'll pardon the pun.'

'Groan,' replied Molly. 'This is what you'll have to put with,' she joked, smiling.

'There's nothing wrong with my jokes,' replied Gabe, pretending to look hurt.

Molly shook her head in jest as she looked back towards Jinny. 'We still have Dixie's car in the garage at the side of the orchard. You can use that.'

'Brilliant! Thank you!' replied Jinny, not quite believing she had landed a home, a job and a car in a matter of hours. Her luck was certainly in.

'Is there anything else you need to know or want to ask?'

Jinny shook her head. 'I can't think of anything.'

'If there's anything you need while settling in, I'll be around this afternoon and Cam will be back soon from his deliveries.'

'And I'll be with you in the morning,' added Gabe.

'Thanks again,' Jinny replied, filled with delight. She was itching to explore her new home and to ring Jay to tell him the good news.

As they all stood, Molly took the signed contract from Jinny and handed her the keys to the cottage. Just at that second Molly's phone rang and she excused herself, leaving Jinny and Gabe alone in the interview room.

Jinny picked up her bag. 'I can't believe I got the job.'

'I hope you settle in okay and—' began Gabe but he was interrupted by Jinny who dropped her bag and gave a tiny squeal. She jumped backwards, flapping her arms in front of her.

'There's a wasp.'

Gabe looked amused as he opened the window wide and the wasp flew out. 'I was going to say, welcome to Heartcross,' he said with a laugh. 'I'm guessing you aren't a fan of flying creatures?'

Jinny knew she had been rumbled. 'I can neither confirm nor deny,' she replied with a wry smile on her face as they headed outside.

A couple of minutes later, Jinny pushed open the rickety wooden garden gate to Bumblebee Cottage. This was her home for the foreseeable and she couldn't contain her excitement as she let go of her holdall and with her arms open wide spun round and round on the small, manicured lawn. She'd done it. All of her hard work had paid off. Jinny's new life was about to begin.

Chapter Five

Taking in her surroundings, Jinny meandered next to the neatly cut lush green lawn with wild pink foxgloves standing tall from the flowerbeds. Admiring the pale-pink roses twisting themselves around the oak porch that flanked the heavy duck-egg blue wooden front door, she walked towards it. 'It's just beautiful,' she murmured. Just outside the door was a doormat with a red heart and littered on either side of the mat were several plant pots of red geraniums and window boxes full of colourful pansies. Bumblebee Cottage oozed warmth and beauty and had clearly been a well-loved home.

Jinny knew that from this moment on she would be in charge of keeping these flowers alive, and thought back with a grimace to the plant on the windowsill that she'd left behind in her old apartment, which was fighting for survival. Noticing the numerous watering cans standing by the outside tap, she knew it was going to be a huge undertaking, but she was up for the challenge.

Putting the key in the door, her excitement heightened. If the outside of the cottage was anything to go by, surely the inside was utterly gorgeous. And Bumblebee Cottage proved her right. Stepping onto the red flagstone floor in the hallway, she saw it was adorable. She was greeted by a cream vase of freshly cut blush peonies. How lovely and welcoming, thought Jinny, placing the keys next to the beautiful blooms and inhaling the scent.

Looking around she noted that the ceiling was low and a coat stand stood empty. There was an old-fashioned cream telephone on a small circular table, the kind Jinny had only ever seen in antique shops or featured in TV programme re-runs from years gone by. She picked up the receiver to hear the dialling tone before placing it back and walking down the hallway. The walls were lined with paintings of horses and foxes, and further along there were pictures of butterflies and birds, a couple of beehives and a photograph of a man dressed in a white beekeeper's suit, who Jinny could only assume was George, the founder of Bees' Knees honey. This cottage was full of character and Jinny felt a sense of homely warmth the second she stepped inside.

First things first, she kicked off her Wellington boots and waggled her toes, thanking the Lord her feet could finally breathe again. Taking a pair of sliders from her holdall she slipped them on. Following the hallway towards an archway she stepped down into the kitchen.

'Wow!' The word left Jinny's mouth in a gasp as she

looked around. This kitchen wouldn't look out of place in *Country Living* magazine. Over her head, various pans hung from the wooden rack on the ceiling, alongside bunches of lavender. There was an impressive stone alcove that housed a racing-green Aga, and two wingback chairs and a small coffee table sat in front of an open fire at the far end of the kitchen. The shelves above the worktops were crammed with plates and floral cups and she ran her hand along the old farmhouse table in the centre of the room before walking over to the Belfast sink that was positioned under the window. She looked out over a magnificent country garden, which she couldn't wait to explore.

Swinging a glance around the room, she noticed there was a door in the corner. Jinny walked over to it and swung it open. 'Oh my gosh, this pantry is larger than my old apartment bathroom.' There were rows and rows of empty jam jars and gingham lids piled up on the shelves that lined the walls. Next Jinny walked over to the free-standing fridge. Back in her apartment there was a double American fridge with an ice machine that was a ridiculous size for just one person as most weeks Jinny struggled to fill up more than one shelf. Just as she moved to pull on the silver handle of the cream-coloured fridge that was humming its own tune, a bell rang out. Then it sounded for a second time. There was somebody at the door. Skipping back along the hallway towards the front door she flung it open to find Gabe on the other side holding up two carrier bags. 'I'm your knight in shining armour,' he said, grinning.

Jinny narrowed her eyes. 'I wasn't aware I needed a knight and if that's the case, where is your armour?'

'It's a figure of speech! I've brought you groceries.'

'Woah!' As she peered inside the bags her mouth fell open and she brought her hands to her chest. There was everything from fresh salad to cheese, milk, fish and potatoes.

Gabe placed the bags on the step. 'Wait there. There's more.'

Jinny watched as Gabe hot-footed back towards The Old Bakehouse and returned a moment later holding in one hand a magnificent Victoria sponge oozing fresh cream from its middle with strawberries decorating the top, and in the other a bottle of chilled Prosecco.

'Is this for me?' asked Jinny, amazed not only at the size of the cake but at how delicious it looked.

'Unfortunately, I can't take the credit for all this.' He handed Jinny a note.

Just a few provisions to help you settle in. Mol x

Jinny came over all emotional. 'This is amazing, thank you.' She took the cake and the bottle from Gabe. 'Would you like to share any of this with me?' she asked, hoping the answer was yes.

'I would, but I have to be somewhere.' He was already walking backwards down the path. 'I'll see you later.'

Jinny wanted to ask if that was a figure of speech too,

but he'd already jumped in his van and was waving at her as he pulled away from the kerb.

After packing away the groceries into the fridge along with the bottle of Prosecco, Jinny put the cake in the middle of the table and headed upstairs to explore the top floor of the cottage.

Each of the three bedrooms were cosy with their floral bedding, matching curtains and quirky soft furnishings. The only dilemma that Jinny faced was which bedroom would she choose as her own? The double bedroom at the front of the cottage that overlooked the green was divine but the double bedroom at the back of the property, which overlooked the gardens and the orchard she was yet to explore, was just as idyllic. Jinny actually went to pinch herself but stopped. If this was a dream she didn't want to wake up.

She couldn't quite believe that she was so lucky. She thought about Felicity's certainty that once you arrive in Heartcross you never want to leave and Jinny realised she might be right as she was already picturing herself growing old in the cottage. There was a tiny bathroom upstairs and a downstairs toilet, a study area, and then Jinny followed another dinky hallway that led to the front of the cottage and into the quirkiest, quaintest living room that she had ever set eyes on. There was a dresser and a bookshelf overspilling with books that were mainly about cottage gardening, chutney-making and beekeeping. A little two-seater settee in worn green velvet that faced an impressive fireplace was covered by a multi-coloured crochet blanket and tapestry cushions. The thought of winter months in front of the roaring fire was already appealing.

Jinny pulled her phone out of her pocket and Facetimed Jay who immediately picked up.

'I GOT THE JOB!' Jinny shouted. 'AND MY NEW HOME IS AMAZING!'

Jay was in his usual place, standing behind the bar, and grinned back at Jinny. 'No way! That's brilliant! Congratulations!'

'You *have* to see this place. The pantry is bigger than my old bathroom. It's full of quirkiness, pots and pans that hang from the ceiling and an open fire, which I already know will be brilliant in winter.' Jinny was speaking so fast that she barely came up for breath.

'Give me a tour. Show me around,' Jay insisted.

Five minutes later Jinny had toured him around the whole of the cottage. 'And work starts in the morning. I'm being shown the ropes by Gabe.' The second she mentioned his name a wide beam spread right across her face.

'And who is this Gabe we are talking about? Because judging by your face…'

'He's pretty easy on the eye but he's my boss and I don't know a thing about him.'

'Mmm, I'm sure with your journalistic skills and determination it won't take long to discover his whole life story.'

'I've left that life behind, remember? But promise me you will come and visit soon.'

'I promise! But I'm going to have to go, the bar's just got busy. I'm so glad you're happy. This is fate!'

After Jay hung up, Jinny was feeling so happy she walked straight back into the kitchen and popped the cork off the bottle of Prosecco. Finding a wine glass in the corner cupboard, Jinny poured herself a large glassful before turning the key in the back door and flinging it open wide. As she was hit by a burst of colour, the sight of the garden made her smile even more. Noticing a pair of old rubber clogs by the back door Jinny slipped her feet from her sliders and into them before stepping outside. This was a classic country garden, with colourful blooms, lavender, heady scents and wayward flowers. Taking the gravel path in front of her through the lawn area towards a gate, Jinny was amazed to see it led through to a walled garden that was full of brightly coloured gladioli, standing tall over the crimson geraniums and blue delphiniums. Up ahead there was a wrought-iron bistro table and chairs under a canopy of wisteria that clung to a brick archway that led through to another area that Jinny could only describe as utterly gorgeous. She had no real clue about the different types of plants and flowers but the sight in front of her was truly magnificent. Flowers stood tall and short in every colour of the rainbow and one thing Jinny noticed was the sight of the honeybees buzzing between them. It must have taken a lifetime to grow a garden as spectacular as this. She carried on walking to discover a tiny wooden bridge over a stream that flowed through the garden. This place was magical. The bridge led through to an orchard, with greenhouses, wheelbarrows and wicker baskets scattered on the ground. As she walked through the orderly rows of trees, she scrumped a plum from a branch and sank her teeth into the delicious fruit. There were windfalls scattered on the ground, masses of strawberries and tomatoes growing inside the greenhouses, and a vast vegetable garden. Jinny noticed another gate a little further with a hanging sign in large bold capitals saying:

DO NOT ENTER. PROTECTIVE CLOTHING MUST BE WORN AT ALL TIMES.

It was at that moment that Jinny properly took in the view and she couldn't quite believe her eyes. The field was full of small white wooden beehives that were in row after row. 'Woah!' exclaimed Jinny. 'This place wasn't called Bumblebee Cottage for nothing.'

'I hope you aren't thinking of venturing in there?'

Jinny turned around to find Molly standing behind her.

'Sorry, I didn't mean to frighten you. I'm just checking everything is okay before I head off for the afternoon.'

'Okay? Everything is just amazing. Look at this place.'

'It is very special, isn't it? Dixie and George were happy for a lifetime.'

As they began to walk back towards the cottage, Molly pointed out different areas of the garden and filled Jinny in on when and why they were established. 'The honeybees love this area.'

'I have to admit I am a little nervous of the bees,' shared Jinny and was relieved by Molly's reaction.

'You and me both,' admitted Molly. 'I go nowhere near them.'

They both laughed.

Jinny liked how easy-going Molly was; her warm personality settled Jinny instantly.

'And Gabe dropped off the supplies okay? I didn't want you just arriving and worrying about food shopping. There should be enough for at least a day or two.'

'I really can't thank you enough. How much do I owe you?' she asked, hovering at the back door to the cottage.

'Absolutely nothing. Call it a moving-in present.'

'Is everyone in Heartcross this super kind? I've never known a place like it. It's full of such lovely people.'

'Heartcross is special. What do you think of the cottage?' asked Molly, pulling out a chair from under the patio table.

'It's just gorgeous. People dream of living in a place like this and here I am. I just can't believe my luck.'

'They do. Sit down, I have something I'm excited to share with you.'

'What is it?' asked Jinny, intrigued, noticing Molly taking something out of her bag.

'Bees' Knees' original recipe book. I thought this would give you a little insight to life as a chutney-maker and supplement your research on the business, which I was impressed by in your interview. I could see from the effort you put in you weren't going to take anything for granted. Bees' Knees is part of the history of this place and we didn't want to see it fold. I'm glad we found a safe pair of hands for the business.'

'This is so exciting. The original recipe book!'

Jinny could tell it was a work of art, old and delicate, and was very careful as she took it from Molly. On the front cover was a hand-drawn illustration of a beautiful garden with bees hovering over a honeypot. Inside, there was a handwritten index in old-fashioned ink, and illustrations in water colours of fruit and bees. She cast an eye over all the different recipes. 'Look at all these chutneys! This is just unbelievable. Spiced beetroot and orange chutney…'

Each recipe looked more scrumptious than the mouth-watering one before.

'That one is our Christmas special,' shared Molly. 'We release it at the beginning of November and it's a huge hit. And our bestseller is redcurrant and red onion relish. It's fantastic with goat's cheese, sausages or cold meats. We sell an awful lot of that in the shop up at Foxglove Farm and in the local delis.'

'This might be a silly question but where do I make the chutney?'

Molly swept her arm towards the country kitchen. 'Right in the heart of Bumblebee Cottage – in the country kitchen. Dixie loved working in that kitchen She was always perfecting new recipes and got us all involved in any new ideas.'

'Dixie sounds like a wonderful woman.' Jinny turned the last page of the book and closed it carefully.

'She was, and when she came up with new ideas she did

exactly what we did to you in your interview. She would make us taste the new recipes and come up with a name on the spot.'

'That was fun,' replied Jinny. 'She and George sound like they were the perfect couple too.'

'They were. Cam and I have a lot to live up to,' replied Molly. 'Do you have a boyfriend? Partner?'

Immediately, Jinny shook her head. 'No, that's the reason I can up sticks at such short notice and start a new life. No commitments, not even a fish.'

Jinny knew why she had neither a boyfriend nor a partner. That was the nature of being a journalist. Unsocial hours, out for nights and days on end while searching out stories, and when her head finally did hit the pillow all she wanted to do was sleep. This change was going to do her a world of good in more ways than one.

'Which means this new life has my full and undivided attention.' Jinny couldn't wait to start her new job.

'And Gabe will be on hand to take you through everything. He'll need to measure you up for your suit too.'

'A beekeeper suit?' queried Jinny.

'The very one,' replied Molly, pointing to a small outbuilding that had crimson roses tumbling over the trellises on each side of the door. 'That's the storage area. Full of maturing chutneys and empty jars and over there the honey is extracted in the Honey Pot,' she pointed in the opposite direction to another building that was nearly hidden by a weeping willow.

Jinny was willing for tomorrow to hurry up and arrive

already. She felt a sudden burst of excitement and knew she would be in bed early so she could start work tomorrow.

Molly checked her watch. 'I need to go. Before I forget, Cam is going to give Dixie's old car a once-over and we can insure it through the business. I'll get Gabe to go through the paperwork with you.'

'Perfect,' replied Jinny. In fact, the whole set-up was perfect, she thought.

Molly stood up, leaving the recipe book on the table. 'Take good care of that. It belongs at the cottage.'

'I will,' promised Jinny, already feeling honoured to be trusted with such an heirloom.

'And before I forget, there's a BBQ next week at the pub. It would be the perfect time to meet the other villagers.'

'Yes, Felicity has already mentioned it. I'm looking forward to it already.'

'You'll be part of the village before you know it.'

Jinny watched Molly disappear around the side of the cottage and heard the gate shut behind her. Pulling the spare chair towards her she stretched her legs across it and smiled at the worn-out clogs on her feet. There was a time when Jinny had been obsessed with the latest designer shoes and handbags and had to have the latest technology, and now here she was, with the sun beating down on her, wearing a pair of vintage dungarees with worn-out clogs on her feet, and for the first time in a long time the pressures of her old job had evaporated and she didn't have a care in the world.

'More Prosecco,' she murmured, standing up and

wandering towards the fridge to top up her glass. Then she switched on the old-fashioned radio in the kitchen and danced her way back into the sunshine. After she had unpacked her clothes and made lunch, she was going to spend the rest of the afternoon with a good book soaking up the rays. Unlocking her phone, she took a selfie featuring the beautiful garden behind her along with the cobalt sky – there was no filter needed here in Heartcross – and immediately uploaded it to her brand-new Instagram account, @jinnysnewlife. She captioned the photograph: 'A brand-new chapter'. Looking around the garden she still couldn't quite believe her luck.

'Welcome to Bumblebee Cottage, Jinny!' She held her glass up and toasted her new beginnings. 'Here's to my new life,' she said, watching a butterfly flutter between the blooms as she took a sip of her drink.

Chapter Six

The discovery of a padded floral sunbed propped up at the side of one of the outbuildings was a bonus. With the sound of the birds singing and the stream trickling at the bottom of the garden, Jinny prepared herself for an afternoon of relaxation. These idyllic surroundings really did beat the din of the office and the sound of the cars in rush hour. Feeling like she'd just arrived on holiday, Jinny had changed her outfit and was now dressed in a bikini top with a pair of denim shorts to soak up the rays. She'd been reading for the last hour but with the combination of the travelling and a couple of large glasses of Prosecco she was beginning to tire. Fighting hard to keep her eyes open and with the warmth of the sun on her face she placed her book down on the edge of the sunbed and it wasn't long before she drifted off to sleep in the privacy of the cottage garden.

Jinny jolted slightly from her slumber and wafted her hand in front of her face. She thought she was dreaming but the strange sensation on her cheek was real, causing her eyes to spring wide open. With a racing heart she made a weird, strangled sound when she came face to face with a pair of humungous eyes staring back at her. A wet tongue swiped right across her nose, causing her to squeal and bolt upright. 'Get off me!' she yelled, stumbling to her feet and losing her balance when Claude took another opportunity to give Jinny a second lovable but wet lick across her face before he woofed excitedly, prancing on his paws while furiously wagging his tail.

'No more!' she stated, wiping the wet patch on her face with the back of her hand. Claude didn't hang around long, bounding to the side of the cottage and barking loudly. The sound of footsteps on the gravel could be heard and Jinny's heart began to beat faster, suddenly realising that if Claude was here no doubt Gabe was likely to appear around the corner at any second. Right on cue, their eyes met.

'I seem to have had a wash I wasn't expecting,' Jinny mused.

'Doesn't he just give the best kisses?' An amused Gabe looked towards Claude and attempted to reprimand him. 'Come here and behave yourself,' he ordered, patting his thigh followed by a click of his fingers. Jinny was impressed seeing Claude dance around Gabe before quickly settling by his side. Gabe patted his head. 'Good boy.'

'I'd thank him for licking me to death but—'

'He must like you,' interrupted Gabe, with a spark of humour.

'Here I am, lying asleep in my private garden, minding my own business and suddenly I get attacked...' Jinny teased.

'I think "attacked" is a little strong. Waking up being smothered in kisses can't be that bad?' Gabe grinned.

A sudden image of being woken up like that by Gabe hit Jinny and she gave herself a little shake. 'I'm living my best life – I have the sunshine, Prosecco, and dog slobber all over my face,' she joked, trying to cover up any hint of her wayward thoughts.

'He doesn't normally give out kisses at such an early stage but you must have caught his eye.' Gabe looked at her with a glint in his eye and the most kissable smile she'd ever laid eyes on.

She wasn't quite sure if Gabe was just being friendly or flirting a little, but she was charmed either way.

'Clearly he has very good taste,' she replied, embracing the playful banter.

With his eyes still locked on hers, Gabe picked up a tennis ball that was lying in the garden border and threw it down the lawn. Immediately, Claude gave out a playful woof and chased the ball before he was distracted by a scent in the bushes, which he began to investigate.

'Do you normally walk into people's gardens without an invitation? Is that what I can expect from village life?' she asked, wondering why he was here.

'I did knock on the front door but there was no answer.'

'Because I was out here.'

His dark eyes were still glistening at her and he was making Jinny feel nervous – but in a good way.

Claude loped back towards them and dropped the ball on the ground in between them. He'd obviously given up on the scent he had been chasing. Immediately they both bent down to pick up the ball and their heads bumped.

'So sorry,' Jinny apologised, feeling like an idiot and rubbing her head.

'You'll have concussion as well as sunstroke at this rate,' he said, sweeping a swift glance over Jinny's body before throwing the ball for Claude again.

Feeling a little exposed, Jinny realised her lack of clothes.

'Exactly how long have you been sunbathing?'

'Not long. Twenty minutes or so?' she replied, covering her chest with her arms.

'Really? That looks like a lot of sun for twenty minutes.'

Jinny looked down at her body and was mortified to discover it was glowing bright red. She quickly checked her watch. It couldn't possibly be that time. She thought she'd only closed her eyes for twenty minutes or so but judging by her watch it had been nearly three hours. 'Shit!' she exclaimed.

'You might want to think about getting some cream on that because it's going to be very sore.'

Gabe wasn't wrong. She could already feel her neck and shoulders tightening as she reached for her T-shirt, which was lying on the back of the sunbed. She should never have let herself fall asleep. 'That's first on my agenda, but what can I do for you?'

'I've come to measure you up for your beekeeper's suit. I'm on my way to town so I'll sort it today.'

Jinny was hoping at some point tomorrow that she would be able to convince Gabe that they could postpone that part of the training until she had the chutney part of the business fully under her belt but that didn't seem possible now as, before she could say another word, Gabe had pulled a tape measure from his pocket.

There was no getting out of it now as Jinny stepped away from the sunbed and stretched out her arms. Holding the tape measure under her armpit Jinny began to giggle and squirm. 'I'm ticklish!'

Gabe grinned as he tried again. Jinny reacted the same.

'I can see this isn't going to be an easy job.'

Jinny was still wriggling. 'Sorry!'

Gabe cocked an eyebrow. 'I'll hold the tape measure a little further away this time.' His eyes shone in amusement.

'Perfect,' she replied, briefly closing her eyes and inhaling his woody, masculine aroma, which made her heart beat a little faster, then breathing out only to find that when she opened her eyes, he was watching her. There was an undeniable spark of attraction between them; she could feel it and wondered if he felt it too.

'There, all done,' said Gabe, jotting down the measurements on his phone. 'I'll be off. There's cream in the top cupboard, on the left of the fridge,' he said, pointing at her sunburn. 'I've been caught out a few times while working in the garden,' he explained when she looked at him in surprise, not expecting him to know exactly where to find things in the cottage. 'There should be some left. See you in the morning.'

'You will,' she replied. 'In the meantime, I'd best go and get that cream.' She turned and walked away with a little sashay, knowing he was watching. She dared to look back over her shoulder and confirmed it, making a burst of adrenalin electrify her heart, something she hadn't experienced in quite a long time. Tomorrow couldn't come soon enough.

Chapter Seven

The next morning Jinny couldn't wait to start her day. She couldn't remember the last time she'd slept through the night and woken up in a good mood to the sound of birds singing through the open window. She'd chosen to sleep in the bedroom at the back of the cottage overlooking the gardens. The room was simple yet charming and characterful with beams running the length of the ceiling. The walls were white with a feature wall of light-pink wallpaper with delicate roses, allowing it to stand out. The bed was positioned opposite the window with a goose-down duvet and matching rose pattern bedlinen, adding elegance and charm with its pale-pink scatter cushions. There was also an old oak dressing table with a chair, and a huge rug thrown over the wooden floor. It was a magnificent room with an equally magnificent view.

Already she knew it was going to be a sunny day ahead.

The sun was beaming through the gap in the curtains, shining a horizontal pattern across the wooden floor. She pushed back the duvet and swung her legs to the floor, and with a spring in her step she opened the curtains and breathed in the fresh countryside air.

'Good morning, Heartcross!' she bellowed.

'Good morning, Jinny, and about time!'

Taken by surprise, Jinny nearly jumped out of her skin. Gabe was standing in the courtyard below, tapping his watch. 'I don't know what time you start work in the city but...'

'What time is it?' Panicking, she looked over towards the clock.

'Nine a.m.'

'Oh my... I'm so sorry,' she shouted through the open window. 'Give me two minutes,' she said, quickly moving out of sight. 'Damn,' she muttered, risking a tentative look in the mirror. Her hair resembled a bird's nest, her nose looked like Rudolph's and overnight it seemed she'd had an outbreak of freckles that were dotted over her cheeks, thanks to the sunshine.

'Ouch!' she exclaimed, trying to tame her hair by dragging a brush through it. Then with a quick squirt of deodorant and a couple of dabs of concealer in an attempt to tone down the redness of her face, she pulled on her shorts and a T-shirt then winced. Yesterday's sunburn was still feeling uncomfortable.

Feeling flustered – this wasn't how she'd planned her first day in her new life, with no shower and no make-up –

she pushed her feet into her flip-flops before hurrying down the stairs and flinging open the back door. 'I'm so sorry – I overslept.'

'Really? I'll be docking your wages at this rate,' joked Gabe, who shook his head in jest. 'This might be acceptable in the city but—'

'I went out like a light,' she interrupted.

'Sleep well then?' he asked.

'Too well, obviously,' she replied grinning.

'Are you ready now?'

Jinny nodded.

'Follow me.' Gabe was already walking across the patio, leaving Jinny to close the door before catching him up. She spotted Claude up ahead taking a drink from the stream before he began woofing at a frog that croaked on a nearby stone.

Gabe was leading them in a direction that Jinny hadn't explored yesterday. In front of them was a tiny stone archway that led through to a courtyard with twisted vines of coloured roses entwined in the wooden lattice roof above their heads. The wonder of the garden took Jinny's breath away. 'It's beautiful.' The words left her mouth on a tiny gasp as she took in the sight on front of her.

'Isn't it just and…' Gabe swooped his arm towards a table. 'Breakfast is served.'

'Have you done this for me?' exclaimed Jinny, suitably impressed. 'I wasn't expecting this.'

Breakfast was a small feast laid out on a red gingham tablecloth on top of a wrought-iron table. There was cereal, croissants, pastries, fruit, and next to the table on a butler's tray was a pot of tea, a jug of milk and a jar of honey.

'Do you do this for every new resident that arrives in the village?'

'Of course not,' he replied, doing the gentlemanly thing and pulling out a chair for her. 'Only for new residents at Bumblebee Cottage,' he added with a smile.

Jinny looked around in awe. This part of the garden almost felt enchanted. Littered with potted blooms, the whole area was colourful. 'This place is amazing. It must have taken many years to nurture and cultivate it into such gorgeous beauty.'

'Many years. I fell in love with this place the moment I saw it. It's something else, isn't it?' said Gabe, catching Jinny's eyes and causing her stomach to give a little flip.

'It is something else,' she admitted, watching as Gabe patted Claude, who had lain down in the shade at the side of the table.

Jinny wondered about Gabe and took the opportunity to steal a sideward glance at him. She couldn't help but notice his tanned face and his beard glistening in the sunlight. He was probably in a relationship – men as handsome as him were never single – but her journalistic tendencies had already clocked that there was no wedding ring, not even a ring mark.

'Tea?' he asked, pouring them each a cup from the teapot.

'This sure beats what I'm used to.'

'And what's that? Milk?' he asked, pushing the cup

towards her then passing her the milk jug, his hand brushing against hers and leaving a tingling pulse racing through her entire body.

Jinny hesitated. 'Cramming into a busy coffee shop and getting a drink that's too hot or too weak, before fighting my way to the Tube.'

'You said at your interview that your previous job involved admin. I'm not sure I could be cooped up in an office all day when you could have all this beauty around you.'

'I quite agree,' she replied, thinking about the frenzy in the office every Monday morning when their team meeting commenced, reviewing the weekend news reports. Jinny still felt a touch of guilt for not sharing at the interview that she had been a journalist and that her father was the proprietor of the most infamous newspaper in the land. But this was her fresh start and she wanted to leave the past behind by working hard and standing on her own two feet. She was also fully aware of her father's reputation and the part she had played, reporting on stories that had caused people upset. Her only regret was not walking away sooner.

'And yes, just boring admin.' The words had left Jinny's mouth before she could stop them. It wasn't as though it was an earth-shattering lie, but she didn't want to spoil the moment by having a conversation about her father.

Jinny wanted to know more about Gabe. 'What made you become a beekeeper? Who wakes up and decides that's their future career?'

'It started off as a favour for Dixie but the more time I

spent here the more I became involved in other aspects of her business. Gardening, vegetable growing, distribution, et cetera.'

'And what happens when I take over all this?' asked Jinny, as it suddenly occurred to her that she might be putting Gabe out of a job.

'I think there'll be enough for both of us,' he replied, pouring her more tea. 'Dixie always had a pot of tea waiting for me every morning and usually a sausage sandwich.' His voice wavered and she was surprised to realise he had teared up at the memory.

Jinny could see how much Gabe missed Dixie. 'Dixie really does sound like a remarkable woman. I've got a lot to live up to.'

'Just so you know, brown sauce on the sausage sandwich,' he added with a grin, as Jinny playfully swiped him with a napkin. 'But you're right. This place isn't the same without her. She was a remarkable woman who lived her best life and was extremely kind to me at a time when —' Gabe stopped himself.

'When…?' repeated Jinny, encouraging Gabe to finish his sentence as she was more than a little curious about what he was going to say next.

But Gabe quickly composed himself and swerved the conversation in a different direction. 'This is a special business because the chutneys are made by hand in the kitchen. Dixie loved it that way, knowing that she had handmade every jar that went onto the shelves.'

'That is some achievement,' said Jinny admiringly.

'It is, and on each jar Dixie would place a tiny sticker with a picture of a bee with a small pink love heart. It was her way of putting her own personal touch on the product.'

'That is so lovely!'

'And I'm proud to say the honey is award-winning. And because the best way to understand the business is to sample what you will be making and selling, I thought before I start showing you the ropes you should try the product. Yesterday was chutney and today it's honey.' He slid the jar of honey across the table.

Jinny picked it up. 'By the way, I love the name "Bees' Knees".'

'And it is exactly that. This honey is the best honey you will ever taste. It can be used to sweeten your dressings or marinades. Stirred into coffee or tea. Drizzled on top of toast or pancakes. Mixed into yogurt, cereal or oatmeal. The list is endless.'

Jinny was amazed. 'I never actually thought about all the different uses.'

'That's not all. Honey can also be used to make skincare products, or put on wounds, or help soothe a sore throat. It's gluten-free and – this fact will blow your mind – honeybees are the only insects that produce edible food for humans.'

Jinny was blown away. 'There's so much to learn.' She opened the jar and Gabe pointed to the croissants.

'Honey buttered croissants. Go on, try one.'

Jinny tore one of the croissants in half and took a bite.

Immediately sounds of approval escaped her. 'I've never tasted a croissant like that before.'

'Cam uses the honey to bake the croissants and they're a very good seller. Put some on the cereal and tell me what you think.'

Jinny tipped a small amount of cereal in a bowl, poured in the milk and added the honey as instructed.

'The best way to learn is by understanding the product – the taste – and loving it. It's all about the passion.'

'It's blooming good,' she admitted, now spooning a huge dollop of honey from the jar and plunging the spoon straight into her mouth. She caught Gabe smiling at her.

'Have you been making all the chutney and honeys since Dixie passed away?' she asked, waving the spoon towards him.

'Yes, with help from Molly. She took some time off work to look after Dixie in her final months and we managed between us. But now she's back working at the vet's we knew help was needed to keep Dixie's heritage alive. I mean, look at this place. Who would not want to live and work here?' Gabe gestured towards the orchards.

Jinny couldn't agree more. The cottage had a sense of calm about it and the beauty of the garden had literally taken her breath away.

'I think I'm very lucky to be here.'

'Rumour has it that once you arrive in Heartcross you never want to leave,' Gabe shared.

'I've already heard that rumour!'

'Please do say if this is a personal question but how are you able to leave your life behind so easily?'

Jinny didn't hesitate. 'Not too personal at all. There just wasn't anything I wanted to hold on to anymore,' she replied, thinking about the job, flat and car that she had abandoned at a moment's notice without a second thought.

'No husband or partner?' he asked, watching her closely.

'No husband or partner,' replied Jinny. 'Just me. How about you?'

'No husband or partner,' replied Gabe with a smile.

'You know what I mean.' Jinny rolled her eyes playfully but noticed that Gabe didn't give any more away.

'Let's finish our breakfast and get you up and running. This morning we'll begin with making the chutneys, then tomorrow we can introduce you to the bees.'

The look of hesitation must have shown on Jinny's face.

'Don't worry, you won't get stung if you're wearing your suit correctly,' he teased, before finishing his croissant.

Jinny scrunched up her face. 'Can I be truly honest with you? I'm not entirely sure if this is going to bode well but… I'm not too keen on bees.'

'I know. I could tell at your interview when you were freaked out by the fly. It's natural to be hesitant at first around the bees but soon it will become second nature,' reassured Gabe. 'Trust me.'

Jinny didn't have an alternative; she had to trust Gabe.

Five minutes later, having devoured another croissant each, mixed honey into their tea and spooned more onto their cereal, their plates were empty and Gabe stacked them on a butler's tray at the side of the table. 'Now it's time for proper work.'

As Jinny stood up, she held up her phone. 'Photo time! Breakfast at Gabe's,' she joked, turning around and holding the camera up in the air, positioning it so Gabe was in the background. But he quickly moved out of the shot before she had a chance to take the picture.

'It's for my new Instagram account,' she shared enthusiastically. '@jinnysnewlife.'

With Gabe obviously reluctant to be in the picture she snapped a photo of the table instead. 'There's not many followers at the minute though. Are you on Instagram?'

'No, I'm not,' he replied.

'Any reason for that?' she asked, thinking he must be the only person she knew not on Instagram.

'I like to live my life the normal simple way and don't need any validation from a world where I know no one.'

'But do you not think social media helps the world go round?' Jinny was intrigued by his unusual stance and wanted to know more.

'I don't feel the need to document my every move and have my life liked by strangers who have never crossed my path. And why do I need to shout to the world what I've eaten for breakfast?'

'But people can connect through social media.'

'I'm already connected with everyone that I need to be

connected with and if I have any news, I use this.' He held up his phone. 'A telephone was invented to talk to people and that's what I do – have conversations. All social media does is increase cyberbullying and lower people's self-esteem.'

Jinny could understand his opinion because that mirrored exactly what her father was encouraging his staff to do at the newspaper, but then there was a flipside too. 'But what about the positive aspects?'

'Are there any?' replied Gabe.

Jinny wasn't a hundred per cent sure but she felt slight tension in the air and had a sudden desire to prove him wrong. 'Of course! It can be used to advertise and promote business, just like what I'm doing now. I'm posting a visual diary. My first day in my brand-new life. Not only can I look back on it in twelve months' time to see how far I've come, my aim is to also to make Bees' Knees known all over the world. I'm going to be famous!' she joked, flinging her arms wide open.

'I love your enthusiasm but there's only one way to do that and that's the old-fashioned way – through hard work and determination.'

'I disagree, and it seems like taking over the business is not the only challenge I have on my hands. I'm going to have to prove to you that social media can enhance hard work and determination.'

'I think we'll have to agree to disagree on that.'

'But the world has to move on,' argued Jinny.

Gabe didn't answer. He looked lost in his thoughts.

There was a strange atmosphere hanging in the air and Jinny began to wonder if there was more to this conversation than what she was understanding.

'Have I said the wrong thing? I didn't mean to upset you,' Jinny said tentatively, not wanting any uneasy tension between them.

Gabe shook his head and pointed to one of the paths. 'Let's get to the kitchen. I can show you this week's orders and you can make your first batch of chutney.'

Jinny noticed that Gabe had swerved the conversation and it left her wondering what had prompted his strong opinions on social media, but she didn't push him and was determined to lift the tension. 'That sounds like a plan,' she said as they weaved their way back from the courtyard through the gorgeous flowers and plants.

'All this must take some watering, I'm guessing?'

'There's a sprinkler system, which is operated from one of the outbuildings.'

'I've only ever had a couple of house plants in my time and they both curled up and died.'

'Thank God we have a sprinkler system then because what you see before you has taken a lifetime to get as established as this.'

Thankfully the smile was back on Gabe's face as he bore left along another path. Claude was ahead of them and woofed when a butterfly fluttered near to his nose before it took off in the opposite direction. The honeybees were out in droves, buzzing around the wilderness garden, and flowers and plants in a multitude of colours danced up to her waist as they ambled along the hexagonal paving stones. 'Can this place get any more magical?'

'It's just something else, isn't it? Those are my favourites.' Gabe pointed to a section of tall pink flowers and with her eyes fixed on the beautiful array of blooms Jinny hit her foot on the stone step in front of her and tripped. Stumbling into the flowers she let out a squeal and grabbed onto a nearby post, her eyebrows shooting up in surprise as the palm of her hand hit a large red button. Time slowed as she heard a hissing sound then all of a sudden water gushed towards her from every angle.

She tried to move out of the way but it was too late. She was soaked.

From under her dripping wet fringe, she dared to gaze in Gabe's direction, only to see he had jumped over a nearby low stone wall and was out of the reach of the water.

'You can operate the sprinkler from that button too!' Gabe was trying to suppress his laughter. 'But I would suggest not pressing it unless you want to get soaked.'

'What's the point in putting it there?'

'It's just the system back-up. On a normal day you would operate it from the outbuilding.' Gabe couldn't hold it in any longer and burst out laughing.

'It's not funny!' she exclaimed, feeling embarrassed as she swiped the water from her arms.

'It's a little funny. Even Claude managed to dodge the drenching.'

'And my flippin' toe, it's throbbing.' Jinny looked down at her flip-flops. 'I didn't see the step.'

'And here was me, thinking you were falling for me.' There was a glint in Gabe's eye as he offered his arm. 'Let me help you. Sit here for a second while I turn off the sprinkler.'

Feeling a fool, Jinny held on to Gabe's strapping arm as she hobbled to the stone wall and took her foot out of her flip-flop.

'An accident on your first day of work,' he said, shaking his head. Taking a long stick that was strategically placed against a tree, he pressed the button from a distance. 'My money would have been on a bee sting, not a stubbed toe, but I suppose there's still time.' Gabe grinned.

'Oh gosh, don't say that.' Jinny was horrified at the thought. 'It'll be just my luck.'

'Hopefully your suit will protect you. How's your foot feeling now? Do you think you can walk or will I have to carry you?' he joked.

That very thought sent a tingling pulse racing through Jinny's body that she couldn't control. Pulling a face, she sarcastically said, 'I think I'll be okay.'

Gabe walked slowly as Jinny hobbled along next to him. He looked sideward at her. 'And really, don't worry about the bees. The key is to stay relaxed and calm and everything will be okay.'

The truth was that Jinny was not just worried about the bees – she was absolutely petrified of them.

'And just so there are no more accidents, can I just point out there's another stone step up ahead?'

Jinny rolled her eyes in a playful manner. 'I can see working with you is going to be a barrel of laughs.'

'Your sarcasm is noted,' he replied. His phone pinged just then and he pulled it from his pocket. He swiped the screen. 'It's Cam,' he said, reading the message. 'He's resurrected Dixie's car.' Gabe's smile was wide. 'I think it's a car that's going to suit your personality.'

Jinny narrowed her eyes. 'What does that mean?'

He shrugged playfully. 'I'm saying nothing except that Cam's just having it valeted and hopefully it will be ready this afternoon or tomorrow morning. He'll go over the paperwork with you so everything that needs to be filled out before you can legally drive the car is signed.'

'Can't wait,' she replied.

They chatted about the business as they walked back through the wilderness garden and followed the path towards the whitewashed building.

'Everything about this business is as organic as possible. We grow the main ingredients on the land here and recycle as many of the glass jars as humanly possible. Chutney has to be matured for at least three months to infuse all the flavours so in here you'll find the existing stock, but it's dwindling, which means you'll need to get ahead of yourself as soon as possible. And not to frighten you too much, but we need to begin making the Christmas stock so it's matured in time to go out onto shelves in late November.'

Jinny was already beginning to feel the pressure. 'It's too early to be thinking about Christmas.'

'Not in the chutney world,' replied Gabe, as he held the door open for Jinny who stepped underneath the trellis of roses keeping one eye on the honeybees that were hovering around the flowers and one eye on where she was walking. Claude seemed to know the drill and positioned himself in the shade underneath a bench outside.

Inside the building was a far cry from the picturesque outside. It was a rickety, run-down building that felt cold and Jinny immediately shivered as the chill air hit her wet skin. There were barrels of apples and crates of all different fruits stacked up against the walls along with shelves of filled jam jars.

'This is where we store the mature chutney. It's quite an easy system. When you make a new batch, they're put onto this shelf and the more matured chutneys are moved down a shelf. The ones right at the bottom are the most mature chutneys, ready to be delivered. Simple.'

'And what about the honey?' asked Jinny, looking around the room and noticing there wasn't any sign of the amber liquid.

'Dixie worked out of the cottage kitchen and keeps her stock in here, whereas George worked over in The Honey Pot and kept his supplies over there.'

Gabe picked up an oversized bucket and handed one to Jinny. 'We'll begin with the simple bestselling chutney until you get the hang of it. We cook up a month's supply over the course of a week, which keeps you ahead of the orders. Now fill that bucket up with apples, taking the ones from the back.'

'What happens during the seasons when there are no apples?' asked Jinny, beginning to carefully place the apples one by one in her bucket.

'You work three times as hard during the season when we do have apples. The more you can get ahead of yourself, the more time you have to play around with new recipe ideas... If you fill the buckets up like that it's going to take you forever.' Gabe picked up another bucket and scooped as many apples in at a time as possible. 'Like this.'

'But what if they bruise?'

'You're about to wash and peel them.'

Jinny looked between Gabe and the bucket. 'We have to peel all these apples?'

'No, *you* do.'

Jinny was horrified at the prospect and looked down at her perfectly manicured hands, the product of trundling off to the beauty therapist every couple of weeks for years. 'You have to be kidding me.'

'I kid you not! Hard graft is what this business is about. You don't work in an office now.' When Gabe's bucket was full to the brim, he began walking towards to the door. 'Come on. Over to the kitchen we go.'

The door swung shut behind him as Jinny attempted to lift the oversized bucket of apples off the floor. Gosh, it was heavy. She walked with tiny steps, careful not to drop the bucket on her toes. As soon as she was outside in the fresh air, she saw Gabe was already in the kitchen. She wasn't going to be beaten so easily. Blowing out a breath, she used all her strength to make it the short distance to the cottage and dropped the bucket on the step.

Gabe smiled and pointed to the aprons hanging on the hooks by the door as she entered. 'Put one of those on. Hairnets are in the left-hand side drawer of the dresser.'

Jinny picked up one of the aprons and smiled – it sported a cartoon bee that was winking above the words: *'Please beehive in my kitchen'*. She looped it over her neck and tied it around her waist before pulling on the hairnet. 'I look ridiculous.'

'It's not a fashion show,' replied Gabe with a slight smirk.

'You're smirking at me.'

'I am not. Pass me the other one.'

Jinny laughed when he popped the apron over his head. 'I'm assuming that was George's apron?'

Gabe smoothed down the apron. He was sporting a naked muscled torso wearing a kilt with the words: *'Is he a real man?'*

Jinny playfully swiped the tea towel at him. 'Are you a real man? What do you have under your kilt?' She gave him a cheeky wink.

'This apron was actually modelled on me,' Gabe said seriously before breaking into laughter.

'Do you have a kilt? Asking for a friend.'

'Maybe, maybe not. Now concentrate.'

'I'm not sure I can,' she mused, perching on the table and watching as Gabe took out two large pans from the cupboard, which he placed next to the Aga. 'Two pans. Start with one batch before moving on to the next.'

Jinny saluted. 'Yes, chef!'

'And get down from the table; it's against health and safety,' ordered Gabe, rolling his eyes.

Jinny jumped down. 'What next?'

'We need the order book – which should be in the top drawer – and the recipe book that Molly gave to you… And do not salute me.'

'Yes, chef!' She saluted again, hurrying towards the drawer and retrieving the order book before grabbing the recipe book. Then she perched back on the table but soon moved when Gabe gestured towards the chair.

'Sorry, sorry,' she said, leaning towards him.

'These are the rolling orders. There's enough chutney prepared for all of these and if a shop wants to change the order there is a back-up supply you can pull from. At the moment, we're looking at the November orders, which need to be made along with the Christmas orders that the shops have already placed based on last year's sales.' Gabe tapped the book. 'The Christmas orders are mainly for residents and some of the smaller delis over in Glensheil and of course the farm shops. Cam was thinking about setting up a website for online orders but that's still in talks at the minute. I suppose it depends on how well you do.'

'No pressure then.' Jinny watched Gabe walk over to a small table and pull open the drawer. He took out a book and placed it on the table in front of her. There were numerous columns scored down the first page and old-fashioned writing in ink pen. 'Is that Dixie's writing?'

'It is. This is your recipe bible, which outlines the exact quantities of each ingredient for the number of jars. Nothing more, nothing less. We're going to start with the classic recipe, filling twenty-five jars.'

'How do I measure everything out?' asked Jinny.

Gabe pointed to the old-fashioned scales on the side.

'All the mod cons,' Jinny joked.

'Dixie believed in the personal touch. First you need to start with the apples. Peel them and then weigh them. The peelers are in that drawer.' Gabe walked over to the cupboard and took out two large bowls, filling one with water and leaving the other empty. He then threw Jinny a pair of pink marigolds. 'You may want to wear gloves. Your hands can get a little sore.'

Jinny looked down at the quantities she needed and separated the apples. 'That's a big pile to peel.'

'It is.' Gabe separated a pile of apples for himself.

'I'll just nip to the bathroom before we get going.' Jinny was still staring at the pile of apples. This was going to be a long, tedious job but in order to make this business successful and give it the personal touch it was famous for, this was what needed to be done.

She'd only left the kitchen for a few minutes but when she returned Gabe looked smug. In front of him was a pile of peeled apples. Jinny pointed in shock. 'How the heck have you done that so quickly?'

'You've either got it or you haven't,' replied Gabe, holding an apple and a peeler towards Jinny. She stared at his pile then hers and was determined to peel them as fast as Gabe.

'Urghh, this is so difficult,' she said almost immediately.

'Have you never peeled an apple before?' Gabe grinned.

'Funnily enough I've never had the need. You can buy them peeled and chopped from the supermarket these days.' She placed down the peeler. 'Come on, there's no way you've used a traditional peeler. These are blunt! What's the trick?'

'Okay, busted. You have trusty Delilah to help you!' shared Gabe.

Jinny blew out a breath. 'Thank God. So, I have an assistant who peels the apples?'

'You have, and she's been in the business for a number of years and never missed a day's work in her life.'

Jinny was grateful. Delilah was sounding like her fairy godmother and she couldn't wait to meet her. 'Where is she hiding?'

'Right here,' replied Gabe, reaching under the table. 'Meet Delilah! Dixie's trusty friend. A hand-operated apple peeler.' Gabe placed it on top of the table.

Jinny's eyes widened; the contraception in front of her reminded her of a vice. 'What is that? It looks like something a mechanic would use.'

'Don't turn your nose up at her just yet! Delilah is going

to be your new best friend. She can peel that number of apples in less time than it took you to use the bathroom. Have a go. Like this.'

Gabe showed Jinny how to put the apple onto the peeler. 'There are three functions: peel, core and slice. Delilah takes five seconds to peel one apple.'

'I think I love Delilah,' joked Jinny, watching in amazement as she took less than five seconds to peel and core and apple, as promised. Once it was done, Gabe threw it in the bowl of water to be washed.

'That actually looks fun,' exclaimed Jinny, taking an apple but struggling to push it onto the hands of the machine.

'That's the tricky part.' Gabe stood and walked around the table towards her. She could feel his presence behind her as he leaned forward and placed his hand on top of hers. 'You need to give it a shove like this.' He pushed her hand and instantly the apple was secure on the peeler. 'Now crank the handle.'

'Okay,' she replied, biting down on her lip as she glanced up at him quickly. He really did have lovely eyes. As she turned the handle, Jinny was amazed. 'This is actually easy!' As soon as the apple was peeled and sliced, she copied Gabe and threw it in the bowl to be washed.

'If you carry on, I'll get the rest of the ingredients from the pantry,' Gabe offered.

As Jinny began to peel the apples, Gabe gathered the rest of the ingredients and lined up the empty jars, gingham lids and labels on a side table. 'All the labels you need are in these drawers and the other ingredients are in the pantry. Each month, you will need to do a shop and bulk buy the sugar, mustard seeds, etc. from the wholesaler. How are you enjoying it so far?'

'I was a little worried when I thought I had to peel all the apples by hand.'

'Delilah can be used for other fruit and veg too. You'll soon be in a routine and you'll have four different chutneys bubbling away on that stove.'

'What made you so good at making chutney?'

'Watching and learning from Dixie. She was the master,' he said, opening up the deliveries diary. 'There are no deliveries until tomorrow so today we can concentrate on making the chutney and ease you in slowly.'

In no time at all, the apples were peeled and Jinny swiped her hands together. 'Delilah is my new best friend.'

'You'll be chatting away to her and telling her all your deepest, darkest secrets before long.'

'It's a good job I haven't got any then, isn't it?' Jinny joked, but as soon as the words had left her mouth, she felt a twinge of guilt. She hadn't been completely honest about her background. Using her mother's maiden name was also playing on her mind, knowing that her driver's licence sported her proper name and Dixie's car needed insuring. She hadn't thought that one through.

'I'm wondering what deep, dark secrets Delilah knows

about you.' She held Gabe's gaze and for a split second she could have sworn there was a fleeting look of concern on his face, which took her by surprise. 'I was joking,' she added quickly, hoping she hadn't overstepped the mark.

'I know,' replied Gabe, walking over towards the Aga and placing the washed apples in the pan. 'Look at the recipe and measure out all the other ingredients, then we throw them all in the pan together, put it on the left side of the Aga and bring it to a boil.'

Just at that moment, his phone rang out and Gabe looked at the screen. 'I need to take this. Can you carry on?'

'Yes, chef!' She saluted, swizzling the recipe book towards her and checking the quantities of the rest of the ingredients.

'Once it begins to boil, stir then move it onto the simmering ring.'

Before Jinny could ask any more questions, Gabe had stepped outside to take the call. It only took a few more minutes to gather and measure the rest of the ingredients and it was soon bubbling away in the pan. Jinny felt a sense of achievement. 'This is so easy!' she exclaimed, whipping out her mobile phone and taking a few selfies. She posed with Delilah then captioned the photo:

Meet Delilah, a woman of many talents

Jinny admired the photograph, adding another with the caption:

My first day on the job! #JinnysNewLife

before uploading both. Then she stared at the screen. 'Oh my word,' she exclaimed, checking her notifications. The account was already gaining some momentum with a few hundred new followers since yesterday.

She began to read some of the comments from the last post.

You go girl!

Good luck with your new job!

You're on fire!

A new life, a new you!

The comments went on and on...

Jinny couldn't help smiling. The new account gave her a lift and a warm, fuzzy feeling inside. It had taken some guts to move her life north but she knew she had made the right decision. Everything was going so well. Heartcross was a beautiful place, the cottage was stunning, Delilah was a peeling machine and Gabe was definitely a bonus.

And there it was again, that instant flutter in her stomach every time he crossed her mind. Gabe was tall, dark and handsome with a good sense of humour, and as Jinny watched him through the window she chuckled at the sight of him animatedly talking on the phone while wearing an apron depicting a semi-naked man. She could tell by the way he fitted into his clothes so perfectly that he was a person who looked after himself. She had visions of him working out in the gym, going on early morning runs, kayaking down the river... Gabe made a pleasant change from the men she used to work with, the majority of them middle-aged overweight chainsmokers who made derogatory comments when any female walked past their desk.

'I am actually living my best life,' she said, switching on the radio before gathering up the apple peelings and throwing them into the bucket ready to take to the compost heap. Once that was done, she took the cloth and danced around the table, wiping down the surface. Feeling she had accomplished something, she poured herself a glass of water while waiting for Gabe to finish his call.

He appeared in the doorway. 'That was the deli over in Glensheil. They need an extra thirty jars by tomorrow. When this happens, you use the mature ones but it means we have to make more up as otherwise there will be other orders not fulfilled.'

'That's okay. We can do that, can't we?'

'This is your time to shine as I have to nip out. Something's come up. Follow the recipe and make four batches. I'll be back in a couple of hours. You'll be okay. Have faith!'

As she watched Gabe disappear, Jinny's mood slumped a little. This was her first day and she was enjoying his company, and now she'd been left alone, thrown in at the deep end.

'Come on, you can do this,' she told herself, clasping her hands and looking around the kitchen. There was one batch already under way. All she needed to do was to go and collect another bucket of apples and repeat the process. 'Easy,' she said, looking at the large pot on the Aga that was beginning to bubble. This moment needed to be recorded. Her very first batch of chutney was about to be made. Reaching for her phone, she propped it up against Delilah and set the timer. As soon as it counted down, Jinny beamed and introduced herself. 'Today is my first day at work and just look at this beautiful country kitchen.' She spun the camera around the room. 'And I'm here making chutney!' she said enthusiastically. 'Look at me go!' Jinny picked up the camera and showed the racing-green Aga with the pan bubbling on top. 'Do pop into The Old Bakehouse in the village of Heartcross where they stock all the chutneys from the Bees' Knees brand and do tell me what you think! I'd love to hear from you.' Jinny gave a little wave and stopped recording. Within seconds the video was uploaded to her Instagram and almost immediately notifications began to arrive. Leaving the phone on the table she picked up the empty buckets and with a spring in her step skipped to the back door to collect some more apples from the shed. Behind her, Jinny heard a loud gurgle, follow by a pop. She turned around but it was too late. Like a rabbit caught in headlights she watched in horror as the chutney began bubbling over. Without thinking, she rushed towards it just as a volcano of chutney erupted in the air, throwing huge fat dollops of chutney all over the kitchen.

'Damn,' she muttered, reaching for the pot.

'No! Don't touch that! It's hot!'

She spun around to see Gabe grabbing a pair of oven gloves before lunging forward to remove the pan from the heat.

'Looks like I turned up just in time,' he said, placing the hot pan on the stand.

'What are you doing back so soon?'

'I forgot my keys but it's a good job I did otherwise you would be burnt, and I would be calling an ambulance. Look at this place.' Gabe looked at the dripping chutney that was making its way to the floor. 'How to lose profit on your first day of work,' he joked, running the hot water in the sink and throwing a cloth into it. 'You didn't move it to the simmering plate.'

Feeling like a failure, Jinny swallowed down a lump in her throat and felt her lip begin to quiver. Out of nowhere she was engulfed with emotion. Usually everything had a habit of falling into place and as much as she hadn't been fond of her previous job, she had been blooming good at it. Suddenly teary-eyed, she cast her gaze to the floor. 'Sorry, I didn't mean to cost the business money.' Her voice faltered on the final word.

Gabe must have heard something was wrong in her tone as he quickly looked over his shoulder. 'Hey, I was only teasing. It's just a few apples.'

Jinny tried to hold back the tears but failed as a tsunami

rolled down her cheeks. 'Sorry, I don't know what's come over me. I thought I'd be good at this and I've messed it up completely.'

'Don't be daft. It's your first attempt. Let's look on the bright side – things can only get better. We all have to start somewhere.'

'But look at all the mess.'

'It's just chutney. If I let Claude in here, he'll soon clean this up.' Gabe grinned. 'Come on, it's not that bad. It's not worthy of tears,' he said tentatively.

Jinny blew out a breath and a small smile crept across her face at the thought of Claude being let loose in the kitchen and lapping up the chutney. Gabe gestured for her to step closer and he enveloped her in a warm hug. Resting her head on his chest she inhaled his aroma. The hug only lasted a few seconds but it felt good.

'I'm sure you're going through a number of emotions at the minute. You've piled a hell of a lot of stressful situations into a matter of days. I was all over the place when I first moved here. I'd left everything I knew behind me – my friends, my normal surroundings, changed job and moved house. Thankfully, Dixie was always on hand with her hugs, which made life a little easier.'

Jinny nodded. She hadn't realised how much it was affecting her. 'I just wanted to be good at this.'

'And you will be. This is nothing. I'll let you into a little secret – on my first attempt I burnt the bottom of the pan. Cooking on an Aga is a little different to a normal stove.' Gabe pointed. 'That's the rapid hot plate, that's the simmering plate. Hence why I said, as soon as it bubbles, move it across. Come on, we can start again.'

Jinny pointed to the door. 'I thought you had to go?'

Gabe glanced towards his phone. 'It can wait. Let's get this cleaned up, then I'll show you exactly what Dixie taught me and, by the end of the day, you'll know you were born to make chutney.' He reached into the sink and squeezed the excess water from the cloth.

'I hope so,' she said, feeling her mood lift. 'And thank you. A hug was very much needed. I didn't mean to cry on you.'

'That's okay. A cry does you the world of good and as long as you're feeling better now, that's all that matters.' Gabe was playful as he swooped his hand through the top of the bubbles in the washing-up bowl and flicked them towards Jinny. 'Unfortunately, Delilah doesn't clean up, so you'd best get the mop from the cleaning cupboard and here's the cloth.' He threw the wet cloth towards Jinny who caught it.

'I'm on it,' she said, feeling more upbeat now Gabe was hanging around.

'I'll go and get the next batch of apples and we can start again.'

Gabe headed towards the door and Jinny watched him for a moment. She liked the way he had just handled the situation, his kindness towards her, and she was intrigued to find out more about him. What was his story? How had he ended up in Heartcross?

Chapter Eight

The next morning, Jinny was determined not to make the same mistake twice so she set her alarm and was up in plenty of time to start work. While she was getting dressed, she thought back to the previous day and how caring Gabe had been towards her when she'd got upset. After comforting her so kindly they had worked side by side, Gabe showing her exactly how Dixie had made the chutneys, everything from the preparation to the spooning of the mixture into the jars. As soon as the mixture had cooled her job was to stick on the labels and add the batch date before storing them in the shed. It had been like a military operation. Peel, wash, boil, simmer and repeat. They'd put on the radio and Jinny sang and danced her way around the kitchen as they worked, much to Gabe's amusement.

Feeling fresh as a daisy, Jinny headed downstairs and wondered what today would have in store for her.

According to the order book she would need to make her first delivery and she was already feeling excited about meeting the locals and getting to know the area. As soon as she opened the back door to let in the early morning sunshine, she was amazed to discover a cardboard box sitting on the doorstep.

She bent to grab the note balanced on top.

Breakfast! I picked up some croissants from next door for you. I'm just on my way to pick up your beekeeper's suit. Back soon, Gabe x
Ps. Dixie's car is ready. Cam will bring it over later.

The first thing Jinny noticed was the kiss and she smiled as she opened the box. Three types of pastries looked back at her and the only decision she had to make right at that moment was which one to eat first. She laid the breakfast out on a floral china plate and made a pot of tea then positioned a jar of honey from the cupboard next to them on the table, on top of a yellow gingham tablecloth that she'd spotted in a drawer. It was the perfect country breakfast and she picked up her phone to take a photograph. Jinny knew the positive influence social media could have on this small business and as there was no current Instagram account for Bees' Knees she could just change the name of the one she had already set up and use it to promote the brand. With it she could give an insight into the daily workings of the business, and if Cam had plans to put the products online then the account would be a useful tool to engage with potential customers, which could rapidly grow sales.

After changing the account name to @beesknees, Jinny uploaded the photo of her breakfast, making the jar of honey the focus and captioning it: *#BuzzingForBreakfast*. Within seconds the notifications began to ping. The day was off to a good start. She tucked in to breakfast and propped Gabe's note up against the jar of honey. This afternoon, as soon as the wheels arrived, she could make a start on the deliveries. She was excited to meet her very first customer. The only slight problem with that was she couldn't leave Molly or Gabe sorting out the paperwork knowing the name on her driving licence wouldn't match the name she had given them. How was she going to explain that? Not wanting to jeopardise her position, she would need to sort this out herself as soon as she had details of the car.

While drinking her tea she searched for The Old Bakehouse on Instagram and gave them a follow. The chocolate shop was also featured and she watched a couple of reels of Cam and Bree baking bread and making chocolate. Their likes were in the thousands. Jinny began to think that she could do something similar with chutney or even making honey. She made a plan to chat to Molly and Cam about it and hoped she could convince Gabe to get involved, knowing that the followers would warm to him immediately, as she was doing.

Just at that moment her phone rang out, the screen telling her it was Jay. She swiped to answer and beamed as the call connected. 'Good morning! There he is, my bestie,' she trilled.

'There she is, Jinny living her best life,' he teased. 'How're things this morning in the Scottish Highlands?'

Jinny told him all about yesterday's breakfast and how the table had been laid in the garden. 'It was the perfect way to start my first day.'

'That sounds like a date to me.' Jay tilted his head to one side while he considered the evidence.

'Of course it's not a date but...'

'But what?' Jay narrowed his eyes. 'I know that look. You find him attractive!'

Jinny pinched her thumb and forefinger together. 'It was a working breakfast so I could sample the honey.'

'Is that what they call it these days?'

'Behave. Anyway, a little disaster struck after breakfast. I overboiled the chutney and had an emotional wobble but all is great again in the land of chutney and today my new wheels are being delivered.'

'Very exciting. You really have landed on your feet. I'm so pleased for you. Ping me over a photo of your new car when it arrives. I can't wait to see it. Ugh, I'll have to go as there's a delivery here, but catch up soon.'

'Thanks for ringing!'

After breakfast, Jinny began to hum along to the tunes on the radio while she labelled the rest of the chutney from the previous day's batch. As soon as they were done, she piled them in the wicker basket by the back door and took them over to the shed to store. Fifteen minutes later, she returned and noticed a beekeeper's suit draped over the patio chair. Gabe wasn't in sight but she knew he must be around somewhere. Lifting the suit and holding it up against her body she saw it was the least flattering outfit she had probably ever owned. Pulling it over her clothes, Jinny caught a glimpse of her reflection in the window. Thank God no one could see her now as she looked like a giant lumbering paranormal monster. There was a separate wide-brimmed hat with a veil, gloves and even boots. The boots fitted perfectly and once Jinny was fully kitted out there was only one thing to do – upload a photo to the Bees' Knees Instagram account.

With her mobile phone in hand, she outstretched her arm to snap the pic, then nearly jumped out of her skin as she checked the image. Gabe was standing behind her in the shot. 'You frightened the life out of me. Where have you popped up from?'

He grinned. 'I was just getting my suit from The Honey Pot. I see yours fits.'

'It does, and thankfully I'm not looking ridiculous on my own.' She ran an approving eye over Gabe, who carried off his suit to perfection, unlike her. 'Oh and just so you know, I've not been slacking this morning. I finished labelling the chutneys from yesterday and they're all stored on the correct shelf in the shed. Thanks so much for breakfast, by the way.'

'You're welcome… and not bad for a city girl.'

'I think there's a compliment in there somewhere.'

Gabe smiled and gestured towards the path into the

garden. 'Let's go and introduce you to the bees.' He began to walk but Jinny remained rooted to the spot.

He turned around and walked back towards her, giving her a playful push in the right direction. 'You'll like this, I promise.'

Jinny raised her eyebrows, not convinced in the slightest. Reluctantly, she followed him through the gardens, making their way towards the hives. She took a sideward glance towards Gabe, studying his face. She wanted to know more about him.

'Tell me about yourself,' she probed. 'Did you grow up in Heartcross? And how did you become a beekeeper?'

'Beekeeping was something I fell into when I met Dixie,' he answered. 'Dixie was a very persuasive woman and I didn't have a clue about bees. That's something we have in common.' A smile hitched on his face.

'I'd rather keep it that way,' she added.

Gabe grinned. 'She reminded me a little of my own grandmother. Dixie had a certain get-up-and-go about her, a kind, genuine woman who went out of her way to help anyone and everyone. That's what I loved about her. Dixie taught me all about the bees and her passion for this business was infectious. Then suddenly I was the new beekeeper.'

'But surely beekeeping doesn't earn enough to live on?' Jinny knew she was firing questions at Gabe in an interview style, a hangover from a lifetime of being a journalist, and a habit she knew she needed to learn to curb.

'I get by,' Gabe replied, not giving any more away. He

looked sideward and caught Jinny's eye. 'And how are you feeling today? Any homesickness kicking in?'

'Embarrassed for crying yesterday. I think it was out of frustration. I wanted everything to be perfect and I took my eye off the ball –'

'The pan,' interrupted Gabe.

'– for a second and looked what happened.'

'You won't be doing that again.'

'I won't and as for homesick, not at all. My relationship with my father can be described as somewhat difficult, even volatile at times. It's either his way or no way and to be quite honest with you, it's been like that since I was a young girl. I was passed from pillar to post growing up, from nanny to nanny, and he was barely around, too busy building his empire.'

'Empire? He sounds like a very important businessman.'

'Yes, he's a workaholic... but at the expense of his relationship with me.' Jinny heard her voice falter. Emotion was creeping up on her again as she thought about the fact that since her mother had passed away, home had never felt like home. It wasn't that she thought her father didn't love her but when she tried to pinpoint a time that he'd actually said those three words to her, she couldn't. 'Sorry, please forgive me...' Jinny brought her hands to her chest and swallowed down a lump. 'It's just... my mother passed away when I was young and it makes me sad to think about all the years I've been without her.'

'That must have been difficult.'

'What about your family?'

'My mum is living her best life in the South of France.'

This was the first real bit of information that Gabe had shared about himself.

'The South of France is beautiful. But why France?' she asked.

'She loves the lifestyle, the sun, the sea and a glass of vino every afternoon in her favourite bistro.'

'Why are you here then? The South of France sounds a little more appealing.'

'Just look at this place. Why would anyone not want to be here?' he replied, walking over the bridge and pointing at the rows and rows of beehives. 'Come and meet the bees.'

Shit a brick, was the only thought going through Jinny's mind as she stared out across the village of bees. She shuddered. Why had she ever thought it was a good idea to come face to face with so many bees on a daily basis? She'd once compared the newspaper office that she worked in to a den of lions but truth be told she'd rather face a pack of lions than this many bees.

'It's all good,' she said, shaking out her arms and trying to keep her composure.

'You okay? You seem to have lost the uncomfortable sunburnt look and gone a little pale.'

'I'm okay,' lied Jinny, her heart thumping. She had never felt so petrified in her life and she'd been put through her fair share of unsavoury situations in her last job.

'As luck would *hive* it, you're not on your own. However, I've forgotten the key to the padlock, so you're going to have to get your leg over.' Gabe had a glint in his eye.

'Now there's an offer. It's been a while,' she joked, holding his gaze flirtily. The gate was just about level with Jinny's waist. 'How the heck am I going to get over that?'

'You must have done the high jump at school.'

'Do you know how many years ago that was?'

'Too many to count,' replied Gabe, dodging a playful swipe from Jinny. 'Stand back.'

Jinny watched as Gabe took a few steps backward then ran towards the gate. He leapt into the air and used his hands to push on the top of the gate before swinging his legs over. He vaulted over with ease and his feet landed with a thud on the ground on the other side.

'I can't do that. You made it look so easy.'

'You can,' encouraged Gabe. 'Take a running leap.'

Jinny looked down at the suit then her eyes darted towards the gate. It was hard enough to walk in the suit, never mind launching herself over a gate. 'Shall I just go back for the key?'

'No, come on. You can do it.'

Jinny blew out a sharp breath then took a run at the gate.

'Jump,' shouted Gabe.

Jinny put her hands on the gate, leapt off the ground, and stopped in mid-air as one leg cocked over and the other didn't follow. 'I'm stuck,' she shouted. 'Help!'

Gabe burst out laughing. 'Swing the other leg over.'

'I can't.' Jinny's legs were flailing in the air. 'My nether regions are stuck.'

Grabbing the back of her suit, Gabe hauled her over the gate and her body fell to the ground, pulling Gabe right on top of her. Their hats had bounced from their heads and their faces were now centimetres apart. For a second they stared straight into each other's eyes before a bout of hysterical laughter escaped from them both and they collapsed into a fit of giggles.

'Am I alive?' asked Jinny.

'You are,' he replied.

'I can't believe you just yanked me over like that.' Beads of perspiration had popped up on her forehead, which she swiped with the back of her glove.

'I can't believe you couldn't get your leg over.'

'Believe me, I've had no trouble in the past with that.'

Their eyes were locked and for a second neither of them looked away.

'You can get off me now,' said Jinny.

'Sorry,' he said, pushing himself up then extending both arms and grabbing Jinny's hands. He pulled her to her feet. He was still laughing as he brushed the soil from his knees. 'Right, follow me,' he said, handing her back her hat.

Gabe strolled confidently into the field while Jinny hesitated, brushing herself down and donning her protective headgear before following him.

'Okay, a little bit about honeybees. All colonies are unique and each beekeeper will have a difference experience,' relayed Gabe, sounding all professional.

All Jinny could think about was that she didn't want any experience with any bees.

'General maintenance requires periodic inspections during warm months to make sure your queen is laying eggs...'

'And she's easily recognisable because she wears a crown?' Jinny was trying to make light of the situation but inside she was engulfed by fear.

'Trust me, you'll know which one is the queen. You also need to make sure your workers are building up honey stores and your colony has enough space to expand. During the colder months, if you last that long –' he grinned at her '– inspections are discouraged to keep from releasing precious heat from the hive. Management time and style will depend on your climate, your hive style and your particular bees.'

'I still don't understand why I need to know all this if you're the beekeeper.'

'Because you need to know and learn everything about the business and be a part of all that Bumblebee Cottage has to offer.' The glint in his eye left Jinny wondering if he included himself in that comment. 'You will get stung at some point,' he continued.

'You really aren't selling this to me,' replied Jinny. The whole of her life she'd avoided being stung by a bee or a wasp but looking at the number of hives it was a dead cert her luck was about to run out.

'A bee might end up in a fold of your clothing, go unnoticed and be unable to get out. Honeybees are mostly docile, and stinging is a last resort, because once they sting, they die.'

'It's in their best interests to keep their distance then.'

Gabe smiled. 'I can guarantee that in no time at all you will love this part of the job.'

'You're deluded,' Jinny murmured under her breath. She could feel herself shaking. She watched as Gabe went over to a large waterproof box but then he turned and walked back towards her, leaning in to sniff her.

'What exactly are you doing?' she asked raising her eyebrows and leaning backwards.

'Smelling you,' he replied, with a grin.

'I've had a shower this morning.'

'I'm glad to hear that you have hygiene standards. I'm just checking that you aren't wearing any perfume as curious bees will fly towards you, making it harder to work.'

Jinny wasn't liking the sound of this at all.

'And remember, gentle, calm movements will help to keep the bees calm. Are you ready?'

Jinny wasn't in the least bit ready but Gabe was still chattering away as he moved back towards the box.

'Bees don't make honey all year round and it won't be until the second year after a hive is established that they have any excess to spare. The amount of honey also depends on where they're located. We're lucky here at Bumblebee Cottage to have an abundance of flowers.' Gabe had stopped outside the first hive and turned towards Jinny.

'Gabe, I'm really not sure about this.' The words spilled rapidly from Jinny's mouth as she watched him place the boards on the ground then reach towards the hive. He glanced over his shoulder to find her walking backwards. He smiled as he reached out for her hand and grabbed hold of her glove. 'You have nothing to worry about. I've got you. Trust me.' Gabe looked deep into her eyes and even though she felt hesitant, she also knew she could trust him. Taking her first steps towards the hive, she breathed deeply.

'Sometimes I use a smoker but today I'm going to use a fume board and the beekeeper's claw,' he explained, lifting the lid of the first hive.

'Woah!' Jinny exclaimed, taking a step back.

'Stay calm,' he encouraged.

Jinny had never seen so many bees in one place. The panic had set in and her heart was racing.

'The bees will begin to move away now. Brace yourself.'

Jinny squeezed her eyes shut. 'I must have been so bad in a past life,' she muttered, taking a tiny peep. As promised, the bees began to swarm upwards, but Gabe didn't flinch. There was a sense of busyness about them and the drone of their combined buzzing filled the air as the bees swarmed out of the hive and flew frantically all around Gabe and then Jinny.

She squealed.

'Stay calm and still. No sudden movements,' Gabe repeated again. 'This is the easiest way to harvest the honey.'

Jinny wasn't convinced. Holding her breath, she watched wide-eyed as the bees continued to circle Gabe's entire body.

'This fume board contains an absorbent material that is sprayed with a non-toxic solution that the bees do not enjoy. So we place the board on top of the honey we wish to harvest so that they move away. Come a little closer. Take a look.'

Petrified, Jinny didn't move. She wanted to be anywhere else but here.

'Look, the bees are starting to move away and vacate the hive, which lets us remove the honey with minimal disturbance.' Gabe gave her an encouraging smile.

She couldn't help but notice his calm nature as he moved effortlessly around the hive and didn't let the bees bother him at all. 'Come on,' he encouraged again, 'take a look.'

As if by magic, the bees began to disperse and much to Jinny's relief, she started to breathe normally again. Cautiously, she stepped forward and grabbed on to Gabe's arm, making him smile, as she peered inside the hive. She wasn't quite sure what she was expecting to see but the reality was different to what she'd imagined. Never before had Jinny thought about how honey was made and now she was feeling undereducated.

She looked up at Gabe. 'Where's the honey? I expected to see lots of runny yellow liquid that we collect in jars.' She knew as soon as the words left her mouth that that sounded ridiculous, and she was proven correct when Gabe tried to stifle his laughter.

'Here's the honey.' Gabe grabbed a frame inside the hive that was crawling with bees. Jinny shuddered as she stood behind him and peered around his body. 'First, we shake off the bees.'

Jinny flinched and let out a strangled noise from her throat as the bees began to fly all around her. 'Stay calm,' ordered Gabe as he held up the frame. 'See, here's the honey,' he said, pointing to the frame. 'You know it's ready to collect when the honeycomb is capped with white wax. That means the honey will have the correct moisture content. Once we've removed the frame, we place it in the collecting box and replace it with another in the hive and put the lid back down. It's as easy as that.'

'Easy as that? It's the most petrifying job in the world.'

'I think there are worse jobs in the world,' replied Gabe.

There was something about Gabe's tone that made Jinny look towards him; she spotted a fleeting look of disdain on his face.

'Such as?' asked Jinny, intrigued by what had just triggered him.

Now walking towards the next hive, he didn't answer.

'Wrestling alligators?' she suggested, flapping her arms around her head to fight off the bees that seemed to be following her.

Gabe looked over his shoulder. 'Stop flapping your arms. You need to be calm.'

'Are you avoiding my question?' she asked, only half-joking as she had sensed that something about Gabe's mood had shifted. 'Come on,' she encouraged. 'What do you think is the worst career in the world?'

Gabe stopped in his tracks and looked directly at her. 'If

you really want to know, journalism is the worst career anyone can choose,' he replied.

Jinny had not been expecting that answer and the revelation took her by surprise. Thankfully the shock on her face was hidden by the veil of the hat as the thought crossed her mind that Gabe might have discovered her previous job and was testing to see if she would come clean. 'I still think wrestling alligators is a more dangerous occupation,' she replied.

'Much the same thing, isn't it?' he said as he opened the lid to the next hive.

'I suppose it is,' she replied. 'Hey, what do you call someone who's investigating alligators?' she asked, but Gabe wasn't playing ball. 'An investi-gator,' she added with a chuckle.

He still wasn't smiling.

She swallowed then bit the bullet. 'What is it you don't like about journalists?'

The bees were still swarming all around them but now Jinny was focused on Gabe. She watched him place the fume board down inside the hive before he turned back towards her.

'They're vultures with no morals,' he replied. There was a certain darkness in his eyes and from behind her mask, Jinny watched him closely.

Jinny was just about to argue the fact that there were good journalists out there but then thought about how disappointed she was in herself for not standing up to her father sooner, but continuing to report on jobs that she knew would cause pain to others. Trying to push those thoughts from her mind, she reminded herself she had at least finally done the right thing.

'What makes you say that?' she asked cautiously, knowing that something had triggered him but not wanting to upset him further.

'It doesn't matter,' he replied.

'I don't want to be stating the obvious here, but it does seem to matter.' Her voice was soft. 'Sometimes it's good to talk about the things that upset us.'

'Let's crack on,' he replied, not opening up any further.

Feeling a pinch of guilt, she nodded. Her relationship with Gabe was one of fun as well as work, and she didn't want the truth of her old employment to upset that.

Once again, the bees began to swarm round them and Gabe took a step back. He handed her the beekeeper's claw. 'Use this. Your turn,' he said. 'Lift the honey board out by using this on the edge.'

'Me?' she replied.

'Yes, you. You can do this,' he encouraged.

Jinny could feel herself shaking as she took a deep breath and took the claw from Gabe's hand. She walked slowly towards the hive. 'I'm not sure I can,' she replied nervously.

'There's nothing to be scared of. You're fully protected so they can't sting you and I'll help.'

Jinny's eyes were fixed firmly on the hive. She could feel herself shaking and her heart was thumping so hard that she hoped Gabe couldn't hear it.

'Try not to focus on the bees – just pretend they aren't there.' That was easier said than done. After all, there were hundreds of bees swarming all around her. But Gabe was standing directly beside her, and she could feel his closeness through the suit.

'Here, grip the claw like this.' Gabe leaned in towards her and took her gloved hand in his. He bent her fingers around the claw and eased her hand towards the edge of the board.

'Eek,' Jinny squealed under her breath.

'It's okay, I've got you,' said Gabe as he caught her eye. Feeling nervous – and she wasn't sure that was entirely due to the bees – Jinny lifted one end of the frame then the other.

'Try not to knock off the honeycomb,' encouraged Gabe.

Gabe took the claw from her hand as Jinny gripped the frame. She stole a furtive glance in his direction. 'I'm actually doing this.'

'You are,' he replied, giving her the tenderest of smiles.

'And look at those honeycombs,' admired Jinny. 'It's a perfect work of art.'

'Isn't it just,' Gabe replied. 'Now gently shake off the bees and place the frame in the box. You can tell that honey is ready as it's capped with white wax.'

Doing as instructed, Jinny replaced the frame and carefully closed the lid of the hive. She felt a sense of achievement and like a little child she gave out a squeal. 'I've harvested my first hive. They are clever little things, aren't they?' she said.

'Very clever,' repeated Gabe. 'Now, are you ready for the next one?'

Jinny couldn't quite believe she was about to say the next words.

'I think I am,' she replied, feeling a little calmer.

Over thirty hives later, the honey-coated frames had all been collected and they walked back through the garden. By the time they'd got to the last few hives, Jinny had barely noticed the bees at all. With Gabe by her side, she'd felt calm and proud of herself. Taking off her hat and mask she smiled at him.

'You look like the cat that got the cream.'

'Maybe I have,' she mused. 'And I survived without a sting.'

'That you did, and you will be pleased to know that you only have to do that two to three times each season, and that's harvest number one.'

Jinny stopped walking. 'So I don't have to do this every day?'

'No, but beehives require management and good stewardship, which takes time.'

They continued to walk towards the locked gate and Jinny gestured towards an overturned crate near to the hedge. 'I can use that to step over the gate.'

'That's what I keep it there for.' He grinned.

'Gabe! You made me...'

'Sorry!' He held his hands up. 'I couldn't resist.'

Jinny shook her head in disbelief as she retrieved the crate and easily manged to climb the gate. 'I'll know for next time.'

They were soon back in the courtyard and Gabe pointed to The Honey Pot. 'That's where the extraction takes place.'

'Sounds painful,' replied Jinny. 'Shall we grab a drink first? I'm feeling a little thirsty.'

'Good idea. I'll meet you back at the cottage.' Gabe headed towards the outbuilding carrying the box of frames.

This place was the cottage that just kept giving. There were nooks and crannies everywhere and despite her initial reservations about the bees, Jinny felt proud of herself for overcoming her fear and not showing herself up too much in front of Gabe.

As soon as she got back to the cottage, she took off her gloves and opened the back door. The first thing she did was check her phone. Once more, the brand-new Bees' Knees Instagram account was littered with notifications and likes of her recent upload. Her followers had increased tenfold and Jinny couldn't quite believe she had begun to successfully build the brand.

Taking the opportunity of being dressed in her beekeeper's suit, Jinny put back on her hat and mask and was posing in front of the flowers that were dancing in the wind behind her when Gabe, minus his beekeeper's suit, came ambling down the path towards her.

'I've been thinking,' she said.

'That sounds dangerous already,' he answered, with a snigger.

'I want to give this business everything I have and I was looking at The Old Bakehouse's Instagram and I saw that Cam and Bree shoot little videos, which creates a great opportunity for lots of interaction for their business. I was thinking we could do the same.'

'No, that's not for me, thank you. Shall we get that drink?' He gestured towards the kitchen and walked away, cutting the conversation off without as much as a discussion.

He wasn't old enough to be part of the generation that didn't like change or had trouble understanding the advances in technology and social media and so she was surprised that Gabe couldn't see the advantage of increasing the profile of Bees' Knees on social media as that could possibly lead to more revenue.

Jinny followed him. 'You can talk to me, you know,' she said.

'About what?'

'About why you don't like social media or journalists.'

For a moment a heavy silence settled over them, things feeling uneasy again.

There was a second when Jinny thought he was going to say something but as the silence grew, he kept his eyes firmly on pouring the drinks.

'Sometimes talking about things can help. A problem shared and all that...'

'It's nothing, just family business.'

Jinny treaded carefully. 'I can see that it's causing you some upset. I hope you can sort it out soon.'

'I've struggled with a situation for a while but there's nothing that can be done about it. There's only me who can sort it but thank you.' Gabe didn't say anything else as he handed her a glass of lemonade, his hand brushing against hers, the feel of his touch sending a shiver down her spine.

They walked outside and before she sat down at the patio table, Jinny wriggled out of her beekeeper suit. 'I know I don't know you well but sometimes it's good to talk. I feel like I owe you and Molly a lot already. You rescued me at such a trying time in my life. It's not easy standing up to your father when he's a difficult man. He told me I'd never be able to stand on my own two feet and that I would be nothing without him.' She waved an arm. 'I don't call this nothing.'

She was hoping that she had shared enough about her own situation to prove she was a genuine person and that she really did want to help but, not wanting to cause any further tension, she smiled and changed the subject. 'I really have enjoyed today, though not so much having to jump over a gate. Do you fancy a slice of cake? There's still some Victoria sponge.'

'You've twisted my arm and thank you. Believe it or not I've really enjoyed today.'

She blushed prettily. 'Glad to hear it.' Once inside the kitchen she batted different scenarios in her head as to why Gabe might not like social media or journalists but all she could do was hope that in time he would trust her enough to open up to her.

'Cake!' she exclaimed, placing a huge slice down on the table in front of him.

'The diet starts tomorrow,' he said with a smile.

'It's always a Monday for me,' she added, sitting down on the chair. She squealed and immediately sprang back up, knocking the drink over, which soaked her T-shirt. Gabe reacted quickly. With an outstretched arm he miraculously caught the glass centimetres from being smashed to smithereens on the ground. He blew out a breath then placed the glass carefully back on the table before giving Jinny a lopsided grin, but immediately he realised something was wrong.

'Ouch! Ouch! It's burning. My bum is on fire.' She was dancing around trying to look at her backside then caught a glimpse of Gabe, who was now laughing.

'Oh my! You've been stung, haven't you?'

'I think so. It really hurts!'

'How have you managed to navigate thousands of bees in one afternoon then…'

But Jinny wasn't listening. 'It's still stinging.'

'No shit, Sherlock. That's what happens when you sit on a bee.'

'I'm hot.'

'I have no words.' He laughed harder.

'I mean it feels hot.' Jinny was stepping from side to side while attempting to waft her backside. 'Do something.'

'Would you like me to take a look?'

Jinny's eyebrows shot up. 'What, at my backside?'

'You just told me to do something. I can pull the stinger out before it releases any more venom.'

'Er, no! It's mortifying enough without you... And just look at me!' She cast a glance downwards.

Gabe took a cautious step back and his eyes swept over her entire body. Jinny could feel the crimson burn in her cheeks intensify and didn't know which was more on fire, her cheeks or her backside.

'I am,' he replied, running his hand through his hair.

Jinny was momentarily thrown by Gabe's hazel eyes staring straight at her.

She looked down towards her sodden T-shirt. 'I'm soaked.' Jinny's wet top was clinging to her breasts. She quickly folded her arms, trying to draw his gaze away from her chest back to her face.

'At least being soaked has taken your mind off the bee sting for a second.'

Jinny went to sit down and shot back up again. 'I can't even sit down.'

'Are you sure this isn't the time to whip your phone out and post a pic?' he joked. 'The amount of likes you gain might take the edge off of it.' The amusement was written all over Gabe's face.

'I'm not even going to rise to that,' replied Jinny. This was definitely not a moment to photograph for Instagram.

'Everyone would *bee buzzing* about it.'

'This is not funny.'

Gabe threw his head back and laughed. 'You have to

admit, it's quite funny. The first couple of days in the business and there's been a chutney explosion, a sprinkler soaking, getting stuck on a gate and now a bee sting. Oh, and you're covered in lemonade, which will attract more bees as they love lemons.'

Jinny quickly surveyed the area, but thankfully there wasn't another bee in sight.

'As first weeks go, it's up there with the best. Surely you can see the funny side?' A wide beam hitched on Gabe's face and Jinny could feel herself beginning to laugh.

'It so stings though!'

'I will take a look if you want me to.'

'I do not!'

'Then in that case, I suggest I take over this afternoon's deliveries and I'll tell Cam to hold fire on bringing the car around. That way you can walk down to Peony Practice – just head out of the gate and turn left – and take the rest of the day off. The doctor can take a look and give you some cream.'

'I think I might just have to do that,' replied Jinny.

'And hopefully tomorrow you'll manage a full day in the job,' Gabe teased.

'I hope so.'

Five minutes later, after a change of clothes, Jinny appeared back in the garden. 'I'll be off. What about the honey boards?'

'They'll keep. Now go and sort out your backside ... something I never thought I'd be saying to you in your first week at work.'

Jinny grinned. 'Me neither. Catch you later,' she said, locking the back door behind her. As she followed the gravel path around to the side of the cottage, she summoned up enough courage to glance back over her shoulder only to find Gabe's eyes still locked on her. They grinned foolishly at each other and Jinny shook her head lightly before turning back around and shutting the garden gate behind her. There was something about Gabe that had her blushing uncontrollably.

Chapter Nine

R *ing... Ring...*
Jinny was woken from her slumber by the sound of her phone ringing. She prised open her eyes and grabbed it from the bedside cabinet. Still half-asleep she swiped the screen.

Jay laughed uncontrollably in her ear. 'I've just read your text from last night. Please tell me you didn't drop your pants in front of your boss.'

'Why are you phoning me at this hour of the morning? And of course I didn't. Even though under different circumstances...'

'Ooh, tell me more,' Jay encouraged. 'Exactly how hot is your boss?'

'Very. But he's my boss. Well, not technically my boss, but teaching me the ropes,' replied Jinny, feeling herself smiling as the words left her mouth. 'Now if you don't mind, I'll ring you back later. I still have another hour of beauty sleep to take advantage of.' Before Jay could say another word, she hung up and slid back under the duvet. Yesterday afternoon had been embarrassing enough, arriving at Peony Practice and having to endure the humiliation of the doctor pulling out the stinger and swabbing the area with antiseptic before sticking a My Little Pony pink plaster on her backside. Jinny wasn't sure which aspect of the whole experience was more embarrassing.

Yesterday, Gabe had taken care of the deliveries and today Jinny was determined to get through a full day of work with no more mishaps. She was beginning to think she was accident-prone. Now wide awake thanks to Jay's early morning call, she reluctantly threw back the duvet, slipped her feet into her slippers and wandered downstairs to make a cup of tea. Noticing a slip of paper on the doormat, she picked it up.

Your carriage awaits! Call in next door when you're up.
Love Molly x

My new car, thought Jinny excitedly, walking towards the kitchen and switching on the kettle. After making a cup of tea and eating a slice of toast she began to panic a little about the car insurance. Everything was going so well here and she knew it was possible that coming clean about her identity would put her job and home at risk, especially after Gabe had shared his intense dislike for journalists. The best thing to do was insure the car online herself as soon as she knew all the details.

Thirty minutes later, Jinny was showered and dressed. Following the gorgeous aroma of freshly baked bread she headed towards The Old Bakehouse. The door of the shop was wedged open and customers was already queuing at the counter. Molly was juggling a baby in her arms and Jinny assumed Cam was the guy wearing the baker's hat.

Molly spotted her. 'Good morning! Cam, this is Jinny. You haven't met yet.'

He looked up from serving a customer and smiled in Jinny's direction. 'Welcome to Heartcross! I'll be with you in a minute,' he called over before carrying on serving the customers.

Molly walked over to stand next to Jinny. 'Lily's having trouble sleeping in this warm weather,' she shared, looking towards her daughter.

'She's so adorable,' replied Jinny, taking her tiny hand in her own and giving it a squeeze.

'Oh, she is, but she has her moments and that's usually in the middle of the night when she's testing whether her lungs still work. But we wouldn't have it any other way,' added Molly, pressing a swift kiss to the top of Lily's head.

Looking down at the gorgeous baby in Molly's arms, Jinny wondered if she would ever be a mother herself. She'd always wanted a family but her body clock was ticking fast and there had never been that special person to make a life with. Of course she'd had boyfriends, but there wasn't one who'd kept her attention long enough for her to commit to. And of course it had been difficult maintaining a relationship in her previous job.

'You're very lucky.'

'Before I forget, Gabe is running a few errands this morning and will be in this afternoon. As soon as we get you insured on Dixie's car you can head out to make the deliveries in the book. There's just a few to local residents and then to the deli in Glensheil.'

'Not a problem at all,' replied Jinny.

'And how's it going so far?' asked Molly, laying the baby down in the pram that was at the side of the counter.

'I'm absolutely loving it. I've made the basic apple chutney and I've been introduced to the bees; next I'm looking over the books and invoices and learning about bottling the honey.' Jinny thought she'd spare herself the embarrassment of sharing that she had been stung on her backside.

'It sounds like we made a good choice and you have everything under control.'

As soon as Cam had served the last customer he turned to Jinny. 'Pleased to meet you at last. I've heard so much about you. How are you settling in?'

'All good, and thank you again for giving me this chance.'

'I left the interviewing in Molly and Gabe's capable hands and they assure me you were the best candidate to carry on my grandmother's business. I have every faith.'

'I won't let you down. I have a few of my own ideas of

ways to promote the business that I would like to run past everyone.'

'Now that's what I like to hear.' Cam reached inside the drawer and pulled out a small bunch of keys that were attached to a bee-shaped keyring. He waggled them in the air. 'But for now, it's time for you to meet Donovan!'

Puzzled, Jinny looked between Molly and Cam.

'Your new car,' explained Molly. 'Named by Dixie.'

Jinny was beginning to realise that Dixie had been keen on naming all bits of machinery.

'He's taxed and he'll take two minutes to insure. We asked Gabe to sort out the paperwork yesterday afternoon but I think something came up,' added Cam, giving Molly a look. The pair of them burst out laughing.

'You know, don't you?' Jinny shook her head and rolled her eyes while smiling. 'Yep, I got stung right on my backside and my first appointment with the local doctor was pulling out the stinger.'

'You couldn't write it, could you?' Molly grinned. 'Let's hope today runs smoothly.'

'I plan for every day forward to run smoothly,' replied Jinny.

'And please look after Donovan.' Cam was talking like the car was actually a member of the family. 'Are you ready to meet him?'

'I can't wait,' enthused Jinny, watching Cam disappear out of the back of the shop while Molly ushered her out onto the pavement.

Jinny looked up and down the road but all she could see was the post van in the distance.

'Just you wait. You and Donovan are made for each other. He's going to be right up your street.' Molly nudged Jinny's arm and nodded towards the small track that led to the back of The Old Bakehouse.

There was a loud bang as a car backfired and Jinny's mouth fell wide open as a fluorescent-green Volkswagen Beetle covered in brightly coloured flowers and bees kangarooed towards them. Jinny couldn't take her eyes off the car. It was the quirkiest vehicle she had ever set eyes on. 'Oh my gosh, would you look at that. It's utterly fabulous! Full of character!'

On the roof of the car was a rack, upon which was a stack of battered old suitcases. Molly pointed. 'You can fit a hundred chutneys in each case. Perfect for deliveries.'

'I just love it!' cried Jinny, watching as Cam pulled the car up right in front of them. He grinned and patted the wheel before climbing out.

'Ta dah!' He flung his arms open wide. 'What do you think of Donovan? He's amazing, isn't he? Vintage!'

'He is just that,' replied Jinny, with a huge beam on her face. She walked around the car taking in the chrome bumper, the huge round lights on the bonnet and the painted flowers. 'Just... wow! He's so quirky. Where does "Donovan" come from?'

'He was named after one of my grandmother's favourite singers,' Cam informed her. 'My grandfather, George, bought this Volkswagen Beetle new just before their very first trip abroad to the South of France. He had grand plans of proposing in the grounds of a palatial château that they'd stumbled across in a magazine—'

'However,' interrupted Molly, 'the proposal took place right across there.' She pointed towards Primrose Park. 'At the bandstand. George couldn't wait – he was too excited – and they travelled to France as a newly engaged couple.'

'Donovan was a huge part of their first adventure abroad and got them back safe and sound. He's been in the family ever since and we could never part with him.'

Jinny could see the happiness in Cam's face when he talked about his grandparents and Donovan. This car held so many memories for the family.

'And that's actually where the idea for the business was born. My grandfather had organised a few days' stay along with a romantic meal in the grounds of a French château that was owned by Margo Laurent—'

'A huge Hollywood superstar,' chipped in Molly. 'It was during that visit that she and Dixie became firm friends and Dixie was actually inspired to write her first chutney recipe in the grounds of the château.'

'Wow,' replied Jinny. Margo Laurent was a legend, a film icon. If she was still working for the newspaper, this would have been the perfect uplifting story to report.

'It's quite something, isn't it?' Molly asked.

'Yes. I can remember my grandmother being sad when Margo passed away,' chipped in Cam.

'I remember,' replied Jinny. 'I read about it in the

newspaper,' she quickly added. 'That must have been around seven years ago now?'

'Yes, that's right,' replied Cam. 'Actually, three years before she passed away, Margo came to visit Dixie here in Heartcross. She stayed at Bumblebee Cottage but it was all kept very low-key as she didn't want any press intrusion. Even though Margo was in her nineties, journalists were still obsessed with her every move.'

'Typical newspapers,' chipped in Molly.

Cam slapped the bonnet of Donovan. 'Anyway, this one became the face of my grandparents' little business empire. He's even paraded in fêtes and classic car shows, not to mention being featured in magazines and a couple of TV shows. Dixie loved this car, treated it like it was one of the family. She talked about that holiday for years. Go on, take a look,' he encouraged, his enthusiasm infectious. 'Get behind the wheel.' He handed the keys over to Jinny. 'That's the ignition key, those are for the suitcases on top of the roof and we could never quite work out what this one is for.' Cam separated a small silver key from the rest. 'But we kept it on the keyring anyway.'

'Are you sure you want to trust me with Donovan?' asked Jinny, knowing this was a huge responsibility. 'And I still need to sort out the insurance.'

'We can do that in a moment,' replied Molly.

'Honestly, you've got enough on your plate. It won't take me long and it'll be easier if I just sort it myself.'

'Are you sure?' asked Molly.

'Of course.'

'And you will take good care of him?' said Cam

'That I will,' reassured Jinny, rattling the keys in her hand. 'Thank you. I really do love him already.'

'Have a quick spin around the green; there's no one about.'

'Are you sure?' asked Jinny.

'It's only a quick lap. He can be temperamental at times but he's very reliable and will treat you well.'

'Can I just get a quick photo first?' Jinny asked, whipping out her phone and posing in front of the bonnet. Molly and Cam grinned at her.

'You certainly do suit each other,' shared Molly.

The photo was instantly uploaded to the Bees' Knees Instagram account and captioned:

My new company car. Meet Donovan!

Jinny was already in love with Donovan. He was indeed vintage and quirky and was exactly what he said on the paintwork: the Bees' Knees. He was the polar opposite to the brand-new convertible BMW with all the latest mod cons that Jinny had left behind. Embracing her new wheels, she opened the door and slipped into the driver's seat, and immediately noticed how immaculate it was inside. She smiled at the dashboard. Donovan was all about flower power, with a vase and a fake flower blooming.

Cam was mouthing something at her through the window and she automatically reached to the inside of the driver's door, looking for a button to lower the window, then grinned, realising there were no electric windows. Leaning over the passenger seat, Jinny used the handle to wind down the small window.

'I've got to go back to the shop and check on Lily. The tank is full. Happy delivering.' Cam waved his hand above his head.

'And I'll wait here until you've driven around the green,' said Molly, still standing in the same spot on the pavement.

Jinny gave her the thumbs-up then put the key in the ignition and pulled on the seatbelt.

'Just give it an extra tug,' shouted Molly.

After Jinny fastened her seatbelt, she adjusted the mirror and turned the key. Immediately Donovan fired up and the old radio crackled. She looked over her shoulder to check the coast was clear. It had been a long time since she'd driven a manual car and the gears were going to take a little getting used to as she clunked her way to first before kangarooing down the road until she'd navigated the clutch. The beam on her face felt huge and soon she was getting the hang of it. She waved at Molly out of the window and within seconds was pulling back up outside The Old Bakehouse.

'That was epic. He's just the best,' cooed Jinny, now standing on the pavement again. 'I can't wait to start the deliveries.'

'I'm so pleased. As I mentioned, today's main delivery is the deli over in Glensheil, which is owned by Tom. The address will be in the back of the order book.'

'I can just check the sat nav—' She stopped in mid-flow then laughed at her mistake.

'You'll find an old-fashioned road map of the town underneath the seat. But Tom's deli is easy to find. Head for the track over the bridge, keep along the main high street then turn left by the gin shop – Glensheil Gin. Follow the back road down past the river and you'll pass the houses on the right. The first set of semi-detached cottages are just so quaint, then you move on to Millionaires' Row. Most have boats or yachts and numerous posh cars on the drive—'

'But I bet none have the character of Donovan,' cut in Jinny.

'That they don't. Then after the last gated property bear right and the deli is up on the left. Now, I'd best get back and relieve Cam of Lily. I start the night shift at the veterinary hospital tonight and my next free day off is next week. If I don't see you before, I'll see you at the pub BBQ.'

'It's in the diary and I'll definitely be there. And where did you say Gabe was? Will he be in later?'

'Just running some errands,' replied Molly, not giving any more away. 'How are you finding working with him? He's so down-to-earth, isn't he?'

'He is, thankfully,' replied Jinny, thinking of all the mishaps in the past few days. 'And he's already passed on to me some of Dixie's working practices, including introducing me to Delilah!'

'The fastest apple peeler in the whole of Heartcross,' said Molly, smiling as she walked back towards the bakery. 'And don't forget to insure Donovan. Any problems, Gabe's number will be in Dixie's old telephone book, in the drawer of the table in the hallway.'

Jinny was thinking fast on her feet. 'Just under Gabe?' she asked.

'Maybe under Gabe Warner.'

They both heard Lily cry out and Molly quickly disappeared inside the bakery.

Once back in the cottage, the first thing Jinny did was make a phone call and insured Donovan, which was thankfully an easy task. She still felt guilty for duping Molly and Gabe about her surname and her past employment, especially after Gabe's revelation about his distrust of journalists. She began to think about his reaction more and wondered whether he had been involved in some sort of bad press that had escalated on social media, as that would account for why he couldn't stand either.

Grabbing a quick cup of tea before she made her first delivery, she settled in the armchair in the living room and as curiosity got the better of her, she punched Gabe Warner's name into Google on her phone. There was no evidence of him being on social media, which didn't come as a huge surprise because that was what he had indicated, and there was no press scandal or any trace of him on the web. Maybe he really was just a private individual who preferred to go about his business without parading his every move before the world. Finishing her tea, she stuffed her phone in her pocket and headed outside. There wasn't a sound to be heard. Jinny was embracing every second of the beauty and solitude of this place. She owed Molly and Cam for giving her this opportunity and could weep with gratitude. This business was in her hands and she had plans, big plans, and was going to work so hard to bring them to fruition.

The morning sun was beating down and Jinny jumped as the sprinklers in the gardens and orchard turned on suddenly. They must be on a timer. There was so much to learn. En route to the shed, Jinny grabbed the wheelbarrow, which would be perfect for transporting the chutneys to the suitcases on top of Donovan.

Proud of having successfully loaded the delivery, she was officially on her way to make her first drop-off. Travelling down the high street, she could see Donovan was turning heads. Tourists were pointing towards the car and waving, so Jinny beeped the horn and waved back at them, loving every moment of the drive.

She was delighted that she'd stumbled across the village of Heartcross. She was enjoying the slower pace of life and actually talking to people, and being part of a community that looked out for each other.

Donovan bumped over the uneven track leading out of the village towards the bridge and soon Jinny was driving through the main town of Glensheil and taking in more of the sights. It was just how she had imagined it would look, a pretty town with views of the River Heart and the stunning countryside with mountains towering in the background. The high street was lined with boutique shops, delis and fancy-looking bistros. She couldn't wait to spend time mooching around the town. Up ahead was a sign for an ice-cream parlour and next door was Glensheil Gin. Jinny slowed down at the traffic lights, indicated left and began to drive up the road that ran parallel with the river.

'Just look at that view,' she murmured. She could get used to seeing that every day. There were boats bobbing along on the water, kayaks sailing under the bridge and children standing on the rocks swooping their fishing nets into the river. It was the perfect summer's afternoon. Glancing sideways, she noticed the gorgeous cottages built in traditional stone with charming gardens. Each house along this stretch had its very own boat dock too. This part of the town had the best of both worlds – the tranquillity of the water and the proximity of the town for restaurants and bars. The perfect combination.

Driving slowly and taking in her surroundings, Jinny couldn't help noticing the towering house on the corner, which wouldn't look out of place in a lifestyle magazine. It was something else. Standing on a huge plot and guarded by electric gates, it must be owned by a well-known business tycoon or a famous person, she thought, because a place like that wouldn't come cheap. Indicating right and turning into the side road, Jinny immediately spotted the deli. It was just as she had imagined, with blue and white striped awnings shielding the front windows of the shop and gorgeous hanging baskets tumbling with purple and white petunias hanging from each side of the door. According to the chalkboard standing on the pavement outside the doorway, they served coffee too, and under the awning were spaced out bistro tables and trendy wrought-iron chairs with padded cushions.

Jinny pulled into the vacant space on the road just outside the deli and cut the engine. She checked her appearance in the mirror. This was her first delivery and she felt a sense of achievement as she smoothed down her hair and applied a little lip gloss. In the reflection of the mirror, she caught sight of a man standing at the ice-cream cart and did a double take before looking over her shoulder. There was Gabe, buying a couple of ice-creams from the cart on the other side of the road. She looked around but he didn't seem to be with anyone. Jinny knew he couldn't be going far with melting ice-creams in each hand. She was just about to get out of the car and shout over to him but he was already on his way down the busy street. Then, as she watched in amazement, Gabe stopped in front of the electric gates of the huge house on the corner of the street. He waved a key fob in front of the pad on the stone column and, as the gates swung open, strolled up the drive and stepped inside the front door.

Locking up Donovan, Jinny took the short walk down the road and stared at the house, which wouldn't look out of place in the Hollywood Hills. She thought it was odd that Gabe was meant to be running errands and he had just disappeared inside the house with ice-cream. Maybe it was a friend's house?

Still perplexed, Jinny walked back to Donovan and was just about to start unloading the chutneys when she was greeted by a man with a portly figure and rosy cheeks. He was wearing an apron and a beatific smile.

'I'd recognise Donovan anywhere. You must be Jinny!' He extended his hand and shook Jinny's. 'I'm Tom, owner of the deli and a huge fan of the Bees' Knees brand.'

'I'm glad to hear it,' replied Jinny with a smile. 'Pleased to meet you.'

'That accent isn't from around these parts. English and southern.'

'London.'

'What brings you all the way to the Scottish Highlands?'

'A change in lifestyle and I'm loving it so far. Can I just tell you, you're my first official delivery.'

Tom smiled. 'Congratulations! You'll love it in Heartcross. Let me help you down with the chutneys.'

Jinny watched Tom whip out a small set of steps from just behind the doorway of the deli, along with a trolley.

'It looks like you've done this before,' said Jinny, taking the chutneys from Tom as he passed them down and loading them onto the trolley.

'Just once or twice,' he replied, with a chuckle. 'Now come inside and have a look around the deli.' Tom pushed the trolley through the door and Jinny followed. The shelves were packed with all different types of chutneys, cheeses and crackers. Then Jinny noticed the whole display dedicated to Bees' Knees with its very own sign letting the customers know this was a local product.

She felt a sudden sense of pride to be the new purveyor of Bees' Knees.

'They're my bestselling products, loved by locals and tourists alike. Dixie will be missed by everyone, but her name lives on.'

Jinny nodded. 'It certainly does. Everyone speaks so highly of her.'

'She and George were a huge part of this community and I believe the competition was very stiff to take over this business, so again, huge congratulations to you.' Tom's face broke into a smile.

'Thank you very much.'

'How are you settling in?'

Jinny smiled. 'It's only been a few days so I'm not quite fully settled. There's still so much to learn.'

After the chutneys were loaded onto the shelves, Jinny hovered by the counter. She hadn't considered how Tom would pay for the order as Gabe hadn't gone through that part of the business with her yet.

'How do you pay me for the stock?' she asked, figuring it was easier just to be upfront about the fact she wasn't sure.

'You send me an invoice at the end of the month,' confided Tom.

'Of course,' replied Jinny.

Tom walked her to the door. 'Have you explored much yet? There's so much to see. The Boat House is terrific and worth a trip, and you must sample the food at the famous Lake House restaurant. Primrose Park is great for a picnic and the gardens at Heartcross Castle are beautiful.'

'The only place I've visited so far is Bonnie's Teashop

but as soon as the weekend comes, I will be exploring every nook and cranny.

'Are you staying at Bumblebee Cottage?'

'I am.'

'A beautiful property and you're lucky to have got it. There aren't many houses that come up for sale in Heartcross as no one wants to leave.'

'I can understand why. It's been lovely to meet you, Tom, and I will see you very soon.'

'Yes, I'd best go and serve the customers otherwise my assistant will be leaving me in the lurch for not pulling my weight. And I'll see you next week.'

'Next week? You'll have sold all those chutneys by next week?' Jinny was amazed.

'You'd better believe it. The tourists love to purchase local products. They're bestsellers around these parts.'

'In that case, I will see you next week! I know this may be a funny request but could I possibly take a selfie of me in front of your very stocked shelves? I'm trying to get different footage in my new role to promote the business on my Instagram account and, as I mentioned, this is my very first delivery.'

'Of course!' Tom beamed. 'Be my guest and do look up the deli on social media and tag us in any posts.'

'I will!' Jinny walked back towards the shelves, posed, beamed, the camera clicked and she instantly uploaded the photo. She captioned it:

Success! 1st Delivery! #BeesKnees

'Thanks so much! I'll see you next week.'

Tom disappeared back behind the counter to help serve the customers while Jinny hovered for a moment on the street outside the deli. She glanced towards the house on the corner before climbing back into the car. There was no sign of Gabe. Starting the engine, Jinny noticed the one-way sign in front of her, which meant she needed to follow the loop round to join the road back past the house on the corner, which would give her the opportunity to take another look. Indicating, Jinny pulled out into the road. 'A beekeeper living in a mansion?' Jinny gave a tiny chuckle. No, Gabe was sure to have been visiting a friend.

Following the one-way system, Jinny was soon driving past the river. Approaching the house, she slowed down and dipped her head towards the passenger window. There was no sign of life but a little further up the road she spotted Gabe walking along the path at the side of the river. She beeped her horn and waved madly at him, now looking in her direction. Indicating, Jinny slowed down Donovan, pulled in next to Gabe and wound down her window.

'You have wheels!'

'Isn't Donovan just fabulous?'

'I knew you'd like him.'

'Like him? I love him!' replied Jinny. 'And I've just made my first delivery.'

'Dare I ask if everything ran smoothly? There were no mishaps, nothing got drenched or required a trip to the doctor?'

'Smooth as a baby's bum.'

'Glad to hear it.'

'And where have you been this morning? Molly said something about running errands.'

'Then that's exactly what I've been doing. I'm just on my way to Bumblebee Cottage. I was going to catch the river boat and walk up.'

'Jump in. I'm going that way.' Jinny gestured to the passenger door then leaned across and pulled up the latch.

Gabe climbed in and pulled on his seat belt. 'Now, before we set off, can I just confirm that you do have a licence and you can drive?'

'Don't you be cheeky.' Jinny looked in her mirror and indicated to pull out. As soon as the there was a gap in the traffic, she put the car into first gear and raised the clutch too quickly. Donovan stalled. 'Damn.'

Gabe snorted.

'Don't laugh. It's because I'm used to driving an automatic and I can't quite get used to the stick thing and the clutch.'

'That stick thing is your gears – and see that there?' Gabe pointed out to the river. 'That's the river taxi and I think it's going to be safer on water.' He laughed as he quickly unclipped his seat belt. Much to Jinny's amazement, he opened the door and hot-footed it across the pavement and down to the river taxi.

'Gabe, come back!' she shouted, laughing.

He looked back over his shoulder. 'Race you! See you in The Honey Pot in ten.'

Jinny was up for the challenge and restarted the engine.

Pulling away from the kerb she kangarooed the car along the street, smiling because she knew Gabe would be watching her.

'The cheek of the man,' she muttered, heading towards the bridge.

Chapter Ten

Abandoning Donovan outside Bumblebee Cottage, Jinny locked up the car and headed towards The Honey Pot. Gabe wasn't in sight and there was no way she could have been beaten by the river taxi. The small building looked as picturesque as the rest of the cottage with its painted duck-egg blue door with the wooden plaque in the middle with the words 'The Honey Pot' engraved along with a couple of bees.

From inside the building the sound of the radio filtered out and Gabe could be heard singing.

'No way!' she said, twisting the knob and pushing open the door to find a wide grin on Gabe's face while he tapped his watch.

'Here she is, the queen bee! What time do you call this?'

'How did you manage to get here first? I don't believe it.'

'You win some, you lose some!'

'Yeah, yeah, whatever,' Jinny marvelled, looking around. 'This place really lives up to its name.'

The brick walls were whitewashed and numerous photos of George were hanging on the wall. There was a freestanding island in the middle of the room with a basin along with a couple of fridges and some sort of machinery in the corner as well as a shelf that housed gingham lids, labels and jars.

'Grab yourself an apron.' He pointed towards two aprons hanging on wooden hooks.

Jinny laughed as she popped one over her head then posed, pointing to the wording on the front of the apron. 'Look, it says, "I am the bee's knees!"'

'Must be true then,' teased Gabe. 'Are you ready to make honey?'

'I'm ready!' Jinny was intrigued. She obviously knew that honey was made by bees but had never thought about the process in any detail until now.

'Let's begin the extraction process. The boards we collected are stacked up here and we take one at a time. What we need first is a hot knife.' He pointed at the sink.

Jinny went to grab one but Gabe caught her hand. 'It's boiling water; you'll scald yourself,' he said, putting on a bright-pink pair of rubber gloves.

'Glad to see you're in touch with your feminine side,' she teased, watching Gabe slip his hand into the water and pull out two knives.

'Always,' he replied, handing Jinny a knife and a board. 'The hot knife is used to cut the wax cappings off the cells of honeycomb... like this. These wax cappings can be used to make candles, so don't throw them away. We store them in here.'

'Candles? That's amazing!'

Gabe pointed to the shelf at the back of the room. 'If there's ever a power cut, we're fully prepared. They're all homemade candles.'

Jinny stared up at the shelf. 'Just look at those! There's another business right there.'

'Dixie used to dish them out to the villagers at Christmas time. There was never any waste. You try.'

With Gabe standing closely by, Jinny began to slice the wax cappings off the comb. 'This is actually fun. There's something therapeutic about it.' It took her a few minutes to remove all the cappings while Gabe did the same on another board.

'Once we've removed all these, we can separate the liquid honey from the comb,' he told her.

'Now that does sound complicated.'

'It's easy when you know how. But let's get the caps off all these boards then we can move on to the next stage.'

They worked in silence at first, before Jinny put the radio on as background noise. After the song finished, the weather and news came on, the newscaster announcing that the sunny weather was going to carry on for the foreseeable future.

'Everything does feel better when the sun is out, doesn't it?' said Jinny.

'It does,' replied Gabe, moving on to the next board.

Jinny noticed that he wrinkled the top of his nose when he was concentrating, which she found very sexy. In no time at all, the capping was safely stored away to make candles.

'What's next?' asked Jinny.

'I need to nip into the backroom to get the honey extractor.'

Jinny watched Gabe disappear through a door into what she assumed was a storeroom. As one of her favourite songs played on the radio she began to jig back and forth while she took a closer look at the photographs on the wall. George was featured standing outside The Honey Pot, holding up what Jinny assumed was his very first jar of honey. He looked proud and that's exactly how Jinny was feeling by following in his footsteps.

Gabe soon returned and stood next to Jinny. 'There's a whole lot of history in this place. I'm surprised I've not seen you whip out your phone and document every second of the day.'

Jinny looked at him. 'Maybe I've been thinking about what you said.'

Gabe raised an eyebrow. 'Which is?'

'You've had me thinking about social media and my Instagram account. So, I've made a change.'

'What do you mean?'

'The second I stepped into Heartcross, I opened up a new account about me and my new life, but you're right. I don't need validation from a bunch of strangers or to share every minute of what I'm doing. It's about being happy within myself, which I am. But I do think it's a great business tool to showcase Bees' Knees products and make wonderful connections and support other businesses in the community. So now I'm focusing on the brand, not on me.'

Gabe narrowed his eyes. 'Did you bump your head when you fell off the gate?'

Jinny laughed. 'My private life is hardly a success story and maybe I was lacking a little in self-esteem and thought attention from strangers would help, but the hit is short-lived. This place brings out the best in me and I believe this business will be a success due to teamwork.' She pointed at herself and him. 'And hard work and dedication.'

'Jinny Smith, it's not often that people surprise me but you have done just that.' Gabe looked suitably impressed.

She smiled at him. 'Glad to hear it. I like to keep you on your toes,' she said, nudging him lightly with her elbow.

'I have to say, you certainly do. You also bring a new energy to this place and I think we make a great team. Albeit you are a little clumsy and have this funny accent going on but there's a genuine honesty about you. I like that.'

Jinny met his eye and instantly felt guilty. She hadn't been totally honest with him and she was beginning to regret that decision. Even though she didn't want to rock the boat, she was thinking it would be better to get the truth about her last job out in the open sooner rather than later; she would talk to him when the moment was right. Already surprised at the relief she was feeling about confiding in Gabe, she pointed at the small machine he had just wheeled in. 'And what is that contraption?'

'This is Alfred!'

'Why does everything need to have a human name?'

Gabe laughed. 'I'm not entirely sure, and I've no clue why he's called Alfred.'

Jinny pointed to the name of the manufacturer on the small label stuck on the side of the machine. 'There's your answer. "Made by Alfred's Machinery."'

'Well, I never realised that.'

'And what does Alfred do?'

'Uses centrifugal force to separate the liquid honey from the comb without destroying the comb.'

'That sounds complicated.' Jinny raised an eyebrow before lifting the lid and staring inside the contraption.

'This means we can reuse the frame. Let's get Alfred loaded up.'

Jinny watched as Gabe placed the boards inside a basket. 'This basket spins and flings the honey out.' He closed the lid and was now standing right behind Jinny. 'Your very first batch of honey! You just need to crank that lever and away you go.'

Feeling Gabe's presence behind her, she reached for the lever. 'It's stuck. I can't move it,' she said, struggling to pull the lever down.

'It just needs a good tug.' He leaned forward and placed his hand on top of hers. 'You need to pull it right back like this.' He kept his hand on top of hers as the machine began to clunk.

She looked over her shoulder. 'What happens now?' she asked as Gabe slowly removed his hand.

'The liquid gets collected in the container and we leave it for a few days to settle, then we can take it over to the kitchen and jar it up.'

'I can't wait to taste it. It's so exciting.'

'I love this process. It's very satisfying when I've looked after the bees all year.' Gabe gestured for Jinny to take a take a look inside the container. Her eyes widened.

'Just look at that. It's amazing.'

'Bees are clever little things and, if treated right, they're nothing to be scared of.'

'A bit like women,' said Jinny with a grin.

'I'm saying nothing.' Gabe looked up from under his fringe and gave her a smile before he emptied the container and started the process again.

'Shall I go and get us both a drink?' asked Jinny.

'That would be good. I'll load up the next batch but then it's your turn.'

Jinny wandered back to the cottage, smiling. She was enjoying spending her time with Gabe; he was easy to be around and he made her smile. While pouring two glasses of orange juice, she heard the letterbox clang and picked up a pile of post from the mat.

There was nothing but junk mail but one leaflet caught Jinny's eye, advertising the 'Heartcross Summer Fair', which was happening in two weeks' time. According to the leaflet there was going to be a best local product competition. Jinny's mind began to whirl. This would be the perfect opportunity to showcase Bees' Knees. Holding the two glasses of juice and carrying the leaflet between her teeth she pushed open the door to The Honey Pot with her foot.

As soon as the drinks were on the table, she wafted the leaflet towards Gabe. 'Have you seen this? Heartcross has a summer fair.'

'Yea, they have one every year, out on the green. It's a great day for all.'

'And this competition – the best local product competition – this would be brilliant for Bees' Knees! We can easily win this.'

'You'll be up against some tough competition there, what with Cam, Drew, Rona...'

'Are you saying I've no chance?'

'That's not what I'm saying, but the competition will be stiff.'

'And a little healthy competition never hurt anyone.' There was determination in Jinny's voice as she looked from Gabe to the photo of George on the wall. 'But we need something different.'

Gabe went and stood next to her. 'What are you thinking?'

For a moment, Jinny stood in silence, her thoughts turning over in her mind. Then a smile spread wide on her face and she suddenly swiped Gabe's arm. 'I've got it!'

'Go on,' encouraged Gabe. 'It's either chutney or honey.'

'That's where you're wrong.' Jinny was waving her hands about with excitement. 'It's going to be both. We can combine the two products for a brand-new product: honey cider chutney! This would be perfect for Halloween and

Christmas. I can bubble the autumn fruits together and concoct the potion. I just know this is a winner! What do you think?'

For a moment they stared at each other in a contemplative silence.

'I think you may be on to something here.'

'Will you help me? In the name of Dixie, George and Bees' Knees?'

Gabe didn't hesitate. 'It will be my pleasure. The farmers' markets are on next week. If I remember rightly there's a local stall that sells cider... or we can have a go at making on our own? I've attempted cider in the past. Primary fermentation should begin in twenty-four to thirty-six hours and should finish in five to nine days but is that cutting it too fine? Either way, we could use shop-bought to practise.'

Jinny clapped her hands together like a demented sea lion. 'Absolutely! I have a good feeling about this. Determination and hard work will get this business on the map. I'm so excited! Wait until I tell Molly and Cam. This way both Dixie and George will still be out in the world – together.'

'You are just amazing,' said Gabe. 'It's a wonderful idea.'

The excitement overwhelming her, Jinny flung her arms around Gabe's neck and kissed him swiftly on the cheek. He gave her a surprised, lopsided grin. 'I'm in no doubt you're going to win.'

'No! *We* are going to win!' confirmed Jinny. 'We're in this together!'

'I'm liking the sound of that,' he replied, lifting Jinny clean off her feet and spinning her round before placing her firmly back on the ground. 'Now, check that honey as we're going to need every drop to put this new chutney on the map.'

Jinny didn't need telling twice. Opening the lid to the extractor she was faced with the gorgeous dark-brown honey. 'It's perfect! We're definitely making the chutney with this batch,' she declared.

'I love it when a plan comes together.' Gabe carefully took the boards from the extractor and loaded in the next ones.

Jinny had a clear agenda for the next two weeks: making the new product, winning that competition and spending as much time with Gabe as she possibly could.

Chapter Eleven

It had been a busy few days and Jinny had spent the first week in the job getting to grips with the business and spending every waking hour working next to Gabe, which she had thoroughly enjoyed. He had been patient taking her through the paperwork, and Jinny realised the business needed bringing up to date with technology, which would make the accounting and invoicing a whole lot easier than the handwritten ledgers it had always relied on.

Gabe had left around his usual time and Jinny was enjoying a soak in the bath with a glass of wine when her phone rang.

'Good evening, Jay!'

'And how has your first week *bee*-n in the land of Bumblebee Cottage?'

'Amazing! There's so much to learn and I have a good teacher.'

'And how is the gorgeous Gabe?'

Jinny was quiet for a second. 'Jay, I'm feeling guilty.'

'What about?'

'The fact I've lied about my surname and about my last job. As each day goes by it's getting harder to say something.'

'Mmm, don't worry. I think you're overthinking it. Someone can't dislike the press that much. Maybe it was a passing comment, or he'd read a bad article, or he was possibly just having a bad day.'

'Possibly. Maybe I am just reading too much into it.'

'Anyone can see you're a genuine person and when you do tell him, he will understand your reasons. You wanted a fresh start. Everyone is entitled to that.'

Jinny hoped Jay was right but there was a still a niggle in the back of her mind.

'Have you found out whose house he was visiting on Millionaires' Row yet?'

Jinny had told Jay about the day she'd seen Gabe going into the property. Now she realised it had totally slipped her mind to tell Gabe she'd seen him and ask him about it. 'No, but like you said, it must be a friend. I mean, that house is huge and there's no way a beekeeper's wage could pay for it. I am curious though.'

'I know what happens when you get curious, so stop right there. Just keep getting to know him and eventually he'll introduce you to his circle of friends and the rest of the community and you'll organically find out who lives in a house like that,' he said, attempting the voice of Keith Lemon.

'Bad impression. Speaking of the community, it's the BBQ tonight at the pub and I'm excited to meet the locals.'

'Is Gabe going?'

'He never said.' Jinny was kicking herself that she'd never asked him. 'I hope so.'

'I can't wait to hear all about it. Have a great night and don't do anything I wouldn't do!'

A couple of hours later, Jinny checked her appearance in the mirror. After discarding numerous outfits, she'd kept it simple and finally opted for a pair of white skinny jeans and a navy T-shirt accompanied by a pair of Converse, combining comfort with not being too over-dressed for a BBQ at the local pub. Molly and Cam had already left for the BBQ and Jinny had arranged to meet Felicity on the corner of the high street in ten minutes' time. She wandered into the kitchen and poured herself a glass of water before studying the contents of the pinboard. There was everything she expected to see – menus from the takeaways in town, the name and number of a taxi firm – and then she saw a square piece of paper and stared. There was Gabe's name with a mobile phone number written underneath. Jinny unpinned the piece of paper and picked up her phone. She stored his number and took the plunge.

It's your favourite apprentice! Just wondering if you're going to the BBQ tonight at the pub? I forgot to ask. You could introduce me to a few regulars.

. . .

Jinny looked at the text and before she could change her mind, she pressed send.

Her phone pinged back within seconds. When she saw Gabe's name light up her screen, her heart leapt.

You're my only apprentice!

He hadn't confirmed whether he was going tonight but his reply made Jinny smile as she headed out towards the high street. It was the perfect summer evening for a BBQ and this was her first chance to meet and chat with most of the locals. As arranged, Felicity was waiting for her on the corner and they were soon walking through the doors of The Grouse and Haggis. Felicity weaved her way towards the bar with Jinny following closely behind.

'Allie, I want you to meet Jinny, she's staying at Bumblebee Cottage. This is Allie. She lives with Rory, the local vet, and her parents own the pub…'

'Hence why I'm working behind the bar,' added Allie. 'I always get roped in.'

'Rory is now in partnership with Molly; they've merged their vet's surgeries,' continued Felicity.

Jinny held her hands up in the air. 'Woah!' That's way too much to remember already!'

Allie laughed and extended her hand over the bar. 'Welcome to Heartcross!'

'And I'm Meredith, landlady, mother to this one, and my

husband Fraser is in charge of throwing the meat on the BBQ in the garden. You must be the one who's taken over Dixie's business. Welcome, welcome, welcome!' she trilled. 'Let me get you a drink. The first one is always on the house. What would you like?'

'Ah, thank you! A glass of Pinot Grigio would be lovely.'

'I'll get you a bottle; it'll be bedlam coming back and forth to the bar and there will always be someone to share it with.'

'That'll be me,' added Felicity, with a grin.

'Thank you again.' Jinny was amazed at everyone's kindness.

As soon they stepped out into the pub garden Jinny could see Allie had her work cut out behind the bar. The gorgeous weather had brought the thirsty revellers out in their droves.

The setting was perfect, with a small terrace area filled with wrought-iron tables and chairs and glorious flowers tumbling from planters in every corner. Fairy lights wrapped around the wooden slats above them and there were steps down to a lawn area. Jinny noticed Molly and Cam sitting under the shade of an umbrella with the children and gave them a quick wave.

'That's my partner, Fergus, and his daughter, Esme.' Felicity pointed over to the table next to Molly and Cam. 'Fergus works at Foxglove Farm with Drew and here's Isla – they own the farm.' Felicity tapped Isla on her shoulder and the other woman spun round.

With a warm smile on her face she said, 'You must be Jinny! Pleased to meet you. I'm Isla. Are you settling in?'

'I am, thanks. I know I've not been here long but I feel like I could stay here for ever.'

'Once you arrive in Heartcross you stay in Heartcross!' echoed Isla and Felicity at the same time, then laughed.

'Come on, let's go and join the others.' Isla headed towards Drew and Fergus. She looked back over her shoulder. 'And I hear you've already got a love interest in the village.'

Jinny automatically thought of Gabe but merely raised an eyebrow. 'Have I?' she said carefully.

'Donovan! Isn't he just so vintage!'

'Ha, yes! He's definitely vintage!' enthused Jinny, thankful that neither of the women could read her mind.

Felicity hung back and whispered to Jinny, 'What was that look for? Who did you think she meant? Gabe?'

'I can neither confirm nor deny,' replied Jinny, knowing that Felicity knew exactly who was on her mind.

'Fergus, Drew, meet Jinny. She's staying at Bumblebee Cottage and is now in charge of Dixie's business.'

After introductions were made and the wine was poured, Jinny felt like she was sitting amongst old friends. The conversation flowed and so did the drinks. Settled at the wooden table not far from the sizzle of the BBQ, Allie's dad, Fraser, was in his element and looked the part, wearing his wife Meredith's apron, which instantly made Gabe cross her mind again. She was hoping he would turn up tonight.

'There are sausages ready,' Fraser shouted triumphantly

as Allie ferried out a large platter of buns and people began to form an orderly queue.

'I love this kind of evening,' enthused Jinny, looking all around. 'It's been such a long time since I've felt this relaxed.'

'Have you always been in the honey and chutney game?' asked Isla, sitting opposite her.

'Only for the last week but I'm enjoying every second,' she admitted.

'And what did you do before?'

'Just admin, boring stuff,' replied Jinny, once again stretching the truth, then noticing that Drew had just swiped a newspaper from the next table and opened it up. She watched him flicking through the pages.

'Absolute dross. Honestly, call some of this stuff news?' he declared.

'Don't get him started,' chipped in Isla, rolling her eyes. 'We have the same conversation every morning when the newspaper pings through the letterbox. I don't know why he keeps ordering it when all he does is moan.'

'This isn't journalism. This is just trash. I mean, look at this...' Drew turned the newspaper towards them all and tapped the article. 'This poor woman has been trying to live her life away from the public eye only to find herself splashed all over the pages because she's put on a little weight. It's bordering on immoral.'

Jinny glanced towards the newspaper. It was clear her father had got his story without her. She shook her head.

'Even Jinny agrees, don't you?'

Jinny was put on the spot and felt ashamed and embarrassed knowing the part she had played in spreading negative news in that very tabloid over the last ten years. This was the ideal moment to share with her new friends exactly who she was and that she wholeheartedly agreed with Drew. She didn't want to be deceitful but she knew she was in a dilemma. She'd kept that information to herself at her interview and owed the truth to Molly and Gabe first.

'I do,' she replied. 'Completely.'

'Have you seen this?' Molly appeared at the side of the table and handed Jinny a poster. 'I just love this time of year! Heartcross Summer Fair.'

'The Summer Fair is just the best day. It's like a bank holiday but just for the villagers of Heartcross. It's all about getting together as a community and—' Felicity began but she was interrupted by Isla.

'It involves drinking all day on the green. You can't beat it.'

'That does sounds like the perfect day,' agreed Jinny.

'There's all sorts going on during the day, but this year there's a brand-new competition for the best local product which will be judged by... well, that's something we need to sort out yet,' Molly quickly added.

'There's only one winner here,' piped up Drew. 'Either my homemade sausages or cheese.'

'I think we have other ideas,' challenged Molly, giving Jinny an encouraging smile. 'The winner's product gets pride of place in one of the biggest supermarket chains in

Scotland and we have every intention of winning this. Isn't that right, Jinny?'

This was the first Jinny had heard about the product being sold on the supermarket shelves, which gave her added determination. 'Absolutely right,' replied Jinny, thinking this would be the perfect opportunity to shine and give something back to Molly to thank her for everything she had done for her.

'Interesting! The newcomer is going to try and give me a run for my money. This will be war,' declared Drew.

'Go easy.' Isla shot him a playful warning look. 'Sorry, Jinny. Drew can get a little over-enthusiastic.'

'Challenge accepted,' Jinny said confidently, extending her hand over the table and shaking Drew's.

'I'm backing Jinny!' replied Molly, giving Drew a wink before returning to her table.

'There's never a dull moment in Heartcross,' said Isla, taking a sip of her drink. 'And a good day will be had by all. Who's for food?' she asked, looking over towards the BBQ. Drew and Fergus were on their feet before anyone could answer.

Jinny placed the poster down and smiled, knowing that she and Gabe were already working on their entry, then reached for the newspaper, which was still lying open on the table. She quickly scanned the article and winced. Maybe it was for the best that she hadn't shared who her father was because looking at the pages didn't make her feel like a proud daughter.

'I'm actually feeling peckish now too,' she declared,

standing up and following Felicity and the aroma of sizzling sausages. 'This looks and smells heavenly.'

'They're Foxglove Farm sausages.' Drew tipped her wink. 'Simply the best.'

'You should know he doesn't like to lose,' confided Isla.

'That makes two of us,' replied Jinny.

'No doubt Cam will bake bread and Bree will conjure up some wonderful chocolate creation. There will be so many entries. I can't wait to see what everyone comes up with.' Isla was next in the queue so she turned back towards Fraser who'd stabbed a sausage and was waving it in the air.

'And here comes your favourite villager,' Felicity whispered, angling her head towards the back of the beer garden

'Huh?' Jinny followed Felicity's gaze and spotted Gabe. An instant smile hitched on her face; he was here.

'And how are you getting on with Gabe? He certainly seems taken with you,' Felicity noted. 'He keeps looking over in your direction.'

'I would say very well. He makes working life at the cottage *very* enjoyable.' Every time she set eyes on him there was some sort of pull towards him.

'Oh, I bet he does.'

Jinny's eyes were fixed in his direction. He was chatting to Molly who deposited baby Lily in his arms. He cradled the little girl, letting her tiny body rest against his chest. Jinny watched him inhale her baby smell and laugh with Molly. He looked like a natural as he rocked Lily to and fro in his arms, and Jinny took a moment to admire how handsome he looked. He was wearing a tight white T-shirt that clung to his biceps perfectly, navy-blue tailored shorts and flip-flops. A second later, baby Lily started to cry, soon building to a crescendo of screaming. Apologetically, Gabe promptly handed Lily back to Molly.

'There's only certain men that can pull off flip-flops,' whispered Felicity. 'And just so you know, you're staring.'

Felicity didn't need to point that out. Jinny knew she was well and truly staring yet she couldn't help but keep flicking her eyes in his direction. Gabe must have sensed someone watching him and looked over towards her, catching her eye. Immediately she felt her heart give a little flutter when he acknowledged her with a lopsided grin.

'He's spotted you,' pointed out Felicity.

'You don't need to keep giving me a running commentary.'

'I'm assuming there's no one special in your life at the minute?'

'Far from it,' Jinny replied without hesitation. For the last twelve months, she had dabbled with internet dating, but as she only swiped right once in every one hundred profiles, it was like playing the weirdest game of Snap ever. Every date she had been on had been a disaster and she'd been close to turning her stories into an article for the newspaper with the bold headline: 'Be Careful What You Swipe For'.

'How old do you think he is?' asked Jinny, turning back towards Felicity.

'Good question. My guess is mid-thirties.'

'Which would make him ten years older than me,' added Jinny.

'Age is just a number,' replied Felicity. 'Take Isla's grandmother, Martha.' Felicity nodded towards a lady dressed in a short-sleeved tunic and sandals with her hair tied up in a bun. 'She's a character – an expert serial dater, usually with men twenty years younger than herself, and she can see into your future. She doesn't give two hoots about what anyone thinks of her. Live life like Martha.'

'No, don't,' chipped in Isla. 'The number of times I can't get to sleep because she's not home.' She chuckled. 'But I can confirm no man is safe around my grandmother.'

They watched as Martha sidled over to Gabe and squeezed his bicep. He took it in his stride as Martha gave him a cheeky wink and carried on walking to the next table before sitting down with Rona.

'I told you no one's safe,' confirmed Isla, laughing.

Everyone was in good spirits. Fraser was chatting to people as he flipped over the sausages and he was soon introduced to Jinny who was next in the queue.

'And how is life so far at Bumblebee Cottage?' he asked, offering her a hot dog.

'I'm absolutely loving everything about it. Everyone has made me feel so welcome,' she replied, squirting the tomato ketchup along the sausage and placing it on her paper plate with a handful of salad from the table at the side of the BBQ.

'Anything else you need, just ask,' said Fraser.

She walked back towards the table. Gabe was nowhere to be seen. He must have disappeared inside for a drink. Felicity topped up the wine as Jinny settled herself on the bench and moved the newspaper and the poster.

Felicity looked around the table. 'I think we should have a toast. Here's to Heartcross's newcomer, Jinny... Jinny...'

'Smith,' Jinny replied, once again using her mother's maiden name.

Everyone clinked their glasses together. Out of the corner of her eye she noticed Gabe heading in their direction but then he was distracted by Fraser shouting over to him.

'There's one hot dog left.'

'And it has my name all over it, thank you,' he said, taking a plate.

Drew gestured towards the spare seat on the bench opposite Jinny. 'Come and join us,' he said. 'How's it going? Or should we be asking, how is your new apprentice?'

Gabe slid onto the bench and placed his pint and plate down on the table. 'It's been an eventful week. This new girl turns up from the city, she has a chutney explosion in the kitchen, sets the sprinklers off in the garden, gets stuck on top of a gate and near enough moons me after being stung on her backside by a bee. How do you think it's going?' he said playfully.

Felicity threw her head back and laughed. 'Bloody hell, you haven't been stung by a bee already, have you?'

All eyes were on Jinny.

'Afraid so,' replied Jinny. 'Right on my backside and then I had to drop my pants in front of the doctor.'

'I didn't see that post on Instagram!' Felicity laughed. 'I found your new account. It's really taking off.'

'Thank you,' she replied.

'You're a natural at taking photographs. You should chat with Allie. A while back she worked in Glasgow as a photographer for a national newspaper. She'd taken a photo at the Summer Fair of Zach Hudson and Rory, her partner...'

Jinny knew the exact photo she was talking about. Zach Hudson was a Netflix superstar and she loved his wildlife documentaries.

'That was here in Heartcross?'

'It was,' replied Felicity. 'How did you come across it?'

Each and every journalist in the land wished that they had taken that photo. It had become an instant success and went viral in literally minutes.

'It was all over social media. You couldn't miss it! And Allie is *the* Allie McDonald?' Jinny glanced towards the back of the pub.

'The very one. Because of that photo and her job at the time, Allie set up a photography centre for disadvantaged kids up on the Clover Cottage estate.'

'Social media does have some advantages, doesn't it?' she said, nodding in Gabe's direction before turning back towards Felicity. 'Good on Allie, that's amazing.'

'You should go and take a look. And what about you, Gabe? Are you following Jinny's antics on Instagram?'

'I have the pleasure of witnessing those antics in real life,' he replied, making everyone laugh.

'It wasn't my fault I sat on a bee,' protested Jinny. 'Or that I've never worked with an Aga.'

'A bad workman always blames their tools,' he teased. 'And the impression I get is that Jinny is very accident-prone. The only way forwards is to wrap her up in bubble wrap,' he jested, smiling warmly at her before he took a sip of his pint.

'That is music to my ears,' chipped in Drew. 'Because if you're so accident-prone, that Summer Fair trophy has my name already engraved on it. If you could leave Jinny in charge of the competition that would be a great help. I want that place on the supermarket shelves.'

Gabe looked puzzled. 'Supermarket shelves?'

Jinny slid the poster across the table to him. 'The best local product gets a place in one of the biggest supermarkets in the land.'

'And not only that,' added Allie, appearing at the side of the table to collect the empty glasses. 'You get a double spread in a national magazine and a write-up in the newspaper.'

'Wow!' replied Isla. 'That would be good for business. This competition will be fierce. Cam is already famous after winning the annual baking competition and Bree will definitely give us a run for our money with her amazing chocolate. Then there's you and Rona with cakes, Eleni from the B&B with her artwork…' Isla looked towards Felicity. 'There's a huge variety of products and I might just enter my very own chicken eggs or even a scarf I've made from the alpaca wool. What about you, Jinny?'

'That's top secret for now but all will be revealed in due course! A double spread and an interview in a magazine would be great exposure for the business. What do you think, Gabe?' Jinny looked across the table towards him. Was it her imagination or had he just bristled?

'I think I'll give that part a miss. I'm not one for the limelight and I'm sure you're capable of being interviewed all by yourself.'

'But it'll be good for business. Imagine people opening up the newspaper and seeing our product. A wider market is what we need.'

'I second that,' added Drew.

Jinny noticed that Gabe had that fleeting look of disdain on his face again, confirming to her that something was going on in the background for him. But not wanting to make a big deal of it in front of everyone, she picked up her hotdog. 'Let's see how good this sausage is,' she teased Drew, sinking her teeth into one end of the bun and immediately hearing a tiny gasp from Gabe.

'Oh my...' Felicity gulped, then attempted to stifle her laughter.

Gabe's eyes shot to Jinny's before his gaze dropped down to his formerly clean white T-shirt, which was now splattered with blood-red ketchup. Jinny wanted the ground to swallow her up.

'I'm so sorry!' She leapt to her feet with a serviette in her hand and began to dab his T-shirt but only made the stain a whole lot worse.

Gabe pointed to her white jeans. 'How much ketchup did you put on that hot dog? I'm not the only one who got covered.'

Jinny cast her eyes downward. 'Blooming 'eck!'

Everyone sitting around the table burst into laughter.

'It's not far to walk home. I'm going to nip back and get changed. What about you, Gabe?'

'I don't think my T-shirt is as bad as your jeans but I keep some spare clothes over at Bumblebee Cottage. I'll walk you back.'

Jinny turned to Felicity. 'I'll be right back.'

'I won't count on that,' she whispered jokingly under her breath.

Jinny was thankful that comment had passed Gabe by as he was looking at the screen of his phone, which was ringing. He silenced the call but his phone began to ring again almost immediately.

'I think someone wants you,' said Jinny.

'I think you may be right. I need to take this,' he replied. 'I'll meet you around the front of the pub in a sec.' Walking away from the table, he answered the call.

'I'll just nip to the bathroom, and hopefully I'll be back soon,' Jinny told Felicity.

'The night is still young and we aren't going anywhere. There's a band playing next and no doubt Fergus will be murdering the karaoke later on,' Felicity said with a shrug.

Jinny laughed, looking towards Fergus who pretended to look hurt. 'I can't miss that then. I'll catch you in a bit.'

———————————

After using the bathroom, Jinny made her way out to the street. She looked around for Gabe, and found him standing with his back to her outside the village shop on the opposite pavement. She ambled across the road towards him then stopped. He was still talking on the phone and the conversation sounded heated. She didn't mean to eavesdrop but Gabe was sounding stressed. His words were getting faster, his hands animated as he spoke. Then Jinny realised he was speaking in French.

'*Pas de mère. Cela fait dix ans et nous avons réussi à rester à l'écart des projecteurs aussi longtemps. Je ne veux pas de cette vie.*'

Jinny's French wasn't up to much but she could ask for a gin and tonic and where the nearest metro station was. But Gabe was clearly protesting about something and she managed to translate the words 'ten years' and gather that he 'didn't want that life'.

As Jinny began to edge backwards, Gabe spun round and met her gaze. He paled. Switching back to English, he said. 'I have to go. I don't want to speak about this now. I'll call you tomorrow.' He hung up the phone and stuffed it back into his pocket.

'I'm sorry about that,' he said. His eyes were downcast and he was avoiding eye contact with her. She didn't need to be a genius to know something was troubling him. There was worry etched all over his face.

Jinny contemplated her next move. Gabe looked like he was in turmoil and she couldn't ignore that. 'Is everything okay? You look a little—'

'I'm fine,' he cut in, then exhaled.

'Anyone who says they're fine is not fine,' she replied tentatively. 'And French... You speak French?'

'I'm sorry, that was a little sharp of me. I didn't mean to snap. I've just got a few things on my mind,' he admitted, raking his hand through his hair. 'Come on, let's walk you home.' Gabe placed his hand in the small of her back and they headed towards Bumblebee Cottage.

'You do look like you have the weight of the world on your shoulders.'

'Sometimes it feels like that,' he admitted. He stopped walking. 'A lot of stuff has happened but it's difficult to talk about.'

'Nothing can really be that bad, can it? Sometimes talking to someone who isn't involved can give you a different perspective on a situation. I can lend a confidential ear.'

Jinny could see that Gabe was out of his comfort zone. Maybe he hadn't had anyone to open up to before except Dixie, who was no longer here. She didn't want him closing down or being guarded but maybe his way of coping was by keeping whatever it was to himself.

They carried on walking down the high street in silence. As soon as they turned the corner, Jinny smiled at the sight of Donovan parked outside the cottage. 'That car makes me feel happy. But I'm learning he can be temperamental… like most men, apparently.'

Gabe rolled his eyes then smiled. 'Don't you mean like most women too?'

'You're smiling!'

'I can't help but smile when you're around. You have a good aura about you.' Gabe patted the bonnet. 'Dixie loved this car. She used to talk to it like it was human. Honestly, most mornings, she'd stand out here with a cup of tea chatting away about anything and everything.' He gave a little chuckle. 'I was quite envious of her carefree lifestyle. She was full of wisdom, never one for judgement and the first person to offer help without question.' There was a faraway look in Gabe's eyes, as though he had first-hand experience of Dixie's unconditional help.

'And Dixie and George's love affair was the kind everyone dreams of. They were a solid, loving unit with the utmost respect for each other, always encouraging one another to continue to grow and chase their dreams. Donovan came a close second in Dixie's heart though,' he added.

'I'll make sure I treat him like he's the only man in the world.'

'He's a lucky man,' replied Gabe, turning towards her and holding her gaze, causing a burst of fireflies to instantly flutter in her stomach.

'Do you need to rush off, or would you like to stay for a

drink?' she asked, pointing towards the cottage. 'There's a few beers chilling in the fridge.'

'Sounds perfect,' he replied, opening the garden gate and letting Jinny walk through first. 'But on one condition.' He paused, leaving Jinny wondering what he was going to say next. 'That I don't end up wearing it! I know how clumsy you are.'

Jinny beamed, glad to see Gabe's mood had lifted again. 'I promise.'

'In that case, I accept. It's a good job I keep a couple of spare T-shirts in The Honey Pot. I'll just go and grab one.'

'And why's that then? Have other tenants splattered you in ketchup before?'

'No, only you've had the pleasure of that one,' he replied with a lopsided grin. 'And you're the only tenant Bumblebee Cottage has had – well, except Bree, who moved in with Dixie for a short time, but now she's living in her flat above the chocolate shop.'

'Living above a chocolate shop. Could life get any better than that?' murmured Jinny, watching Gabe walk off towards the outbuilding.

The second Jinny was inside the cottage she hotfooted it upstairs to change her jeans. As she pulled on a pair of shorts, the conversation that had taken place outside the pub was firmly on her mind. She didn't like to see anyone upset and Gabe was definitely agitated by the phone call. She repeated the words that she'd heard in her mind and quickly typed them into Google Translate on her phone and stared at the screen.

No, mother. It's been ten years and we've managed to stay out of the spotlight for so long. I don't want this life.

Exactly what spotlight was Gabe talking about and why was he frustrated with his mother? Jinny had a long list of questions that she wanted to ask but she didn't want to drive him away. Even though her curiosity was in full throttle, gaining Gabe's trust as a friend was first on the agenda. Hopefully, he would open up in time and she would be able to help him.

Back downstairs, Jinny took a couple of cold beers out of the fridge and mustered a platter of cheese, crackers and chutney. Wandering outside, she placed the tray down on the patio table. With the sun still high in the sky and the trees providing a light breeze, Jinny sat down and took a sip of her beer. Glancing across towards The Honey Pot she noticed Gabe through the window.

Her eyes stayed firmly focused in his direction as he pulled the ketchup-splattered T-shirt above his head. Jinny lost herself for a moment. His features were perfect, slim and muscular. She glimpsed his strong arms, his biceps, his broad, tanned shoulders... She swallowed. Damn, that man was in good shape.

Dear God, you have answered all of my prayers.

She blinked slowly, taking in the view, feeling like it was a scene from a movie. Why the hell did this man not have a ring on his finger? He pulled a clean T-shirt over his head and smoothed it down then turned around and looked straight at her. It was too late; there wasn't time to look away. He'd caught her watching. Jinny bit down on her lip to supress her smile, aware she was acting like a schoolgirl with a crush. But she couldn't help it. She found him damn attractive.

As he moved away from the window, Jinny closed her eyes and tilted her face up to the sun. She was surrounded by silence, which was a welcome change. She loved the calmness of this place.

'Penny for them?'

She looked up to see Gabe standing nearby. 'Listen. All I can hear is the rustle of the trees and the buzzing of the bees.'

'This place is something else,' he said, pulling out a chair and sitting down next to her. His leg lightly brushed against Jinny's, causing her pulse to race. They both stared out over the beautiful garden and soaked up the calm and tranquillity.

'Beer?' she said, sliding a bottle towards him. 'And some cheese and crackers, obviously served with the best chutney in the land.'

'Not with ketchup? I'm disappointed,' he said with a glint in his eye.

'Definitely no ketchup,' she confirmed, sliding a plate towards him. 'Help yourself.'

Thankfully, Gabe seemed to have forgotten his troubles. Taking his phone and wallet out of his pocket, he put them down on the table.

'What are your thoughts on the job so far?' he asked, swinging a glance towards her.

'It's the best job I've ever had… and with the best boss.'

'Flattery will get you everywhere.'

'How long have you been here now?' asked Jinny.

'Just under ten years,' he said. 'But it still seems like yesterday that I arrived. I've never tired of this place.'

'And you've been beekeeping for all that time?'

'I have indeed. I was here before The Old Bakehouse reopened, and the chocolate shop wasn't even thought of. It's a job I enjoy and I like the solitude of the place.'

'Is this your only job?' Jinny couldn't help asking. She was intrigued by Gabe.

'Looking after the gardens and orchards, trawling the farmers' markets, completing the invoices and accounting, and delivering the honey keeps me very busy.'

Jinny couldn't argue with that. 'Lucky all the regulars are good friends. Everyone's been so welcoming. It honestly feels like I've known these people for years.'

'It's a very supportive community. Everyone looks out for everyone. Have you left many friends behind?'

Despite living in a busy city like London and working at the newspaper, Jinny didn't have a huge circle of friends. That's why she had taken the plunge and begun drinking in the local waterholes on her own, hoping it might lead her to meet new people. And it had. She'd very quickly stumbled across Jay working behind the bar. She'd had the day from hell, cooped up in a car trailing after a famous TV presenter on her father's orders as he believed the man was having an affair, and Jay had made her smile about something or nothing. He was her level of kooky and they instantly became friends. For Jinny, it had always been quality over quantity when it came to the friends that mattered.

'My best friend, Jay. He works in a bar though so it's a little difficult for him to get time off to visit.'

'Three friends you should always have: a barman, a lawyer and a hairdresser.'

'Definitely, and I do miss him but we've spoken loads since I arrived.'

'And your father? You said things were difficult, but do you think he might come and visit?'

'That's a difficult one.' She wanted to open up about her father to Gabe but needed to hold back until she understood the reasoning behind his loathing of journalists and social media.

'Life would have been so much easier with my mum around.' She heard her own voice quiver. Fanning her hand in front of her face she swallowed down a lump in her throat. 'Oh my, this happens every time I talk about my mum.'

Gabe reached across and touched her arm, the feel of his hand sending a shiver down her spine. 'It's okay. Emotion is a funny thing. I often find when I think of certain things from the past tears involuntarily spring to my eyes.'

Jinny met his eye. 'I can relate to that.'

Gabe nodded in agreement. 'I hear you. I know first-hand the devastating effects it can have on a child not having a mother.' His voice was soft but he didn't elaborate, and for a second he looked a little lost in thought, his eyes suddenly watery. She knew his mum was living in France and was curious to know who he had been talking about, but she didn't want to send him running for the hills, which he would if she pushed for answers.

'I heard you speaking in French before,' she said, leaning across and placing a cracker and a slice of cheese on her plate. 'Were you speaking with your mum?'

'Yes,' he confirmed. 'She only ever talks to me in French.'

'You sounded pretty good at it.'

'It's my first language.'

'Ah, that must be why I struggled to place your accent when we first met. It's very unique.'

'French with a little Scottish twang creeping in.'

'You grew up in France?'

'I did, and came to Scotland just under ten years ago.'

'That must have been a huge change.'

'Definitely colder,' he admitted with a smile.

'Here.' She offered him the plate of cheese and crackers and they began to tuck in.

'Heartcross rescued me at a very difficult time. This place...' She gazed around the stunning garden. 'Is just the place to get my thoughts and future in order. My mum would have loved it here. She was always a country girl at heart but moved to the city with work and met my father. As they say, the rest is history.'

'It must be difficult not being close to your dad.'

This was the ideal time to share more about her past and hopefully Gabe would see how genuine she was as a person and that, whatever the reasons for his dislike of journalists, she didn't share the same morals as her father.

'It is. Even worse, he was also my boss.'

'Very difficult then. No escaping him at work or at home,' Gabe observed, giving her a sideward glance.

'Exactly. My dad is set in his ways – a workaholic – and over the years my frustrations with him have heightened. My colleagues at work never really took me seriously because I was related to the boss and he made a point of dishing out menial jobs to me to prove there was no favouritism. There was also other stuff that I didn't agree with – company policies – and after ten years, I finally cracked, walked out and within half an hour stumbled across the ad for the accommodation and business here in this little piece of paradise. Forty-eight hours later, I left the not-so-bright lights of the city, and look at me now.'

Gabe let out a low whistle. 'You don't do things by halves, do you? And what does your father say about it all?'

Jinny rolled her eyes. 'He told me I'd be back with my tail between my legs.'

Gabe looked amazed. 'You upped and left within forty-eight hours, giving up everything you knew. That shows real determination. It's a long way from London to the Scottish Highlands and I have to say, I'm not sure if I'm in awe or if I think you're absolutely bonkers.'

'Yeah, it's about… 568 miles,' Jinny said.

Gabe eyed her. 'I think it's awe. Your drive is very inspiring, Jinny Smith.'

'It's also a long way from France to the Scottish Highlands,' she said. This was Gabe's opportunity to share with her why he'd upped and left France but she noticed he steered the conversation right back in her direction.

'What if you'd walked out of the frying pan into the fire?' he asked.

'It really couldn't have been any worse than what I had: a job I detested surrounded by beer-swilling colleagues that smoked, made crass jokes—'

'Sounds like you were living the dream,' Gabe cut in, grinning.

'Hardly!' Jinny laughed, then swept her arm in front of her. 'I'm so glad I made the call to Molly. Just look at this place! I have a quirky car, a beautiful cottage and this scenery is stunning.'

'I second that,' replied Gabe, giving her a look that once again caused her heart to give a tiny flip. She wasn't quite sure if he was referring to the scenery or her but she was hoping it was the latter.

Gabe was so easy to talk to and it was such a relief to be able to chat without thinking someone would report back to her father about what had been said. 'And I know I'm only twenty-six but honestly, I felt stifled. There's nothing worse than feeling there's no way out and always having to toe the line. I've never been allowed to do me.'

'You really don't look the type of person to toe the line.'

Jinny raised an eyebrow. 'Tell me more,' she said, smiling but with a serious undertone. She wanted to know exactly how Gabe viewed her.

'There's a quirkiness about you and you know your own mind. There's two things I pride myself on: being a good judge of character and not suffering fools. I think that goes for you too.'

Jinny flushed. 'And how many fools have you come across?'

Gabe took a breath. 'I learned a valuable lesson a long time ago about people… Ten years ago, to be precise.'

There was a sudden look of contempt that flashed across his face and his eyes darkened. Jinny could see he had been deeply hurt by something. This was the most information that Gabe had shared with her and she hoped he would share some more.

'Uprooting yourself from everything you know takes some balls,' he reiterated, trying to steer the conversation back to her.

'Is that what you did?' she asked, steering it right back to him.

'Something like that.'

Once again, he looked saddened but still didn't give much away.

'Have you ever talked about what's going on with you to anyone?' she asked tentatively.

'It's difficult to talk about,' he admitted. 'I've always kept things close to my chest.' He exhaled. 'Most people are out for themselves with little regard for how their actions might affect others. Call it self-preservation, but the only person that you can rely on is yourself… and Dixie,' he added with fondness.

'You can count on me,' she said softly.

'Thanks. That's good to hear.'

They were both silent for a second and took swigs of their beer.

'Isn't it a sad and lonely existence, not letting anyone in?'

'Sometimes, but it usually takes me a long time to let someone in. To be honest with you, there hasn't been anyone I've wanted to open up to, but you never know what's around the corner or when that could be about to change.' He looked at her with such warmth that Jinny's skin flushed with goosebumps.

'You're right there. This time last week I was working in a boring office with a painful commute to work and this week I'm making chutneys and about to enter a winning chutney in the Summer Fair and take Heartcross by storm.'

Gabe laughed. 'I love your optimism! You've only been at the job one week and you're already planning to take over the world.'

'I have plans! Big plans!' Jinny grinned. Finishing her beer, she asked. 'Would you like another one?'

But before Gabe could answer, his phone started ringing. Gabe reached out to pick up the phone and Jinny noticed the name flashing on the screen was 'Eliza'.

Gabe silenced the call but it quickly rang again.

'You can take that, if you want.' Jinny gestured towards the phone, curious to know who Eliza was.

'It's okay,' Gabe replied, as they both heard footsteps crunching along the gravel path.

They looked up and waited to see who would walk around the corner.

'Hello,' a voice shouted. Looking over the gate was an elderly gentleman wearing a flat cap. His wizened face was a map of wrinkles accompanied by a warm smile. In his hand, he was holding a newspaper.

Jinny got to her feet. 'Can I help you at all?' she asked.

'I don't think we've had the pleasure. I'm Hamish, owner of the village shop.' He tipped his cap then thrust his hand forward.

'And I'm Jinny. Lovely to meet you.'

Hamish nodded towards Gabe then held out the newspaper. 'Habit,' he said, taking off his cap.

Jinny took the newspaper from him. 'I don't understand,' she said.

'Every weekend, I still drop off Dixie's newspaper without fail. I've done it for so many years that I can't seem to get out of the habit. And here I am again.' Hamish's voice wavered and Jinny touched his arm.

'It must be difficult not having her here anymore.'

Hamish nodded. 'We used to have a tipple and put the world to rights. I suppose you don't want the newspaper. I was just on autopilot... again.'

'You're very welcome to come and join us,' offered Jinny. 'We can definitely put the world to rights.'

Hamish smiled. 'Thank you, Miss Jinny, but it's a beautiful evening so I think I'm going to take a walk through Primrose Park.'

Jinny could see that even though Hamish was trying to put on a brave face he was missing his friend. 'I would love to still have a newspaper each weekend, if that's okay by you. How much do I owe you?'

He gave a little chuckle. 'Dixie hasn't paid for a newspaper for years. She always provided the tipple and the odd jar of honey.'

'I can do that too.'

Hamish tipped his cap and nodded towards Gabe. 'That would be grand. Enjoy your evening. This garden is a wonderful place to be on such a beautiful summer's evening.'

And with that he turned, leaving Jinny with her hands on her heart as she watched him walk back down the gravel path.

'How absolutely gorgeous was that man, bringing his friend a newspaper for all those years? But how utterly heartbreaking that we have to lose loved ones and good friends.' Jinny sat back down and placed the folded newspaper on the table. It was a newspaper she recognised instantly and even though she had vowed she would never read her father's paper again, here it was, staring her in the face. She opened it up. The headline was bold:

VIVIAN BAMFORD: THE SMILE THAT SAID IT ALL

Instantly, the name struck a chord with Jinny. She dragged her mind back to her first day of work at her father's newspaper. The whole office had been in a frenzy, the phones constantly ringing as the news had hit that the world-famous actress was dead. She remembered the story well and there had been many conspiracy theories about her death. It was rumoured she'd got behind the wheel of her car under the influence of drugs and alcohol and, if Jinny remembered correctly, the car had crashed in the South of France. Vivian's face had been on the cover of every magazine, splashed over every tabloid and broadcast on multiple TV specials about her life and films. The whole world had been in mourning.

Thinking back, Jinny was surprised to remember that her father had been holed up in a meeting room for the whole day, instead of demanding his team cover every aspect of the story. But then, he did eventually order a four-page dedication to her life to be printed a few days later – possibly the nicest thing her father had ever done.

'She was taken too soon. Can you actually believe that was ten years ago?' Jinny tapped the newspaper and looked towards Gabe. 'What an interesting but short life she had. It was rumoured she had connections with royalty – dated a prince they said. And always had a long list of famous men hanging off her arm. Her films were amazing. Growing up, I admired everything about her. And the clothes she wore… She was a fashion icon.'

Gabe was staring at the headline and Jinny did a double take when she noticed that his face had paled, his eyes full of tears. His phone rang again. Once again Eliza's name flashed across the screen. Gabe stood up and picked up his phone and wallet. He swallowed. 'I'm sorry. I have to go.' His voice was almost inaudible. He looked drained of every ounce of energy.

Jinny was taken aback. 'Are you okay? Is it something I've said?' Jinny couldn't understand what had just happened. One minute they were laughing and joking and the next Gabe looked upset and was running for the hills.

'No, but I really need to go.' His phone was still ringing but he silenced the call once again. 'Journalists have a lot to answer for.' Gabe pushed his chair under the table. 'I'll see you in the morning.'

Perplexed, Jinny watched Gabe disappear out of sight. She heard the ring of his phone again but this time he answered it, and she could hear him speaking in a low, serious tone before his voice petered out. Puzzled, she sat staring at the bold headline. She was sure that the front cover had sparked his change of mood. Jinny skimmed the article, which was accompanied by pictures of a magnificent château in the South of France that was rumoured to have been Vivian's home before she died. For once, Jinny was impressed; there was little about Vivian's personal life and it seemed her father's newspaper was capable of printing a story that didn't involve exposing someone's secrets to devastating effect. This was a well-written piece celebrating the life of Vivian Bamford and Jinny couldn't see why Gabe would react to it as he had.

She leaned back in her chair, thinking about how she'd opened up to Gabe about the difficult relationship she had with her father. She'd learned very little about him in return, beyond the fact that there was something that was causing him pain. Jinny didn't like to see anyone struggling, especially when she knew first-hand that having a friend to talk things through with was worth its weight in gold.

But there was one thing that she did know. Regardless of what was causing Gabe's dislike of the press, she didn't have a cat in hell's chance of him opening up if she shared the fact that Ralph Birdwhistle, the owner of this very newspaper, was her father.

Chapter Twelve

One hour later, Jinny was curled up on the settee in the front room and still couldn't get Gabe's rapid departure out of her head. With her laptop balanced on her knee and the newspaper to the side of her, she googled Vivian Bamford. The look on Gabe's face when he spotted Vivian on the front page was implanted in her mind.

Jinny exhaled, thinking back to the night before the story had broken. She could remember it quite clearly as she had been anxious about the next day – her first day working for her father. When she finally got to sleep, she remembered being woken by the sound of her father's voice. His phone call was on speaker and she instantly recognised the voice of his right-hand man from the newspaper – her godfather, William Goddard.

'We need to stop print immediately and get that headline changed.' Her father's voice was agitated despite the fact that he was giving clear, concise orders. 'Do you understand me?'

'Yes, I'm just getting my coat on,' replied William. 'I'll phone you as soon as it's done.'

'Make sure you do. We do not, and I repeat *do not*, want that story to get out because questions will be asked.'

'I understand the potential consequences,' William affirmed. 'I'm leaving for the office now.'

At the time, Jinny had taken the brave move of tiptoeing to the top of the regally arched stairway. Barely daring to breathe she crouched down, her eyes on the half-open living room door. She knew something big was breaking. Through the banister she could see her father was wearing his coat and shoes, meaning he'd only just arrived home. She held her breath, not daring to make a sound as he peeled off his jacket and threw his car keys down on the coffee table before walking towards the fireplace. That was strange in itself. He barely drove himself anywhere as he had a full-time driver on staff. His head was bent low and with both hands resting on the mantelpiece of the huge stone fireplace he let out a long, shuddering breath then looked at his reflection in the mirror.

'Jesus Christ,' he muttered, loud enough for Jinny to hear.

She had no idea what had happened, but there had been an urgency to his voice and it unnerved her. Jinny knew if he caught sight of her it would make things ten times worse but she was rooted to the spot, watching as her father poured himself a large tumbler of whiskey from the decanter on the sideboard. In one large swig the glass was empty, and he made a strangled sound as the amber liquid burned the back of his throat. Immediately he refilled his glass, switched on the TV, sat down on the chesterfield, then fired up his laptop. There was nothing more to see and Jinny slowly tiptoed back to bed.

The next day Jinny had arrived at the office to discover a mass frenzy. Every journalist seemed to have a phone clamped between ear and shoulder, taking notes with one hand and verifying facts on a computer with another. Filing cabinet drawers were being opened and slammed shut, with the whirl of the printer and the drone of the air conditioning adding to the din. It was only then that Jinny had seen the bold headline on the front of *The Daily News* that Vivian Bamford, the most famous actress in the world, was dead.

The last thing she remembered about that day was the look that William had given her father as they left the office that evening. At the time she'd thought it was a look of reassurance after a hard day, but after ten years of working by their sides, Jinny now realised that it had been a look of guilt. And there it was again, that feeling in the pit of her stomach that there was a story to investigate here. There was something about the death of Vivian Bamford that seemed to rattle or upset everyone, including Gabe.

Jinny began to search the internet. It was full of information about Vivian, which wasn't a surprise. Her films were listed, her reviews always outstanding as everything the woman touched turned to gold. Back in the day there had even been reports of film companies fighting for her to appear as their leading lady and offering her obscene amounts of money. Jinny spent half an hour flicking from one article to the next but there was nothing that explained why Gabe had reacted the way he had when he saw the newspaper.

How did Vivian Bamford die? Jinny hit return and stared at the screen then sat up straight.

She read headline after headline, growing more confused. According to some reports, Vivian had died in the South of France, while others suggested it had happened in England. No one seemed to be able to confirm the exact location, which was strange. She zoomed in on the date of the newspaper article in front of her, realising it had been published exactly ten years ago today – the 2nd of August.

Jinny was sure she was on to something, but still couldn't make a connection to Gabe so she typed his and Vivian's names into the search bar and waited in anticipation. But absolutely nothing came up that connected them.

In fact, according to the internet, Gabe Warner didn't exist.

With curiosity still getting the better of her, Jinny decided to check if she still had access to the newspaper database – an archive of all the front covers the newspaper had ever printed. With the date staring her in the face, she knew exactly which issue she was looking for.

Jinny typed in the details then paused, knowing there was a possibility that her father might be notified that she had accessed the files. For a moment her finger hovered over the key but then she pressed enter. Her curiosity was too great to stop now.

The all-too-familiar screen asking for her login and password appeared and she quickly typed them in before she could change her mind. She was in. Next, she typed in the date she was looking for. Immediately, the front cover popped up. She zoomed in on the article and began to read.

According to *The Daily News*' take on the accident, Vivian Bamford had been killed in a car crash while she was travelling in the South of France. It was just an accident – a tragedy – and the moving article went on to highlight what a global treasure Vivian was, with further pages written by Jinny's father dedicated to the actress's life and career. He'd included all her achievements along with photos of Vivian holding her awards and BAFTAs. There was no mention of any next of kin she might have left behind but there was a photo of her standing next to an Aston Martin outside a magnificent château – the same picture as in the article in today's newspaper.

Jinny leaned back in the chair. This was a woman who had been at the top of her game, leading a glamorous lifestyle and rich beyond her wildest dreams. The headline was indeed correct – Vivian had been taken too soon. She closed down the archive and logged off her laptop. Maybe she was overthinking it, letting her old investigative mind run wild because the internet hadn't thrown up anything peculiar except the conflicting reports on the place of Vivian's death. Jinny folded the newspaper and placed the laptop on the coffee table. It must have just been a coincidence that something significant had also happened in Gabe's life ten years ago. Jinny felt disappointed in herself for snooping and delving into other people's business. Gabe would trust her in time and tell her when he was ready. He'd made it quite clear he wasn't a fan of journalists for whatever reason so she needed to step away from that role once and for all. That was her old life.

Swinging her legs to the floor, she stood and walked across to the window, noticing Molly and Cam ambling up the road. Molly was pushing the pram and Cam was giving a very tired-looking George a piggyback.

She turned and picked up a framed photo on the dresser. It showed Dixie and her husband George with two young boys who she assumed were their grandkids. They were standing near what looked like a lake. Taking a closer look, she noticed that one of the boys resembled a young-looking Cam. He was standing proud, holding a fishing rod and wearing shorts and Wellington boots. The smiles on their faces said it all. Jinny placed the photograph back on the dresser and thought about her own mum. Jinny was twenty-six and still missed her every day. Ralph wasn't one for showing any emotion so the loss of her mother was something she had never discussed with him. In fact, Gabe was the first person other than Jay that she'd ever felt comfortable opening up to about it.

Replacing the photo, Jinny ran her fingers across the

spines of the books then took out a blue velvet photo album that looked somewhat regal. On the front was a small love-heart lock, which bound the album firmly together. It needed a key to open it and immediately Jinny thought of the extra key on Donovan's keyring. After retrieving the keys from the kitchen table she placed the key in the lock and turned it.

Click. It sprang open.

Sitting back down, Jinny balanced the album on the arm of the chair, opened it and smiled. The first photo was of Dixie and George. He'd scooped her up in his arms, the caption underneath reading:

The day we moved in to Bumblebee Cottage

They looked so young, carefree and very much in love. She turned the page and there was Donovan. Dixie was behind the wheel, her smile wide. The caption read:

Setting off on our very first road trip

Jinny remembered that Molly had told her that they'd driven all the way to the South of France and that's where the idea of Bees' Knees had been born. She turned the page to find a photo of Dixie and George sharing a picnic on the side of the road. Another showed them paddling barefoot in a stream. They really had been on an adventure together and each photograph told a story, their smiles radiating such happiness.

'The summer of love,' she murmured.

On the next page was a recipe that had been scribbled on a piece of cream embossed paper, with a gold heading reading: *Château de Laurent*. The recipe was for apple chutney. Jinny wondered if this was the very first recipe that Dixie had come up with. After all, Molly had mentioned that Dixie had invented it on her grand adventure in France.

The pictures in the album were of a beautiful château surrounded by a maze of immaculate and stunning gardens and grounds that extended along a river. There was endless manicured box hedging, elaborate geometric shapes and startlingly scenery. The whole place was dreamy – a picture postcard. The last photo was of Dixie and George sitting at a table in the garden with the château directly behind them.

'Dramatic and breathtakingly beautiful,' Jinny murmured. 'And where it all began.'

Staring at the photo, she realised there was something very familiar about that château; it felt like she had seen it before. Jinny tapped the photograph.

She *had* seen it before… and only moments before!

Quickly reaching for her laptop she scrolled back through her search history and pressed enter. Jinny's pulse was racing as she scrutinised the screen. There was Vivian Bamford, standing in exactly the same garden, in front of the exact same château as Dixie and George. Jinny's heart began to race, her thoughts tumbling over each other as she quickly typed *Dixie* and *Vivian* into the search engine.

Nothing.

Next, she typed *Vivian Bamford* and *Bumblebee Cottage*.

Again, nothing.

There was something inside Jinny that was telling her this was not just a coincidence but she had no clue what the connection was beyond the fact that the two women had visited the same château. She exhaled. What exactly was she missing here?

Chapter Thirteen

B y three o'clock in the morning, Jinny was still tossing and turning. Reaching for the glass of water on her bedside cabinet she took a sip then sat up in bed and began to scroll through Instagram. She smiled at an image of Jay dressed up in a blue sequinned jumpsuit and wearing a long blonde wig, clearly enjoying himself at an Abba tribute night. That was the only thing she missed about her old life – their mad nights out. Jinny noticed the photograph had been posted only twenty minutes ago, which suggested Jay might still be very much awake, if a little inebriated.

She dialled his number and put the phone on speaker. Jay picked up within three rings.

'Honey, honey, oh I love you, ah ha,' he sang. 'See what I did there? Abba night combined with bees!'

Jinny chuckled. 'You are not funny! Actually, that was a little funny...'

'Gimme, gimme, gimme a man after midnight,' Jay carried on singing. 'There was be a time when I couldn't quite openly sing that in public.'

'And how is your love life?' asked Jinny.

'Probably as non-existent as yours.'

'I'm saying nothing,' replied Jinny.

'Oh my *g-o-s-h*,' Jay said, stringing out the word. 'Please tell me you have been pollinated by the beekeeper?'

'Jay! Don't be ridiculous. It's still early days. But he *is* very handsome…'

'Is that why you're ringing me at ridiculous o'clock? I thought your late-night calling would have stopped now you've changed jobs.'

Jinny had often rung Jay in the early hours when she was onto a story and couldn't sleep as she knew she could trust him one hundred per cent with any information she shared. She hesitated, knowing that what she was about to say sounded ridiculous, but there was still that tiny niggle that something wasn't quite as it seemed.

'Jinny!'

'Listen to me, Jay. I need you to tell me the honest truth about what you make of this…'

Jinny relayed the story of how Gabe had upped and left quickly after seeing the front page of the newspaper and how Vivian Bamford had been at the same château as Dixie and George.

'Surely that's not a coincidence?'

Silence.

'Are you still there? You haven't passed out on me, have you?' asked Jinny.

'I've got no chance of that now you have me intrigued,' he replied.

Jinny could hear some rustling at the other end of the line. 'What are you doing?'

'Organising my snacks and climbing into bed. Let me put you on speaker.'

Jinny shook her head, picturing the scene.

'Okay, what's the château's name?'

'Château de Laurent,' Jinny said, hearing Jay tapping on his laptop.

'It's pretty famous, you know. Owned by Margo Laurent.'

'I know. Margo was a friend of Dixie's. They met when Dixie and George visited the château on their first trip abroad and she's even been to visit her here at Bumblebee Cottage. But what's the link between Vivian Bamford and Margo Laurent?'

'Call yourself a journalist—'

'An *ex*-journalist.' she interrupted, laughing.

'The link is simple. They were both in the entertainment industry – granted it was decades apart – and my guess is that their paths crossed and Margo invited Vivian to hire out a wing of the château. And as far as Dixie and George were concerned, it was a place they stumbled across on holiday and that's just a coincidence.'

'Possibly, but what's the connection with Gabe?'

'Absolutely nothing. No connection whatsoever. He's just minding his own business and something has sparked a painful memory from the past. Maybe it's an anniversary of something. Who knows? I don't think there's a connection at all. But I have to say this château looks amazing. Whoever owns it now is very fortunate.'

'Mmm, I'm not convinced. I feel like I'm missing something.'

'You, my dear, are buzzing around the wrong honeycomb. Mark my words.'

'I'm overthinking things?'

'I hate to say it but yes. Just get to know Gabe. Be his friend. If there's something more, trust is the only way to go. Let him know you're there for him and he'll open up to you in his own time.'

'I know, I know.'

'Oh, and Jinny…'

'Yes?'

'Go to sleep!'

Jay hung up the call, causing Jinny to laugh. She didn't take offence, as it was Jay's preferred method of ending a call when he'd had enough of her. And granted, it was the early hours of the morning.

Pulling the duvet up to her chin, she turned on the alarm before switching off the bedside light. There were only five hours of sleep left to grab before Gabe arrived in the morning. He wouldn't usually come on the weekend but the farmers' market was on the third Saturday of the month, which was tomorrow. She gave one last thought to the article that had sparked her investigation tonight. There was no doubt that the easy-going, jovial atmosphere she'd enjoyed with Gabe had somewhat plummeted when he saw it. There was more to it, she just knew it.

Chapter Fourteen

The second Jinny opened her eyes, she had the feeling she was being watched and, bolting upright, she was indeed met with a pair of eyes firmly fixed on her.

'Jeez, Claude! You frightened the life out of me. Where have you come from?'

As soon as Claude saw her move, his tail wagged furiously and before she knew it, he had launched himself straight at her and was licking her face. She manged to wrestle him and push him away before he rolled over, waving his legs in the air. Jinny ruffled his stomach. 'How have you even got in here?' Then she remembered she'd been that occupied with searching for information, she'd gone straight up the stairs to bed, leaving the back door wide open.

Swinging her legs out of bed, she pulled on a hoodie and hurried down the stairs with Claude bounding after her.

'Good morning,' sang Gabe, sinking his teeth into a hot,

buttery slice of granary bread. 'Fresh from the bakery – do you want some? Oh, there he is. I wondered where you'd got to, Claude. And there's tea in the pot,' he said, pointing at the table.

'I woke to find myself being watched, followed by yet another slobbery kiss, and now you seem to be in my kitchen, making toast.'

Gabe pointed to the door. 'I thought you were up. The door was wide open. That's what Dixie used to do.'

'I must have left it open last night.'

'You look exhausted. Did you not sleep well?'

Whatever had put Gabe in a reflective mood last night seemed to have passed so Jinny wasn't going to spoil things by admitting she was shattered because she'd been up all night investigating Vivian Bamford.

'I did,' she replied, telling a white lie.

'Honey…'

'I think it's a little too early in the relationship to be calling me honey.' Jinny grinned, pouring a mug of tea.

'Honey for your toast, I meant.' He pointed to the jar in the middle of the table. 'I've got a couple of things to do in the greenhouse and I'm sure there's an order that needs delivering this morning.'

'I'll check that out,' replied Jinny, taking a bite of her toast. 'If I remember rightly, it's local.'

'All deliveries are local.' Gabe laughed.

'But not for long because soon we will be in the supermarkets!'

'That's what I love about you, always the optimist.'

'There's no point being any other way.'

'You finish your breakfast and I'll meet you out front in about thirty minutes,' Gabe said, looking up at the clock.

'Perfect.'

As he started walking towards the back door, he called Claude to heel from where he was sprawled on the red stone tiled floor. 'And I'm sorry, I didn't mean to intrude.'

'You didn't. Having tea and toast waiting for me in the morning... I could get used to that,' she said, unable to control the dreamy smile on her face.

'Maybe you should leave the door open more often.' Gabe grinned as he slipped out of the back door into the morning sun, leaving the aroma of his woodsy aftershave behind.

'Maybe I should,' Jinny replied, but only once he was out of sight.

Twenty minutes later, after a quick shower, Jinny swiped her clothes from the wardrobe, plumping for a lightweight, colourful summer dress. Sitting down at the dressing table, she tied her hair up in a bun then stared at herself in the mirror. How things had changed. The cottage already felt like home and even though she had only been in Heartcross a short time, her old life was beginning to feel like it had happened a lifetime ago. After applying a small amount of make-up followed by a squirt of perfume, she pulled on a pair of ballet flats then made her way to the shed to collect the orders.

Gabe was standing next to the van outside The Old Bakehouse, waiting for her. This morning he had the casual look going on: denim shorts, loafers and a soft white T-shirt, with a pair of sunglasses pushed up on his head. He waved at Jinny before rushing towards her to help when he noticed her arms were laden with a tray of chutneys.

'Where is this order for?' he asked, opening the van door. 'We can deliver them on the way to the market.'

'No need. Today's order is right here.' She nodded towards The Old Bakehouse.

'I'll drop them in then. You climb into the van. Oh, should I mention what we're up to today, with the honey cider chutney?'

Jinny shook her head. 'No, let's keep it a secret. We don't want to share with anyone what product we'll be entering in the competition. We need to keep the other competitors on their toes.'

'Gotcha,' he replied, smiling as he disappeared into the bakery carrying the tray.

A couple of minutes later, Gabe climbed into the van next to Jinny. 'Are you ready? Your very first trip to the farmers' market.'

'Buzzing!' she replied.

'You've really taken to village life, haven't you?'

'I like to think so. Between the villagers and the bees, I feel like I've made thousands of new friends overnight.'

'A thousand and one,' confirmed Gabe, his eyes sparkling as he gave her a captivating smile.

'That's good to hear,' she replied, with a warm, fuzzy feeling inside.

Gabe began to drive the van through the village towards the track that joined the road to take them over the bridge. A little further up was the main road through Glensheil and Gabe pointed to a small deli on the left of the street, which displayed an extravagant array of goodies. There was an expensive glass case filled with cured meats, everything from pastrami to chorizo, along with jars of pickles, oils and condiments. 'Dixie fell out with that deli.'

'Really? Why?' asked Jinny.

Gabe took a swift glance out of the window as they drove past. 'Because the owner decided to start making his own chutneys to sell in the shop.'

'Did Dixie not like the competition?' asked Jinny.

'She didn't like the fact that he was spooning her chutneys into his jars and charging more!' Gabe raised his eyebrows.

'No way!'

'Yes way. She only found out because someone mentioned it tasted the same as hers so she sent Molly in to buy some and tasted it for herself. All hell broke loose.'

'Some people!' Jinny laughed, wondering why anyone would go to such lengths.

They travelled down a side street, which opened up into a small square. Gabe parked the van and they both jumped out. There were rows of stalls filled with local produce –

bundles of carrots, beets and asparagus, shiny tomatoes and baskets of fruit.

'This looks amazing,' Jinny said admiringly, looking all around her.

'Have you written down a list of ingredients you want to put in this award-winning chutney?'

Jinny waved a piece of paper in the air. 'I have! My first ever recipe,' she said proudly, handing the paper over to Gabe.

She watched him as he ran through the ingredients before he handed the piece of paper back.

'The first thing we need is the cider.'

'Over there.' Jinny pointed to as stall a little further on. 'That looks like just the thing.'

'Apples, pears, onions, bay leaves we can source from the cottage—' added Gabe.

'And of course, the honey,' interrupted Jinny.

'Prunes we can get from here.'

Jinny was enjoying herself. Gabe was in a good mood and the more she thought about it the more she was mortified that she'd attempted to investigate him online. Jay was right; the best way to build trust with anyone was to let the friendship develop naturally.

'It's so colourful,' exclaimed Jinny as they began to walk around the market. The produce at the nearby vegetable stall looked divine.

Arriving at the cider stall, Gabe pointed at the bottles on the table. 'It's up to you to decide which one you think is best.'

'I haven't got a clue!'

'You'd better start tasting then,' encouraged Gabe.

'If I didn't know better, I'd think you were trying to get me drunk.'

The man behind the stall greeted them and immediately lined up numerous samples. He gave them a quick run-through of their origin and ingredients before Jinny set off on the task of tasting each one.

'They all taste too good to me, which means I might have to have another sample of each...' Jinny joked once she'd sipped each of them.

Gabe laughed. 'You can't be drunk in charge of Delilah later,' he mused.

'Aww, you pair have a daughter. How lovely. And what an unusual but gorgeous name. How old, may I ask?' the stall owner queried.

Jinny grinned and was about to put the record straight that Delilah was an apple-peeling machine that was donkey's years old when Gabe jumped in and answered the question. 'Delilah's in her twenties.'

The man's mouth dropped opened. 'You don't look old enough.'

Jinny linked her arm through Gabe's. 'He's kidding! But I'll take the compliment.' She pointed. 'Two bottles of that one, please.'

Gabe handed over a couple of notes and the man handed over the change and a carrier bag.

'However you pair are living your life, you keep it up because it's doing wonders for you both. Those smiles are radiating happiness and if you don't mind me saying, you make a lovely couple.' He tipped his cap. 'Have a good day.'

Jinny giggled as they walked away. 'He actually thought we were a couple, with a daughter of twenty! I'm only twenty-six!'

'And you're looking good for it,' replied Gabe, looking towards her.

She liked the way he pushed his fringe to one side, out of his eyes, showing more of his face, which was tanned from the sun. For a moment she wondered what it would be like to truly be on the arm of Gabe Warner.

Gabe must have sensed she was thinking about him, because he looked at her and smiled, sending a swarm of fireflies swirling at top speed around her stomach. She could feel the sexual chemistry between them and as they reached the next stall she stole another furtive glance in his direction. There was something she liked about the thought of being in a couple with Gabe, but she had to remind herself it was early days and even though there had been an instant attraction – on her side, at least – she still knew very little about him.

'Can I just clarify something?' he asked.

Jinny looked up at him and nodded.

'Are we actually going to make chutney with that cider?'

'What else are you suggesting?'

'That we drink it. It's such great weather for it.'

'I'm sure we can drink one bottle but I need the other

one as I want to have a go at making the new chutney this afternoon. I want to win this competition.'

'Let's live a little.' There was a mischievous look in Gabe's eye that didn't pass Jinny by.

Gabe was right; this was what she had craved – happy, carefree days – and what a perfect opportunity to find more out about him. She was a firm believer that things happen for a reason.

'Yes, let's,' she replied. 'We may as well live dangerously!'

She had a lot to thank Bumblebee Cottage for.

Chapter Fifteen

'We're not drinking any cider until we've made a batch of chutney,' Jinny insisted, pushing Gabe gently towards the door of the kitchen while he was trying to walk towards the sunny patio.

'Okay, I give up. Chutney first but drink after. Even though I'm feeling a little peckish.'

'Once we're done, I'll whip us up a bite to eat.'

'Okay, I'm in,' Gabe said, following Jinny into the kitchen. 'Let's have a look at this recipe.'

Opening up Dixie's recipe book, Jinny placed it down on the table. Next to it she put the notepaper with her handwritten recipe. 'What I've done is tweaked one of Dixie's recipes to bring it into the here and now.' Jinny tapped the recipe in the book, then the piece of paper.

'You have been busy, haven't you?'

'What do you think?' asked Jinny, looking between Gabe and the recipes.

Gabe was scanning both. 'All good ingredients there but I think there's something missing to give it that kick. We don't want this to be bland. We want the judge to sit up and take notice.'

'What are you suggesting?' asked Jinny, intrigued, wondering what else could be added to the mixture.

'I'm not sure. I'll have a think. We're aiming for the autumn market, aren't we?'

'A chutney for all seasons, ideally, but yes, I think that's a good place to start.'

'I'll go and collect the apples and pears,' said Gabe, heading towards the door. 'And have a think about what Dixie would sprinkle to add a little bit of magic.'

'And I'll set up the kitchen and begin chopping the onions.'

'There're loads in the pantry.'

Gabe disappeared towards the shed while Jinny pulled out the pans from the cupboard and retrieved Delilah from the pantry.

Within five minutes Gabe had returned with a bucket overflowing with apples and pears.

'I think we have enough cider to make a batch of ten jars. I just need the cider vinegar.'

'Far shelf in the right-hand cupboard,' Gabe replied, leaning against the kitchen table.

Jinny shooed him in that direction. 'Go on then.'

'Since when did you get bossy?' he replied light-heartedly, laughing as he headed to the cupboard.

'We need honey.'

'Got plenty of that.'

'And prunes, bay leaves, salt and fresh ginger.'

Gabe came back with his arms laden with ingredients. 'Have to say, I'm not a big fan of prunes.' He wrinkled his nose in disgust.

'You won't taste them,' she replied, counting the apples and realising the cap was loose on the bottle of cider. 'Oh no. I think he's given us a bottle that's been drunk out of.' Jinny picked up the bottle in dismay and inspected it.

'No way. That's out of order. What are we going to do now?' Gabe was trying to stifle his laugher.

Jinny narrowed her eyes and walked straight over to him. She leaned in close and took a big sniff.

'What are you doing?'

She pressed her finger on his chest. 'You've had a little tipple! I can smell it.'

'I haven't. It must be the samples we drank.'

'Smell me,' she insisted.

With a look of amusement Gabe leaned inwards and inhaled. 'You smell of Chanel No. 5, very nice. A little over the top for making chutney though.'

Jinny raised an eyebrow. 'You know your perfumes, but that's not the point. I don't smell of cider and I drank more samples than you.'

Gabe leaned in again, this time coming even closer, his eyes locked on hers, his lips mere centimetres away. Her whole body gave a tiny shiver. He pulled back slowly.

'Yep, you're right; you don't.'

'But you do!'

Gabe's eyes looked towards the plastic cup on the worktop.

'How have you managed to take a sneaky drink without me noticing?' She slapped his chest playfully. 'No more until we've made this chutney, you hear me?'

'Spoilsport.' He looked at her with adorable puppy eyes. 'But I have to say, you have great taste in perfume.'

Jinny bit down on her lip to suppress her smile. 'Get to work,' she ordered, and Gabe saluted. Jinny quite liked flirting with him.

Gabe and Delilah were hard at work peeling and slicing the apples while Jinny stoned and chopped the prunes. Once all the fruit was washed and chopped, they added the rest of the ingredients to the pan and placed it on the rapid hot plate on the Aga.

'Are we ready to make honey cider chutney?'

'We certainly are! But as soon as it starts bubbling, move it to the simmering plate.'

Ten minutes later, the chutney was simmering away on the Aga and Gabe pinched a little on the wooden spoon.

'What do you think?' asked Jinny, noticing the scrunched-up look on his face.

'I hate to say it but it's missing something. It's a little bland.'

Jinny took the spoon from him and tasted the chutney. 'You're right. It needs that extra oomph.'

They both stared at the simmering pan. Gabe walked over to Dixie's recipe book and began turning the pages. 'It's missing that autumn winter feeling.'

'What would Dixie have added?'

'I'm just thinking about that,' replied Gabe with a look of concentration on his face. 'We can taste the honey and the cider but we need to make this chutney stand out from the crowd.'

'I agree.' Jinny watched Gabe walk over to the pantry and run his finger along the line of herbs and spices standing to attention on the shelf. 'We have the ginger...' He was lost in thought for a moment. 'Think...' he said. 'It needs...'

'Cinnamon is always a good winter warmer,' suggested Jinny.

'Good suggestion but we need a little more than that. I think we need allspice... Yes, that's exactly what we need to bring the flavours out but there's still something missing to bring out the extra zest.'

'How about a bit of candied orange peel? That always reminds me of autumn.'

Gabe spun round. 'That's it!' A wide smile spread across his face. 'That will blend the spices together more.'

'Teamwork!' Jinny high-fived him, leaving him looking amused. 'Let's get it all added.'

Gabe passed over the allspice and watched as Jinny grated the zest of an orange.

'This is going to taste so good.'

'I certainly hope so!'

After Jinny added the rest of the ingredients and mixed them into the simmering pan, Gabe took another taste. 'It needs a little more allspice.'

Jinny spooned in some more and waited for Gabe's verdict.

'That's it!' he exclaimed. 'Spot on!'

Jinny couldn't wait to try and as she sampled the mixture she felt confident that they were on to a winner. She couldn't have done it without Gabe's help.

'I wonder what Dixie would think about this new recipe?'

'I'm sure she would have loved it.' Gabe moved over to the table and picked up his ringing phone. 'Damn. I forgot I'm meant to be somewhere after lunch. I'm really sorry but I'm going to have to leave you to it.'

'Is it important? You can't go now. This is our first batch of our chutney.'

'I'm so sorry but I'm afraid it is,' he said, edging backwards towards the door.

Jinny was hit by a wave of disappointment. She had been hoping to spend a little more time with him.

'But I'm free later on. I'll make it up to you. Dinner tonight?'

Jinny's mood lifted. 'Where? What time?'

Gabe quickly turned back towards her and placed a swift kiss on her cheek, taking her completely by surprise. 'I'll let you know. It's a date!'

'It's a date!' she repeated, a huge smile spreading across her face. She wondered where he was off to in such a hurry but that thought was short-lived because all she could think about was the fact that they were going out to dinner tonight. Hopefully, that meant she was going to find out a little more about him. If so, it would be an ideal time to tell him who she was. She could feel the chemistry between them and wanted everything out in the open. Jinny had everything crossed that he would be understanding.

'And don't burn the chutney!' he shouted back over his shoulder. Then he was gone.

The pan was still bubbling and Jinny moved it across to the simmering plate before lining up the jars. Then she took another taste. 'This is good,' she said, over the moon with their attempt. All she had to do now was hope that the taste and the Bees' Knees backstory would win over the judge.

Her phone beeped. It was Jay.

How's life in Heartcross? Are you staying out of trouble?

I am. Took your advice and am chilling... Having dinner with Gabe tonight!

You go girl! (Heart Emoji) x

Chapter Sixteen

Once again, Jinny looked at the note in her hand.

Meet me at the Honey Pot at 7pm.

The note had been pushed through the door around 4 p.m. while Jinny was soaking in the bath. For the last hour she had been frantically rummaging through her clothes, trying to find something to wear for the evening, but nothing seemed suitable. In the end, she plumped for a pair of cropped jeans with a white blouse and a pair of ballet flats. Plain and simple.

Jinny checked the time – it was just before 7 p.m. – and with a fizz of excitement she locked the back door of the cottage and followed the hexagonal paving slabs towards The Honey Pot.

The whole day had been perfect and Jinny had enjoyed every second of it but she was feeling a little apprehensive about coming clean about her real identity. She hoped Gabe would see that she hadn't condoned her father's actions at the newspaper and that it had actually been the reason she had walked away.

Approaching The Honey Pot, she found the door ajar and pushed it open, looking around. She couldn't see Gabe but noticed a trail of paper bees on the ground. With a huge beam on her face, she brought her hands up to her heart and followed the trail towards the back door, past the work station where they'd extracted the honey. Jinny had never been through this door – she'd just assumed it was a storeroom – and what she saw there was a sign pinned to it saying '*Open me!*' So that was exactly what she did.

She was amazed to discover the door led to a beautiful semi-enclosed courtyard. There was a bistro table and chairs positioned to take in the view of the flower garden and orchard in the distance. Flower boxes, hanging baskets bursting with colour and a trellis with climbing vines with vibrant pink flowers decorated the area entirely. With the sunlight filtering through the trees, it was the perfect evening. But still there was no Gabe.

Jinny looked all around and noticed the line of bees steering her to a set of wooden steps, which led to a first-floor balcony. She followed the trail; her heart was thumping and she forced herself to breathe calmly. Reaching the top of the stairs she discovered a roof terrace. Colourful triangular bunting hung on the rails of the wooden balcony and the entire place was swathed in fairy lights. Jinny stopped dead in her tracks. In the middle of the open-air decking were two chairs on either side of a table. A white linen tablecloth had been decorated skilfully with the same paper bees, and dozens of tea lights dotted the floor. Jinny looked around and spotted Gabe sitting on a wooden bench in the corner. Her heart started beating nineteen to the dozen. He looked drop-dead gorgeous.

'What took you so long?' he said, standing up with a smile.

'What's going on? What is all this?'

'Dinner,' he replied.

The air was charged between them.

He took Jinny's hand and led her to the settee. 'Take a seat before dinner is served.'

'You've cooked dinner?'

'I would like to take credit for that one but no, I asked the chef from The Lake House to cook us up something delicious.'

Jay had mentioned The Lake House when Jinny first looked into Heartcross, and she'd since learned that the only way to the restaurant was by boat. It had been frequented by numerous famous people, including royalty, in its time.

'You're pulling out all the stops. What exactly is the occasion? I know it's not my birthday.'

'When is your birthday?' he asked, holding up a bottle of chilled Champagne.

'Officially the worst birthday in the world: Christmas Day,' she replied, rolling her eyes.

Gabe walked over to the balcony. 'Come and take a look

at the view from up here . . . Yes, Christmas Day must be one of the worst birthdays in the world.'

Jinny placed her hands on the wooden rail and took in the view. From up there you could see the full length of the gardens with the mountain towering in the distance. She breathed in the fresh air.

'Did you get joint presents or separate ones?' he continued.

Jinny took a moment to think of her father. Christmas had always felt lonely to her. There had been no siblings to play with and she couldn't go and visit her friends or have a party because Christmas was always about family. She'd usually ended up being dragged to William's house, where her father would drink whiskey and Jinny spent the whole day watching TV.

'Usually joint, and usually money,' she replied. 'I can't even remember a present from my childhood, which sounds particularly sad, doesn't it? It was never an exciting day. This year I have every intention of enjoying myself. I can imagine Christmas Day in The Grouse and Haggis surrounded by good community cheer.'

'I have a feeling this Christmas will be a good one for you.'

Feeling his presence so close to her and the way he looked at her gave Jinny that jittery feeling in the pit of her stomach, every inch of her body erupting in goosebumps. The way he looked at her, she knew there was something between them, and it wasn't just her who felt it. Then Gabe popped the cork from the bottle and it flew over the balcony. Jinny gave a tiny squeal and raised her hands in surprise. She giggled as they looked over the balcony and watched the cork land in the courtyard. Being in Gabe's company was just easy; she felt extremely relaxed and comfortable.

With the most gorgeous smile, he handed her a glass and filled it up. 'Here's to a wonderful evening.'

'I see you've plumped for the real stuff.' She was suitably impressed. 'That's some extravagance on a beekeeper's wage.' She chinked her glass against his. 'To my new home, Bumblebee Cottage, and to the village of Heartcross. And to the fact that I've made my very first chutney recipe. I can't believe it!'

'You have!'

'I can't wait to enter it into the competition. This year, the Summer Fair; next year, supermarket shelves… then the world! What I love about this place is how welcoming everyone is. I thought I might feel like an outsider but that's not the case at all.'

'It is a lovely village, with a brilliant community. I ended up here because Dixie promised that everyone would welcome me too. And they did. The community made things so much easier during the most difficult time of my life.'

Jinny reached and squeezed his hand. 'Do you want to talk about it?'

Gabe swallowed. 'I think I do. I was actually hoping we could talk about it tonight. I know my behaviour has been a little erratic and I want to be completely honest with you.'

Gabe gestured towards the table, then politely pulled out a chair for her. 'You're the first person I've wanted to be up front with outside my usual circle. I don't know what it is about you, but…'

Jinny listened intently. She liked that Gabe felt comfortable enough to confide in her.

'Having you around really has lifted my spirits.'

'What do you need them to be lifted from?' she asked.

'A deep slump,' Gabe admitted. 'You being here has made me realise a few things. The first being that I might have created my own suffering by dwelling on the past too much.'

'The past is something we can't change but we can learn from it. Look at me. Since arriving in Heartcross I've become a different person. I wasn't happy with life but from the moment I arrived at the bottom of Love Heart Lane I've been determined to look at each day as a gift. This whole place makes me feel happy. I mean, it's got everything a girl could ever wish for.' Jinny held his gaze as the feeling of the first flush of love washed over her.

'I want to know everything about you, Jinny Smith, and I need to be honest with you about a few things that have shaped my life. Wait here.'

Jinny watched him disappear down the wooden stairs and return moments later holding two silver cloches. 'We have a mixed seafood starter, all from The Lake House bay. You do like seafood, don't you?' Gabe suddenly looked panicked. 'I never thought to check.'

'I love it, and this looks amazing. Thank you.' Jinny was

impressed; there were scallops, mussels, lobster, and a side salad accompanied by crusty bread.

He placed the food on the table. 'Today was fun – the farmers' market and of course the cider.'

Jinny noticed how relaxed he looked. 'Yes, there was a little bit left for me to enjoy after the chutney was made and your disappearance.'

Gabe seated himself back at the table. The eye contact between them was strong, and their legs touched under the table as they began to tuck in.

'There's something I want to be honest with you about, because you'll find out sooner or later and I want you to hear it from me.'

Jinny's heart was hammering against her chest. She didn't have a clue what Gabe was about to say but he was clearly leading up to something big. 'Does this have anything to do with your dislike of journalists? Because if so, there's something I need to be honest with you about too.'

'It is, but can I go first? What I'm about to tell you – and believe me when I say this – I've never shared the whole story with anyone except Dixie. It's a difficult one to share and you might be wondering why now. But the timing just feels right for me on so many levels.' His voice cracked.

Jinny gave him an encouraging smile. 'It's okay. Take your time. I'm listening,' she replied reassuringly. She could see whatever Gabe was about to tell her was causing him a lot of pain.

'When I heard Bumblebee Cottage was being rented out,

and the position of chutney-maker was being advertised, I was apprehensive, wondering who I might have to work with. And then you turned up in your flowery dungarees, got yourself sunburnt to a crisp, set off the sprinklers and got a sting in your backside in a matter of days.' He chuckled. 'What was there not to like? You were different and warm-hearted, even if you did take too many photographs...'

'Which you don't like.' Jinny could kick herself for interrupting.

'And you deserve to know the reason why.' Gabe took a sip of his drink and Jinny noticed him blink away a tear.

'I felt a connection with you the second I saw you outside the teashop. And then I couldn't quite believe it when you showed up at the interview. I was sorry to hear about your relationship with your father and how you had to give up everything to move here and set up a brand-new life, but it also made me admire you.'

'Thank you,' replied Jinny. As soon as Gabe had finished whatever he was going to say she would tell him everything about her father.

'My gut feeling is usually right and I think you are a genuine, decent person. I know I'm stating the obvious here but you're also utterly gorgeous.'

Jinny's eyes widened at his words and her smile hitched wider. 'You're not that bad yourself.'

'Dixie told me that someone would cross my path and bring life back to me... if I let them.' He blew out a breath. 'Sometimes you have to let people in and I think I'm ready to do that. Ten years ago, Heartcross was my brand-new start, and that's thanks to Dixie. I was at breaking point with no one to turn to.'

Jinny curbed her journalistic instinct and didn't interrupt.

'Jinny, I've not been entirely truthful and I'm feeling guilty about that. I don't want to hide who I am from you.'

'What are you hiding?' Jinny asked.

'Ten years ago, there was…' He paused. 'I have a…' The words didn't come out.

'Take your time,' reassured Jinny. 'It's okay.'

'Jinny! JINNY!'

Jinny swung her head towards the balcony, instantly recognising her father's voice but utterly confused as to why she was hearing it now, in this crucial moment with Gabe. What was her father doing here?

'Jinny, I know you're here!' Her father's voice was getting louder.

Jinny remained seated. The last thing she wanted at this very moment in time was any sort of confrontation from her father.

Now up on his feet, Gabe looked over the edge of the balcony and Jinny followed to stand next to him. Her father was pounding through the gardens of Bumblebee Cottage and it was only a matter of seconds before they came face to face. Looking over towards Gabe, the butterflies and goosebumps had now evaporated and Jinny was swathed with anxiety.

As Gabe locked eyes with her she saw that he was shaking, his face pallid.

'What is it, Gabe? Are you okay? You look like you've seen a ghost.'

'R-Ralph Birdwhistle,' he stammered. 'What the hell is he doing here?'

'He's my father.' The words left Jinny's mouth and she could see the instant contempt on Gabe's face. His jaw was rigid, and hurt, anger and disappointment were written all over his face.

'Please tell me you're joking. Your name is Smith. You said so, at your interview.'

'It's my mother's maiden name,' she confessed.

'You've set me up.' He raked his hand through his hair. 'You have, haven't you? How could I have been so stupid?'

'Gabe, I don't know what you think is going on here but I promise you I've not set you up in any way. It's not what you're thinking.' Jinny spoke calmly even though inside she was a confused mess and her heart was beating nineteen to the dozen. 'Why would I have set you up?'

'Oh my God, you're a journalist. You're one of *them*. You were sent here to get the story.' He swung his arm wide and gestured towards the orchard where her father could still be heard calling her name.

'I've not been sent here to get any story. I'm here for me.'

But Gabe wasn't listening. 'And to think I was about to tell you everything. It's been ten years and still you people can't leave it alone. How the hell have you tracked me down?'

Jinny was bewildered and she began to feel herself shake. 'I don't know what you're talking about. Gabe, I promise you I don't know what is going on here. Talk to me.'

Gabe huffed. 'You people are all the same. You just don't know when to stop wrecking people's lives. I'm disappointed in myself. You actually had me fooled. I thought you were genuine. I liked you! How stupid was I to let my guard down?'

Immediately Jinny noted the past tense of 'liked'. She was close to tears. 'Please, calm down and tell me what's going on.' She reached out for his arm but he pushed her away.

'Are you a journalist? Do you work for *The Daily News*?'

'I was and I did, but not anymore. Gabe, you can trust me.'

Gabe wasn't willing to listen. 'You and the likes of Ralph Birdwhistle are not welcome here. This was my safe place and all because of a story your father pursued relentlessly. Who has to die this time? Now leave me alone.'

Gabe gave her a look that shook her to the core then walked away. The view of him leaving blurred as tears filled her eyes. Jinny was at rock bottom.

Chapter Seventeen

Jinny walked from The Honey Pot towards the cottage, confused and upset. All she could think about was going after Gabe and trying to get to the bottom of what had just happened. But with her father standing by the back door of the cottage that wasn't going to happen any time soon. Jinny wanted answers and she had a long list of questions to fire at her father.

He didn't greet her with any warmth.

'There you are. Do you ever pick up your phone? I've been calling you for the past half hour.'

'I left it on the kitchen table. What are you doing here?' she asked, looking over her shoulder, but Gabe had vanished.

'You know what I'm doing here. I've come to take you home.'

Jinny stared at him.

'Why would you want to take me home?'

'You have a job and an apartment back in London.'

'This is my home now.'

'You've been here a little over a week. Look, people in the office think you're on holiday so there will be no embarrassment when you come back. They don't need to know you've had a tantrum.'

Jinny was not going to rise to his belittling. 'You're not listening to me. I am not coming back and I don't care what people in the office think.'

She knew exactly how this conversation was going to go and she wasn't in the mood to keep going over old ground. At this moment there was only one conversation she wanted to have with her father and one question that needed answering.

'How do you know Gabe Warner?' she blurted out, watching him carefully.

Her father looked perplexed. 'What are you talking about? Who's Gabe Warner? Never heard of him. Listen, would you mind if I have a glass of water? I've come a long way.'

Jinny gestured towards the patio chair, unlocked the back door and walked into the kitchen. Returning outside and placing two glasses and a jug of water on the table, Jinny sat down and watched him help himself to water.

'Dad, I don't believe you.'

'I have no clue what you're even talking about.'

'You must know Gabe Warner.'

Ralph shook his head. 'What is all this about?'

Jinny couldn't hold back and began firing names at him.

'Dixie Bird, Margo Laurent...' Jinny noticed her father's eyes widen.

He slowly placed the glass down on the table. 'I don't know these people.'

'Margo Laurent may have been before my time but even I know who she is.'

'I meant I don't know her personally. You're trying to convince me you no longer want a job in journalism, yet here you are having a good go at trying to interrogate me.'

The front page of the recent newspaper flashed through Jinny's mind. 'Did you know Vivian Bamford?' Jinny watched her father swallow and felt uneasy.

Ralph didn't answer immediately, staring coldly at Jinny. 'Why are you asking all these ridiculous questions?' he snapped.

Jinny saw her father was flushed. 'Vivian Bamford,' she repeated.

Her father was now smouldering with rage 'Of course I know of Vivian Bamford. Who doesn't? She was one of the world's biggest superstars. You only had to put her face on the front of the newspaper and it would sell in the hundreds of thousands.'

Jinny felt sick to her stomach as she heard the tenor of her father's breathing change. Her heart was thumping but she wasn't going to back down. In such a short time Gabe had begun to mean something to her and she wanted to get to the bottom of what was going on and help him in whatever way she could.

'And?'

'And what? I don't know what you want me to say here.'

'Do you know anything about Vivian's death?'

Immediately, Ralph scoffed then took a huge gulp of water. 'Don't be ridiculous. I've no idea what is going on here but I'm not listening to any more of this nonsense.' And without another word, he stood up to leave.

'I'm staying at Starcross Manor for a few days. You know where I am once you feel you can talk to me in a civilised manor.'

Jinny threw her arms up in the air. 'And the same goes for you. You always taught me that if there was a sniff of a story don't give up until you've told that story. And there is definitely something here. Margo Laurent, Gabe Warner and Vivian Bamford are connected. I just need to figure out how.'

Ralph stopped and turned around. 'I would suggest you leave it well alone.' There was a look in her father's eyes Jinny didn't like.

For a second they stared at each other before Ralph carried on walking. The crunch of the gravel was followed by the slam of a car door and then there was a screech of tyres as Ralph pulled away from the cottage. Frustrated, Jinny hurried to the living room. She was angry, confused and her thoughts were all over the place. What exactly was her father telling her to leave alone? Jinny grabbed a pile of notepaper and a pack of sticky notes. Drawing two large circles on the paper Jinny scribbled the words *Bumblebee Cottage* in the middle of one piece of paper and on the other wrote *Château de Laurent*. On the sticky notes Jinny scribbled everyone's names, including her father's, and stuck them all around the diagram.

What was the connection between all these people? Jinny was determined to uncover what was going on here. The truth couldn't be hidden for ever.

Chapter Eighteen

Jinny sat up in bed and calmed her breathing. She'd just woken from the most vivid dream, where she was being chased by a swarm of bees through the orchard. Gabe was standing in front of her yelling at her to go home and never come back. Giving herself a little shake, reality came crashing down all around her as she glanced over at the diagram and the names she'd mapped out last night.

What a mess. She'd arrived in Heartcross for a fresh start and just as she'd thought her relationship with Gabe was progressing to the next level, her father had turned up and smashed it into smithereens. Her first plan was to find Gabe and tell him everything. Surely he would be able to see that she wasn't involved in whatever was going on.

As she took a minute to rally herself, her phone rang. Thankful it was Jay's name flashing on the screen requesting a Facetime call, she quickly picked up.

'What a night. You aren't going to believe what happened here,' Jinny said.

'Tell me everything.'

After explaining the weird events of the night before, Jinny sighed. 'What the hell is going on here, Jay? I'm convinced it's somehow linked to Vivian Bamford but I'm not sure how and haven't got any proof; it's just a gut feeling. And there's no way Gabe is going to talk to me or confide in me now.'

'You might as well try as you have absolutely nothing to lose. He's had time to sleep on it, to calm down, and who knows what this morning will bring.'

'I don't even know whether he'll come into work today.' She glanced at the clock. 'And I've got a couple of hours until I find out.'

'If he doesn't turn up then go and find him. Ask Molly where he lives.'

'I can't. Wouldn't she think that was strange?'

'Possibly. Oh! Didn't you see him at that house on the corner? Maybe try there?'

'Are you encouraging me to go digging?'

'It's not just women who can change their minds, you know.' He gave a little chuckle. 'And I can see that look in your eyes. Whatever I say to you, you'll do what you want.'

'I was listening until last night. Gabe and I were getting close and now it's all ruined.'

'Have faith. Secrets don't stay secrets for ever and the truth will out.'

'That's very true. Ugh. I came here for calm and now

look – I've managed to get in the middle of a right fine mess.'

'I've got a feeling Gabe will come good. Let me know what happens. Ring me later.'

Jinny nodded and hung up. She wished she had Jay's optimism because the way she was feeling right now, she wasn't convinced.

Throwing back the duvet she swung her legs to the ground. Even though she'd barely eaten last night, she didn't fancy breakfast. Remembering the promising start to last night's meal she couldn't help wondering what direction the night could have taken if her father hadn't turned up. Opening her internet browser, Jinny re-read the article on Vivian Bamford, but there were still no clues jumping off the page. Hopefully, Jay was right and Gabe would have calmed down and she could get some answers as to what was really going on here.

About to take a shower, Jinny noticed her trainers in the corner of the room. It had been a while since she'd been running and after opening the curtains, she realised it would be the perfect morning to hit the pavement in an effort to clear her head and get everything in perspective. After quickly pulling a brush through her hair and twisting the strands into a bun, Jinny grabbed a bottle of water from the fridge and was ready. She slipped out of the back door and hid the key under a plant pot that housed salmon-coloured geraniums, then limbered up, welcoming the cool early morning breeze. As she made her way down the path, Gabe and her father were still very much on her mind.

'Good morning!' trilled Felicity, jogging on the spot outside the cottage gate. After quickly fiddling with her watch, she pointed at Jinny's trainers. 'Are you running?'

'I thought I'd attempt to do a couple of miles. It's been a few weeks but with scenery like this, I'm going to make the effort a little more often.'

'It's a good way to start the day, and working in the teashop is no good for my waistline. I'm just on my way back but try the route along the river path. At The Boat House, jump on the river taxi and it'll drop you by the lighthouse at the far end of Glensheil town. Then you can follow the road along the river towards the bridge and back along the track into the village. I love the short boat trip when the weather's like this. I'll let you get on, but if you fancy a run any time, give me a shout.'

'Thank you, I will,' replied Jinny, thinking that route would be perfect because it would take her right past the house where she'd seen Gabe.

Jinny watched as Felicity reset her watch and carried on running, before turning in the opposite direction and heading down the high street towards the river path. The village was already busy with dog walkers and hikers heading towards Love Heart Lane to take the stile towards the mountain pass. She smiled and acknowledged everyone that crossed her path and as soon as she reached the road that led to the river, she slowed down, put her hands on her hips and gulped in the air. Realising how quickly her stamina had slipped, she was determined to get five kilometres under her belt. As she walked briskly towards the jetty, she was greeted by a smiley man. 'Welcome to the river taxi.'

'I think I've seen you somewhere before,' Jinny said, recognising him.

'I'm Roman, partner of Ella, who works at The Lake House and is best friends with Callie who dates the chef, Gianni. We were about to introduce ourselves at the pub BBQ but it was at the very moment that you decided to cover Gabe in ketchup!'

'Ah ha, don't remind me…'

'Where are you going this morning?'

'Felicity mentioned I could take the boat and get off near the lighthouse, then follow the river path back over the bridge.'

'You can, and it's an easy route to follow. Keep running towards the castle on the hill and the mountain – you won't get lost.'

It suddenly occurred to Jinny she'd left the cottage with no money. 'Actually, I think I might be swimming across the river. I've forgotten my purse.'

Roman stepped to the side and tilted his flat cap. 'You can have the first trip on Heartcross.'

Jinny touched his arm lightly in thanks before she stepped on board. 'Thank you.'

'The best seats are over there.' He pointed. 'You can see the view for miles.'

Sitting down, she watched a few other passengers climb on board before Roman walked to the front of the water taxi and started the engine. She sat back and looked towards the bridge that separated the village of Heartcross from the town of Glensheil. The castle on the hill was stunning, watching over the town. As the boat set off in the opposite direction the water was calm and already there were tourists in kayaks and rowing boats bobbing about in the distance. She noticed a small sandy bay on the other side of the river, which looked idyllic – perfect for rowing across to and having a picnic. Jinny had a long list of things to explore in the village but first she needed to put things right with Gabe. She was really hoping that by the end of the day they would be back on track. She'd already checked her phone umpteen times this morning but there had been no texts from him.

It didn't take long for the water taxi to reach the other side of the river and stop at the lighthouse. Waving goodbye to Roman, who was advising a couple of tourists of the best landmarks to visit, Jinny stepped off the boat and took a swig of her water. Taking a deep breath, she set off again, running along the path at the side of the river.

Soon she recognised the road that she was on and knew that just around the next bend was the house where she had seen Gabe. Looking ahead, she crossed over the road to avoid a woman who was being dragged along by an overenthusiastic Labrador then began to run around the next corner. She navigated the cars as she ran across the next junction and there it was, the house on the corner. Jinny slowed down and looked up the drive but there was no car parked there and the curtains were shut. Focusing in front of her again, she squealed as her body was thrown backwards and she stumbled, falling to the ground with a bump. Immediately, a startled postman stretched out his arm to help her up.

'Are you okay?' he asked apologetically as she got to her feet.

'Yes, apart from feeling a tiny bit embarrassed about falling on my backside in the middle of the street. I'm so sorry. It was all my fault. I wasn't looking where I was going,' she confessed, feeling a fool as she began to brush herself down then felt a smarting pain in the palm of her hand. There was a trickle of blood where the stones from the ground had scraped it.

'You're bleeding,' observed the postman.

'It's nothing.'

'Here, let me help.' He reached inside his bag and pulled out a packet of antiseptic wipes and a box of plasters.

'I'm impressed. You're like a walking pharmacy.' Jinny gratefully took a wipe from the packet and cleaned away the tiny pieces of grit that had crept under her skin. She winced slightly before placing a plaster over the cut.

'You'd be surprised how many times a letterbox has decided to trap my hand, or a gate latch has nipped my finger. You need danger money in this job but I have to say it makes a change being run over by a runner. Usually I'm being chased by a dog. I'm Ash, the postman, by the way.'

'I think the uniform gives it away,' she said with a smile. 'I'm Jinny and I'm sorry I knocked a couple of letters out of your hand.' Jinny bent down and picked them up.

'I've seen you somewhere before,' claimed Ash.

'Bumblebee Cottage. You've taken over Dixie's business, haven't you?'

'That's right,' Jinny replied. 'I have.'

'My girlfriend works in the chocolate shop, Layers Treats.'

'That must be Bree. Small world.'

'It's great. Most days I get free chocolate and Cam always throws a cup of tea my way along with a croissant.'

'Whereas I can eat my bodyweight in chutneys and honey if I'd like.'

'Have to say, I think I prefer chocolate,' he replied, smiling.

'I bet you get to meet some interesting people on your round.' Jinny looked towards the house on the corner.

'I do, though usually it's little old ladies who want to mother me. Ach, I don't mind.'

Jinny handed the letters back. Taking a quick glance at one of the envelopes, she saw that it was addressed to a 'Galliard Laurent'.

'Thank you,' he said, looking down at the letters then putting them in the post box attached to the electric gates of the big house. 'I must get on, but no doubt we'll bump into each other again.' He gave her a grin.

'I'll look where I'm going in future,' replied Jinny, smiling. Ash walked on and Jinny set off running again, turning the name on the envelope over in her mind. 'Galliard Laurent,' she murmured. Then it hit her like a tonne of bricks, and she stopped mid-stride.

Laurent.

Like *Margo* Laurent!

Taking a breather, she placed her hands on her hips and swung a glance back towards the house. The adrenalin was rising inside her, the same feeling flooding her veins that she always used to get when she knew she was onto something while chasing a story. The first thing Jinny was going to do when she got back to the cottage was google *Galliard Laurent*.

With her thoughts in overdrive, Jinny powered her legs and headed towards the castle. As she got to the high street, Jinny decided to run through the grounds of Starcross Manor, which guided her through the woods to Primrose Park. From there, she came across a duckpond, which led to a wooden bridge. She made her way up to the crest of the hill, towards a small church. Catching her breath at the weathered wrought-iron gates, which created an impressive entrance to the attached graveyard, she glanced up at a statue before pushing open the gate and taking the paved footpath through the well-maintained gardens.

The whole cemetery was alive with colour and Jinny took a moment to admire a gorgeous rose bush at the side of a bench. There was a gate at the far end which she guessed would lead her back to the end of the lane by the Clover Cottage Estate, then she would be almost home. She nodded to a couple who were tending to a grave and, as she made her way to the opposite entrance, she read the names on the gravestone and noticed a small dog running towards her. She bent down and scooped up the tiny poodle to find a thankful woman hurrying towards her. 'Thank you so much. Honestly, I turn my back for a moment and she's gone.'

'No problem,' said Jinny, handing the dog over before ruffling the pom-pom on top of its head.

As she carried on walking, Jinny glanced at an overgrown grave in the corner and stopped dead, confused by the name that was staring back at her: Gabe Warner. Her heart racing, she stepped closer to take a proper look. According to the headstone, Gabe Warner died in the 1800s.

She quickly dialled Jay.

'I'm not sure if you've pocket dialled me as all I can hear is heavy breathing,' he answered jokingly.

'I've been running, you loon.'

'This exercise lark is overrated.'

'Jay, stop babbling. Gabe is dead.'

'Woah, what happened? Are you okay? I wasn't expecting this. You were only with him last night.' Jay was talking so fast that his words were spilling over each other.

'According to the gravestone I'm looking at right now, Gabe Warner died in the 1800s.'

For a second, silence hung in the air as Jay processed her words. 'So… what you're saying is your Gabe—'

'Not quite *my* Gabe…' she interrupted.

Jay ignored her. 'Your Gabe is alive and kicking but you've stumbled across a gravestone with the same name?'

'Exactly that, and I've also just seen a letter addressed to a Galliard Laurent posted into the post box of the big house on the corner where I saw Gabe with the ice-creams.'

'How have you seen that?'

'Long story short, I bumped into the postman and knocked a couple of letters out of his hand. I saw the name when I handed them to him, and watched as he dropped them in the post box.'

'You're kidding me. Is Galliard Laurent related to the Margo Laurent that George and Dixie knew?'

'I'm not sure yet. That's what I need to find out,' she said, still staring at the gravestone. 'I'm definitely onto something here.'

'Okay, Miss Marple. I'm going to leave it in your capable hands but how is any of this connected to Gabe? The one that's alive and kicking?'

'I've no clue about that either yet. Is it just another coincidence that I've stumbled across a gravestone with the same name?'

'You're the journalist. You tell me.'

'Ex-journalist,' she asserted. 'I'll ring you later.' Jinny ended the call. There was an hour before Gabe turned up for work and she was determined to put things right between them.

As she ran back towards Bumblebee Cottage, Jinny mulled things over. Feeling like she was playing a weird game of murder mystery, she kicked off her trainers the second she arrived home, poured herself a glass of water and fired up her laptop. She quickly jotted down a number of questions on a pad. The first question was: who the hell is Gabe Warner, really, and what brought him to Bumblebee Cottage?

Chapter Nineteen

To begin, Jinny checked the electoral roll for Gabe Warner. Currently there was no one of that name living in the vicinity. Next, she typed Margo Laurent's name into the search engine.

According to Google, Margo had been married to Frank Laurent, who'd died at the age of fifty-four, and they had one daughter, Julia. Jinny typed in Julia's full name and hit enter. According to an article that she quickly skimmed over, Julia lived in the South of France and had stayed away from any sort of fame. She owned a florist's shop, which was quite close to the Château de Laurent where she had grown up. But Jinny knew there was nothing particularly strange about that. She'd reported on stories in the past where children of famous people craved a normal life out of the limelight, especially when they went on to have children.

'Children,' she repeated her own thoughts out loud. 'Did

Julia marry?' Jinny began tapping away. It was possible that Galliard wasn't Julia's child because if she'd married, any offspring would have likely taken her husband's name, as was usual for that generation. Jinny quickly discovered that though Julia had never married, she did have one offspring – Galliard. Jinny's heart was racing as she began to search the electoral role for Gaillard … who popped up immediately. He was indeed registered as living in the house on the corner of Millionaires' Row.

'The grandson of a famous actress who knew Dixie and George is living up the road in Glensheil,' she murmured to herself. Jinny knew that Gabe must know Galliard because she'd seen him entering the property but *how* did they know each other? Maybe they had been introduced by Dixie? Or maybe their mothers knew one another, if they both lived in the South of France?

Jinny crossed her legs and balanced the laptop. There were still a few pieces of the jigsaw missing and Gabe's reaction to seeing Vivian Bamford on the front of the newspaper was still playing on her mind too.

She began to type.

Is Vivian Bamford related to Galliard Laurent?

According to Google the answer was no.

Does Vivian Bamford have any famous relatives?

According to Google the answer was no.

Did Vivian Bamford live at Château de Laurent?

According to Google the answer was yes, for a short time.

Has Vivian Bamford starred in any films alongside Margo Laurent?

According to Google the answer was no.

Has Vivian Bamford ever been married?

According to Google the answer was no.

Jinny was beginning to feel like she was at dead end. She knew she was missing something and cast her mind back to her very first day of work at the newspaper, willing herself to remember anything else that could possibly shed some light, but however hard she tried, there was nothing.

Next, she typed 'Gabe Warner Heartcross'. The search threw up that there was a cobbler named Gabe Warner living in Heartcross back in the 1800s, but other than that there was nothing.

Jinny leaned back in her chair and took a sip of water. Noticing the time, she realised she had been searching for over an hour and Gabe hadn't turned up for work, which was a little disappointing because she really wanted to speak to him about last night.

Turning back to her search, she decided to find out more about Galliard. Just like his mother, he had avoided the limelight and the information available about him was sparse. She clicked on the images tab at the top of the page and immediately it brought up images of Margo. There were photos of her films and her receiving awards, and pictures of the château. Then one photo caught her eye. Margo was standing in front of a theatre with a young woman and a boy who was pointing up at the sign outside the theatre. Jinny clicked on the picture and read the paragraph underneath.

It's the opening night for A Family Affair *staring Margo Laurent who was joined by her daughter and grandson.*

As Jinny zoomed in on the photo her eyes widened, the hairs on the back of her neck prickled and her pulse began to race. Her eyes were locked with a pair of eyes she'd come to know so well since arriving in Heartcross. There was no doubt that the young face staring back at her was her Gabe Warner, except according to the caption he *wasn't* Gabe Warner.

He was Galliard Laurent.

Chapter Twenty

'Have you been smoking something?' Jay sounded serious.

'Don't be ridiculous. Its only nine a.m.'

'And if it wasn't?'

'Shut up! Of course not. Have you been listening to me?'

'Oh yes, I've been listening. You're trying to convince me that the grandson of a world-famous actress is the beekeeper at Bumblebee Cottage.'

Jinny could hear Jay laughing at the other end of the phone.

'I am telling you Gabe Warner is Galliard Laurent. Either that or he's been cloned. Maybe an identical twin, who knows, but Jay, I'm being serious.'

'I can tell you are but I just don't get it. Why would he need to change his name? It's his grandmother who was world famous, not him. And I'm not being funny but that family would be loaded. He really wouldn't need to work as a beekeeper.'

Jinny could see exactly where Jay was coming from. 'He's pinched a dead man's identity and is living up the road in a mansion and working as a beekeeper at this cottage. I need to know why and I need to know how – if at all – my father is involved in any of this.'

'I have to say, you're certainly keeping me on the edge of my seat with these updates,' admitted Jay.

'And something is still telling me that Vivian Bamford is somehow connected to all this, but I can't quite fathom that part out yet. But I think Gabe was going to tell me everything last night, before my father turned up.'

'I think you might be right,' agreed Jay. 'What's the plan of action now?'

'I'm going to make the chutneys, deliver an order, and if Gabe—'

'Galliard,' corrected Jay.

'Gabe, or Galliard, hasn't appeared or texted by then I think I'm going to drive over to the house and see if there's any possibility he'll talk to me.'

'And how are you feeling about him, given your new discoveries?'

There was no denying Jinny still thought Gabe was the handsomest man to walk this earth. But neither of them had been entirely honest with each other and was there any coming back from that? Only time would tell. She knew her feelings were as strong as ever and she hoped his were too. Whatever his reason for changing his name, it must be a good one – or maybe it was as simple as just wanting a fresh start, the same way she had. But why?

'I still feel the same,' she admitted. 'Let's hope he's willing to talk to me.'

'Good luck!'

Ten minutes later, Jinny found herself wandering into The Honey Pot. With her phone in her hand, she took the plunge and sent Gabe a text.

Are you coming in today?

She wasn't expecting a reply and jumped when Gabe replied almost instantly. His answer was short and to the point.

Not today.

Jinny's heart sank a little. Last night, Gabe had gone to so much trouble to make her feel special and she remembered how her heart had skipped a beat when she'd opened the door. She made her way through the small patio area then climbed the steps to the first-floor balcony. To her amazement, everything had been tidied away but lying on top of the table was the most beautiful bouquet of hand-tied peonies that she had ever seen. Picking up the flowers, she admired the elegance and intricate beauty of their cascade of fragrant pink petals. These were her favourite flowers. There was a note attached and her heart began to race when she saw her name on the envelope. The words written inside were:

New beginnings for you. Meant to bee!

Jinny clutched the note and took in the aroma. Gabe must have been back at some point during the evening to clear everything away. She was in a dilemma. She didn't know what to do. Had he intended to give her the flowers before he discovered who her father was? But if that was the case, then why had he left them now for her to find? With the flowers in her hand, she returned to the cottage and arranged them in a vase of water. It was fast approaching ten o'clock and she made up her mind that after she had made today's batch of chutneys, she was going to drive over to the house and plead her case: whatever he thought her guilty of, it wasn't true.

It was four o'clock in the afternoon by the time Jinny had made the day's chutneys and taken care of the deliveries. She was now parked on a street near Gabe's house, questioning whether it was a good idea to actually go and knock on the door. Her first challenge was to get through the electronic gates. If she just pressed the buzzer would he even let her in?

Jinny gave herself a good talking-to.

'Don't be a chicken. What's the worst that can happen?'

Gabe was going to have to talk to her at some point; they worked together. Taking the plunge, she climbed out of the car and began walking up the road. As luck would have it, the gate was open when she approached and she saw a delivery driver walking down the driveway. Jinny took her chance and stepped onto the drive, wishing the delivery driver a good afternoon and praying her voice didn't actually sound as much like a chipmunk on helium as it did in her head.

As she stood nervously on the step, gazing at what seemed an unusually large front door – everything about this house looked humongous – she seriously questioned whether this was a good idea. But before she could talk herself out of it, she pressed the oversized brass doorbell with her sweaty palm.

'I'll get it,' she heard a voice she didn't recognise call out, and within seconds the huge oak door swung open to reveal a boy who looked around ten years old. Before Jinny could say anything, the boy called out, 'Mum, Dad, there's someone at the door.'

'I'm really sorry,' Jinny said politely. 'I think I have the wrong house.' Gabe had told her he didn't have a wife – and as far as she knew he definitely didn't have a son.

'Did the delivery driver forget something?' A woman's voice carried from another part of the house.

'No, it's just some lady,' replied the boy, slipping away

into a side room as the woman appeared at the end of the hallway.

Jinny was just about to apologise and explain that she had the wrong house when Claude came hurtling towards her and jumped straight up at her. The woman now standing in front of her was stunning. She was slim, with brunette hair that bounced halfway down her back, and wore a long summer dress in turquoise, which complemented the colour of her eyes.

'Claude, get down. I'm so sorry.'

Jinny was frozen to the spot, feeling numb to her core. What was going on here? Just when she thought the situation couldn't get any more confusing, she noticed another figure walking towards the front door.

Gabe.

Jinny's mouth fell open then closed. She could feel herself trembling. Yesterday, Gabe was preparing romantic meals and flirting with her but here he was playing happy families with someone else. What holy mess was he attempting to drag her into?

'It's not the delivery driver.' The woman looked over her shoulder at Gabe whose eyes had firmly locked on Jinny's. She swallowed as dread rose through her whole body. The man she was feeling the first flush of love for had a wife and son that he had failed to mention. She took a step backwards. 'I'm so sorry,' she stuttered. 'I've got the wrong house. *My* mistake.' She gave Gabe a stony look as she emphasised the word.

She'd wanted to believe he was different from the men

she had been attracted to in the past, as each one of them had let her down one way or another, but Gabe's actions had taken the wind out of her. It turned out he hadn't been honest with her either. She felt sick.

She turned and walked towards the gate, which immediately swung open.

'Which address were you looking for?' the woman shouted after her.

But Jinny didn't trust herself to speak. She carried on walking and hoped her shaky legs would make it to Donovan before they buckled underneath her.

Chapter Twenty-One

Gripping the steering wheel, Jinny drove down the road and headed towards the bridge. 'Do not cry, do not cry. You barely know this man. He's not worthy of your tears,' she repeated over and over again, trying to keep her emotions under control.

But it didn't matter how hard her head was telling her not to think about Gabe, her heart was telling her something totally different, and it won the battle. Jinny began to cry. Tears were still blurring her eyes as she drove up the high street and finally parked Donovan outside Bumblebee Cottage. Taking deep breaths, she tried to calm her frantically beating heart.

'He has a wife and a son,' she said out loud, still trying to comprehend what had just happened. Risking a tentative look in the mirror, she saw she now looked like an 80s rock star, black mascara streaking her cheeks. She quickly attempted to wipe it away before climbing out of the car and glancing over at The Old Bakehouse. Thankfully there was no one around to see her distress, because all she wanted to do was run and hide for the rest of the day.

Hearing her phone ringing from the depths of her bag, she rummaged inside. There was a sudden feeling of hope that it would be Gabe, but seeing her father's name flashing across the screen she was reminded that he was still up at Starcross Manor.

'Could my life get any worse?' she mumbled to herself as she threw the phone back in her bag and turned around, walking straight into Felicity.

'How was your run?' Felicity trilled, swinging a carrier bag.

Jinny looked up and met Felicity's gaze.

'Woah! Are you okay?' asked Felicity.

Jinny could feel her lips beginning to tremble again. She was doing her very best to hold it all together but the tears once again got the better of her.

'You're not okay. I can see you're not.' Felicity touched Jinny's arm. 'Has something happened? Are you homesick? Sometimes it creeps up on you and when you're least expecting it and consumes you.'

'I'm definitely not homesick,' replied Jinny, although she was thinking that being back in London might be a better option right now. What a fool she'd been to begin falling for Gabe.

'Do you want to talk about it?' Felicity's tone was warm and caring. 'I also have chocolate!' She held up the bag in her hand. 'And not just any chocolate... Layers Treats chocolate and a bottle of homemade lemonade.'

'You've twisted my arm, thank you.'

Once inside the cottage, they sat down at the kitchen table and Felicity emptied the chocolate from the carrier bag. 'Take your pick. Oh, look at those beautiful flowers. Peonies are a favourite of mine too.'

Jinny swallowed a lump in her throat. 'Sorry, I don't mean to cry on you.' She was wishing with all her heart that she didn't have any feelings for Gabe but the pain hammering against her chest was telling her otherwise.

'In my experience, chocolate makes everything better. And honestly, if you don't want to talk about it, I can take one for the team and eat all of this. I just want to make sure you're okay. Anything you do say won't go past these four walls, I can promise you that.'

Jinny was a good judge of character – or so she'd thought – and she could see Felicity was a kind and caring individual. She also couldn't deny that she needed a friend right now.

'It can be difficult when you first arrive, especially when you're alone. It's moments like this when you need a good friend.'

Felicity's words resonated with Jinny. In London she'd made superficial friends at work and at the gym but there were no real close friends in her life apart from Jay.

'I think I may need exactly that,' replied Jinny, giving Felicity a watery smile. 'I came here for a completely fresh start but it all seems to be going wrong.'

'Nothing can be that bad. Why don't you talk me through it?'

Jinny broke off a chunk of chocolate and devoured it within seconds. 'This cottage and the job are the best bit. Waking up to the view of the orchards and Heartcross Mountain is just divine and I smile every time I open the curtains. It certainly beats the view of a high-rise car park and the constant beeping of car horns.'

'There you go then. That's a positive.' Felicity smiled warmly. 'Like you, I left my home in search of a fresh start when things got too hard for me to handle. Looking back though, I realise I should have talked about how I was feeling at the time instead of running away to London in the middle of the night on New Year's Eve and then not returning for years.'

Jinny raised her eyebrows.

'I came back when my grandmother was poorly but it was too late; she'd already passed away.'

'Was that Bonnie?'

'Yes. I took over her teashop with Mum when a winter storm hit, the bridge collapsed and I was stranded. But it was the best thing that could ever have happened. I upset a lot of people when I left – Fergus, Isla and Allie most of all – and the reason I'm telling you this is because whatever's going on, you don't have to feel alone. What you'll find out about Heartcross is that we all rally together in anyone's time of need. We're your friends now and we'll be here for you no matter what.'

Jinny liked Felicity. She was warm and honest and very

easy to talk to. She had just shared some of her own past, but Jinny wasn't sure if she should spill all her worries because she didn't even know where to start, especially as Gabe was known to the villagers. She wondered for a second if Felicity knew he was married and had a son – but surely the villagers would know that if he'd been here ten years? That wasn't something you couldn't hide. Jinny was confused. She didn't know what to think.

'Is it work? The cottage? It is a huge thing moving miles from home.'

Jinny dabbed her eyes with a tissue and blurted, 'I don't have the best relationship with my dad,' taking herself by surprise. 'And he's here, in Heartcross.'

'I'm sorry to hear that,' replied Felicity, sympathetically. 'Is that one of the reasons you left London?'

Jinny nodded. 'We don't see eye to eye on a lot of things – and I worked for him as well. I just felt it was time I stood on my own two feet.'

'What sort of things don't you see eye to eye on?'

'Mainly his morals.'

Felicity broke off another chunk of chocolate and slid it across the table. 'Morals in what way?'

The newspaper was on the table so Jinny reached for it and opened it up, putting it between them both. 'I was a journalist, reporting on stories I didn't agree with. I used my mother's maiden name when I arrived here. My real surname is Birdwhistle.'

Jinny could see by the look on Felicity's face that the penny had dropped.

'You're related to Ralph Birdwhistle, multi-millionaire tycoon, owner of…' Felicity looked down at the newspaper. 'Owner of *The Daily News*? He's your father?'

'The very one,' replied Jinny, feeling a weight lift off her shoulders as she shared that information with Felicity.

'Well, I never. I hope I'm not speaking out of turn when I say he has a very controversial reputation.'

'Oh, believe me, I quite agree.'

'And what about your mum?'

Jinny swallowed. 'She passed away. It's just been me and Dad for a long time, and as I've got older, we've butted heads constantly. My career was chosen for me and my dad was someone whose choices you didn't question.'

'Until now,' supplied Felicity.

'I'm sure he loves me in his own way but he can be very stubborn and he just doesn't know how to say "I'm sorry". I mean, it's so easy; it's just two words and those two words can make everything okay.'

'I agree, but that's possibly a generational thing. My granny was also stubborn as hell.' Felicity gave a smile. 'What do you feel he needs to say sorry for?' she asked tentatively.

'For never listening to what I actually wanted to do.'

'And what did you want to do?'

Jinny thought for a moment. 'That's a difficult question because I actually don't know. People look at me and think I have it made – my father is wealthy, we lived in a huge house with a maid, a butler and a driver, I never had to tidy my room or wash dishes, and when I was eighteen, he presented me with my own apartment and a fancy car.'

'And now you have Donovan!' cut in Felicity, lightening the mood. 'Who needs a fancy car?' she said with a smile.

'And I love Donovan. The quirkiness of him and his fantastic backstory more than make up for the convertible I've left behind. That makes me sound so ungrateful.'

'No, it doesn't. It shows that you're standing on your own two feet and beginning to appreciate what's around you.'

'On my first day at the office our driver went past the bus stop. It was the school holidays and there were my friends waiting to catch the bus to the local theme park. I could see them laughing and joking and I wanted to be with them. I didn't want a job. I wanted to go to university and figure out for myself my own career path. I feel like I didn't get to choose, and maybe that's why I resent my father for making me go into the family business.'

'Have you told him all this?'

'Trying to talk to my father is a challenge in itself. He doesn't listen. He only talks *at* me, if that makes sense?'

'So what's changed? Why are you standing up to him now?'

'Because my father's newspaper reports on stories that I don't agree with and I was sick of being forced to write clickbait pieces. People are entitled to their privacy and he pushes the boundaries too far and it hurts people. And for what? To sell more newspapers, to make more money obviously, but it's wrong and I don't want to be part of it.'

'You sound to me like you have your head screwed on.'

'Something inside me was telling me there was only one person who was going to change my life and that was me.'

'And here you are. Heartcross is the right place to mend any problems. What are you going to do about your father? He's staying at Starcross Manor, you said?'

Jinny nodded. 'I'll have to go and see him but I'm not going back to London. I want to give this place a go.' The second the words left her mouth, her thoughts turned to Gabe. She wished things could be put right between them, but how was that even possible now? All she could do was try and put him out of her mind and not let him affect her fresh start in Heartcross. The only thing she had done wrong was keep to herself who her father was and what she had done for living. What Gabe had kept to himself was on another level.

'Talk to him. Tell him how you feel. I know he's your father but maybe you don't know how it is for him.'

Jinny paused for a second. 'What do you mean?'

'You talk like he's a workaholic and lives to work. He's successful, yes, but maybe that's his way of coping. Has he had anyone in his life since your mother passed away?'

Jinny thought for a moment. 'If he has, he's never brought them into my life.' Now she had said those words out loud she realised he was always on his own at events and she had never seen another woman on his arm.

'There's a possibility he's still suffering from a broken heart and the only way to ease the suffering was by throwing himself into work.'

'Possibly,' replied Jinny. Felicity had given her food for thought because she was right. People deal with grief in many ways. Maybe her father had just lost sight of what was right and wrong with no life partner to share his days with. 'But he should still know that some stories should not be reported on, especially those that could wreck lives and affect people's mental wellbeing.'

'Agreed. So have that conversation with him.'

'I will, and thank you.'

'That's what friends are for. Are you feeling a little better?'

'I am.' Jinny was thankful that Felicity hadn't judged her in any way whatsoever and she hoped this was just the start of a wonderful friendship. Because that was what she needed – to surround herself with good girlfriends.

'I need to get back to the teashop but anytime you want to pop in, please do. And I'm always up for a gin and tonic in the pub.'

'I will, and thanks again.'

Watching Felicity disappear through the back door, Jinny thought about how there were always two sides to a story, which led her to wonder what Gabe's side of the story was and why he was keeping the fact that he had a wife and son to himself. There was only one way to find out... Jinny was going to ask him outright once she got her thoughts in order.

Still thinking about her mum, Jinny grabbed the small photo album – the one sentimental thing she had brought with her from her apartment – and sat in the armchair in the living room. As she began to turn the pages, each photo triggered a memory of her mum and she had to blink back the tears. Even though her mother had also been a journalist, she'd always got the work–life balance right and made time for Jinny.

The last photo in the album was a picture of Jinny on her first day at work. She was standing in between her dad and her godfather William in the reception area of the newspaper headquarters. She could remember the photo being taken. It had been just before midday when her father and William emerged from the boardroom. It seemed her father had forgotten she was there, as he'd left her sitting in his office where he'd instructed her to wait. William had insisted on the picture and it had appeared the next day in *The Daily News* with an article telling the world that Jinny Birdwhistle was now part of her father's newspaper empire. What they failed to report was that for the next few years she would be nothing but a runner – running around making tea, ordering lunches and acting as a general dogsbody.

She cast her mind back to the moment after the picture was taken, when her father and William had returned to the boardroom, whispering to each other and looking like they had just got away with murder.

Jinny sat up straight as the word *murder* turned over in her mind. She shivered as Gabe's voice now echoed through her thoughts.

Who has to die next?

Surely her father and William couldn't have had

anything to do with the actress's death? It had just been a car crash. An accident. If there was foul play involved, every newspaper in the land would have reported on it. Jinny felt her heart beat faster as she quickly slid the photo album onto the coffee table and fired up her laptop. Once more she accessed the newspaper's online database. This time she was looking for something else when she delved into the archives, remembering how her father had ordered William to get the front page headline changed the night before Vivian's death was reported. Entering the date Vivian Bamford had died, she waited in anticipation for the page to load and was soon gazing at that day's cover.

According to the file there had been amendments before it went to print and those changes had been made by William, but the file showing the different versions was password protected.

'Damn!' she exclaimed, placing the laptop on the coffee table before getting herself comfy on a cushion on the floor. Cross-legged she began to think. She knew she had three attempts before an email would land telling the administrators that there had been a failed attempt to access a file.

The first attempt was a confident one as Jinny was certain it would open the file.

Plumping for her mum's birthday, Jinny took a deep breath and briefly closed her eyes as she hit enter.

Access denied.

Next, she punched in the date her father was declared

the new owner of the most famous newspaper in the country.

Two red bold words flashed on the screen again.

Access denied.

'Double damn.'

Jinny had one last attempt. This code could have been generated by either her father or William. She was no mathematician, but the odds were stacked against her. In for a penny, in for a pound... This time she entered her own birthday.

She waited.

Jinny's eyes widened as the page began to load. She was in! As the original front cover was displayed on her screen, the bold headline took Jinny completely by surprise.

VIVIAN BAMFORD LIVES A LIE

Jinny's eyes quickly flitted over the article that they had pulled before printing. *The Daily News* was outing Vivian Bamford as a lesbian. As soon as she read the article, Jinny understood the potential harm of what had been written. Ten years ago, the world had been a difference place, with even more stigma and ignorance about being gay than existed today. This article could have had a huge effect on Vivian, impacting her personal life, her earning potential and any future casting for roles. Her father's newspaper had been breaking the story to the whole world and from what Jinny was now reading in the editorial notes it was going to be a surprise to every reader of the newspaper... including Vivian.

The evidence included a photograph showing Vivian in the driver's seat of a car, her lover in the passenger seat. The photograph had been snapped from behind the vehicle, which could only mean that they were being followed by a journalist from her father's newspaper. The car was stationary at the traffic lights and the two women had leaned across and embraced, the picture telling its very own love story. She knew her father would have revelled in one of his journalists having landed this story, the earning potential for his newspaper phenomenal. But after Vivian died, why had he left the story of her private life untold?

Jinny re-read the article, which was brutal. It had delved into the heart of her personal life, claiming every relationship she had had with a man was merely a farce, suggesting that she used her single status to create excitement and often a frenzy amongst the male population, who thought they might still be in with a chance of sweeping the Hollywood superstar off her feet, when in reality they had no chance. This article could have ruined Vivian.

She noticed the other woman in the photograph hadn't been identified. Jinny knew that bit of missing information would have riled her father. The article stated that the women met at a restaurant – there were other photographs attached to the file showing how Vivian had been ushered through the back door of the restaurant by her bodyguard – and she'd spent over three hours inside before she was photographed leaving the restaurant with her mystery woman and driving away.

Jinny quickly re-read that part of the article. The restaurant was one she knew quite well – a Michelin-starred restaurant with an extremely good reputation – as it was near where she and her father had lived at the time.

Jinny felt a niggle. Something wasn't adding up. She flicked back to the front page that was actually printed on the day that Vivian died, and re-read the article, which claimed she had died in a car crash in the South of France. But if she was leaving a restaurant in London when the accident happened, that couldn't have been possible.

There was no way Vivian could have hopped, skipped and jumped into another country unless she took a private plane, but that seemed unlikely. The plot thickened.

'Who are you?' she murmured, looking at the other woman in the photograph. Where was she now? Jinny searched every newspaper headline on that day and for the following week but there were no stories of Vivian being involved with a woman – and no other newspapers had run the story in the years since. Maybe her father had realised at the time that the story he was about to break would cause only pointless damage after her death . . . but Jinny wasn't sure she believed that. She knew that, for her father, a story was a story.

She continued to scroll through the original article, noticing that the manager of the restaurant had declined to comment on whether Vivian had frequented his establishment and with whom. 'Someone at least with morals,' murmured Jinny, finally shutting down the file and closing the laptop. Her thoughts were scrambled. There were so many questions she wanted to ask – and by her reckoning, only two people knew the answers. She checked her phone but there was nothing from Gabe, which was not unexpected but still a disappointment. Where the hell was he? Surely if there was an ounce of him that cared, he would be here trying to put the record straight?

Chapter Twenty-Two

Jinny felt dispirited, and the hot weather wasn't helping. Neither was the anxious feeling in the pit of her stomach. She hadn't seen Gabe for three days and was feeling frustrated by his absence. The last time she'd felt anything close to this heartbreak was back in her early twenties when she'd had a serious relationship with a guy she'd met in the local coffee shop. It lasted a couple of years until his job took him abroad and he hadn't looked back.

Jinny checked her watch. In the next thirty minutes she was due next door at The Old Bakehouse. Molly had dropped her a text inviting her round for dinner and, as much as Jinny knew she wasn't feeling her best, anything was better than sitting at home and clock-watching, wondering if Gabe would appear anytime soon.

With a bottle of wine in hand, Jinny locked up the cottage and walked the short journey round the back of The Old Bakehouse. Seconds later, she stepped into yet another beautiful garden. Molly and Cam were sitting at the patio table but were up on their feet as soon as Jinny walked around the corner.

'Here she is! How has your day been?' asked Molly, giving Jinny a hug and taking the bottle of wine from her.

'Just the best,' replied Jinny, trying to deflect from the worst day ever.

'We've invited Gabe too. He should be here soon.'

The mention of his name made Jinny's heart beat faster. 'Gabe?' She was surprised. 'Has he been poorly? He's not been around for a few days.'

'Jinny! I'm so sorry. I forgot to mention he was taking a few days off. It had completely slipped my mind what with doing the night shift at the vet's. I'm fit for nothing.'

Jinny wondered if the days booked off had been pre-planned because it was the first she'd heard anything about it. 'Has he been doing anything exciting?'

'Family stuff, I think?' replied Molly. 'I feel awful now. Have you coped okay by yourself?'

'Absolutely,' Jinny replied. 'Everything's under control. I've got myself into a little routine. And where are the children?' she asked, looking around, hoping she could spend the night cuddling a baby to keep her occupied if Gabe turned up.

'Isla's given us a night off. They're sleeping over.' Jinny registered the excitement in Molly's voice as she added, 'Because we want to talk to you about something. But let us get you a drink first while Cam throws some meat on the

BBQ. He's picked up the finest steaks from Foxglove Farm. Wine, Prosecco, gin?'

'A glass of Prosecco would be lovely . . . and the finest steaks – are we celebrating?' Jinny sat down at the table while Molly brought out a wine cooler with a bottle. She filled a couple of glasses and clinked hers against Jinny's. 'Possibly could be,' she said, not giving anything else away. 'But let's talk about it once Gabe arrives.'

Cam had disappeared back into the kitchen and now brought out a salad, a basket of bread, an array of cold meats and chutney. He sat down and opened a can of beer. 'Of course, we've opted for the very first chutney recipe that Dixie concocted – the original apple.' He gestured to the jar on the table.

'I found the original recipe card written on notepaper from the Château de Laurent. The extra random key on Donovan's keyring opened a locked photo album I found on the bookshelf.' Jinny brought her hand up to her chest. 'I feel like I've been intruding now,' she admitted.

'That's what that key was for! The little album! We should have guessed.' Molly smiled at Cam.

'Did you ever get to meet Margo Laurent?' Jinny couldn't help blurting out, looking towards Cam. Over the last few days, every waking moment that wasn't consumed by the business had been spent glued to her laptop finding out as much as she could about the Laurent family.

'I did, a few times, the first being when I was a boy. I have to say I remember an early occasion very well. I honestly thought the Queen had come to visit. She dressed to impress and as soon as she walked into the room, heads would turn. Then I remember seeing her… it must be around ten years ago, just before she passed away. She came to visit Dixie out of the blue.'

'Really?' asked Jinny, sitting up straight. 'Can you remember exactly when that was?' As soon as she asked the question, she knew it sounded a little forthright. 'I just meant, did she come for any particular reason?'

'I remember my grandmother was surprised to see her, which suggests it wasn't an arranged trip, and Margo looked frail. Her clothes hung from her tiny frame yet she still held herself with such grace and wouldn't be seen without her oversized sunglasses, which just screamed famous Hollywood actress. She was gone within twenty-four hours and it was only about a month later that she passed away. I assumed she had come to say goodbye.'

'Okay if I change the subject here? We have important things to discuss!' Molly jumped in. 'Namely, any ideas for the village competition?'

Jinny grinned. 'I have but it's top secret, even from you guys. The only other person who knows is Gabe and I'm hoping I do Dixie proud.'

'Gabe is always singing your praises,' Molly said.

'Really?' asked Jinny.

'Oh yes, every time we see him he gives us an update. He's very impressed with your work ethic, your deliveries are on time, the kitchen is always spotless, your communication with customers is likeable and professional…'

'My ego will be sky high if you keep bigging me up,' replied Jinny with a smile.

'And when he talks about you, he has a sparkle in his eye. We haven't seen that before.'

While all this was lovely to hear, Jinny felt a wrench in the pit of her stomach after what had gone on a few days ago.

'You pair do bounce off each other and work well together. I hope I'm not speaking out of turn when I say this but everyone noticed the sparks of electricity flying between you at the BBQ. You could have lit up the whole of Scotland.'

'Everyone?' asked Jinny.

'Isla, Allie, Rona... even Martha hinted she could see your lives mapped out together. Martha is clairvoyant, you know—'

'Clairvoyant in this village mostly means nosey and into everyone's business,' chipped in Cam with a cheeky grin, and felt the wrath of Molly playfully hitting his arm.

'Martha predicted a wedding,' shared Molly.

Jinny spluttered as she took a sip of her drink.

'She can see big things for the business, your wedding car is Donovan and there's a huge ceremony at Starcross Manor. She wasn't sure why but she also felt certain it would be reported in every newspaper in the land.'

'Because she's deluded,' Cam muttered, as Molly swiped his arm again.

'It's not often Martha's wrong. I mean, look what she predicted for us. A letter, a goodbye, a baby girl whose name begins with L and a whole lot of scandal. She wasn't wrong about any of it.'

'I thought a man like Gabe would be taken?' said Jinny, testing the water.

'Absolutely not,' replied Molly, smiling in her direction. 'Whoever snaps him up will be a very lucky woman.'

Jinny was a little confused. Molly and Cam had known Gabe for a long time, so either he'd pulled the wool over their eyes or she'd got the situation very wrong. But if that was the case, why hadn't he come after her to explain?

'You're frightening the poor girl to death. Look at her face.' Cam nudged Molly.

'Sorry, I just love a good wedding!' added Molly pointing to the BBQ and turning towards Cam. 'I also like a good fire, but I don't want my meat cremated.'

Cam was up on his feet and quickly transferred the cooked meat onto the grill at the top of the BBQ, away from the direct heat. He spun round and pointed to the side of the house with his two-pronged BBQ fork. 'Here he is. Great timing.'

There was no mistaking the crunch of the gravel. Jinny's pulse began to race. She quickly gulped back her Prosecco for Dutch courage and then refilled her glass to the brim without anyone noticing.

'Sorry I'm a little late. It's been one of those days.' Gabe appeared around the corner carrying a box of beers in one hand and a bottle of wine in the other.

'It certainly has been a few of those days. Good to see

you,' chipped in Jinny, knowing her tone sounded a little frosty. 'Molly said you've been off doing family stuff.'

'Yes, I have,' he replied, holding Jinny's gaze for longer than necessary before turning back towards Cam and Molly and smiling. 'I've brought beer and wine.'

Jinny was still staring at him. He looked absolutely gorgeous, which wasn't unexpected, but what was unexpected was the way he was acting like nothing was wrong after having disappeared off the face of the earth for the last few days without even a single text.

'I'll take them from you, mate,' said Cam. 'I'll just get you a cold one from the fridge.'

'That would be great. It's such a lovely evening for it.'

Jinny watched Molly stand up and kiss Gabe on both cheeks. 'Are you okay?' she said softly. He nodded and Molly squeezed his arm, leaving Jinny wondering what all that was about. She studied him closely.

'And how are you?' Gabe asked, turning towards Jinny.

'Fine, thank you,' she replied politely.

Gabe leaned in and kissed her on both cheeks, taking her completely by surprise.

'Been busy over the last few days,' she added, making sure Gabe knew he hadn't been missed, which was so far from the truth.

'I'm just going to grab some plates from the kitchen as I think the food's almost done,' announced Molly, leaving the pair of them alone for a moment.

'Great timing,' replied Gabe, pulling out the chair and sitting down next to Jinny.

She looked at him. 'I don't believe this. You disappeared for three days and didn't even bother to check up on me.' She was hurt and frustrated. 'What the hell's going on?'

Gabe looked towards the door then back at her. 'We do need to talk. It's been a difficult few days.'

'Hasn't it just,' she replied.

'But I can tell you now, it's not what you think.'

'I'll be interested in what you have to say.'

'Likewise,' he replied.

'Surely you can't compare me not telling you who my father is to you lying about who you are. I know you're Galliard Laurent.' Jinny stole a furtive glance towards him, waiting for him to say something else.

Silence.

Gabe stared at her.

'How did I get you so wrong?' she asked.

'You didn't. You haven't. And if you were any sort of journalist, it would be you apologising to me.'

'What the hell is that supposed to mean? Why would I possibly be apologising to you? I've not taken a dead man's name off a gravestone.' Jinny knew she hadn't got concrete evidence of that fact but stumbling across the gravestone with the same name didn't seem like a coincidence to her.

Gabe's eyes widened. 'I promise it will all make sense when I explain. I just couldn't talk to you in the last few days because I've had things going on and other priorities I've needed to focus on.'

The conversation was shelved for the time being when Molly appeared in the doorway holding a tray of baked potatoes wrapped in foil. Jinny didn't dare take a sideward glance; she could still feel Gabe's eyes looking in her direction.

'What are you pair talking about?' asked Molly innocently. 'Is it top secret?'

'Maybe,' replied Jinny, daring a quick glance towards Gabe.

'Jinny won't share with us what she's thinking of entering in the competition.'

'And neither will I.' Gabe smiled at Molly. 'I have to say I think it was a genius suggestion and you won't be disappointed.'

'Any hints? It has to be a chutney. A new chutney or a combined recipe?'

'Molly! Stop pushing.' Cam handed Gabe a beer and sat down next to Molly. 'You can see it's all in hand so there's no point spoiling the surprise.'

'How about a name for the product? That's not giving too much away, surely?' Molly had a huge grin on her face.

'Maybe we should name it after where it all began. Chutney de Laurent.' Jinny turned towards Gabe and watched as he slowly turned his head towards Molly and the two exchanged a loaded look. Her jaw dropped a little as she eyed them carefully. 'You know, don't you?' Jinny looked at Molly then back at Gabe.

Molly nodded. 'You two need to talk.'

Gabe placed his hand on top of Jinny's but she didn't pull away.

'We wanted to chat to you tonight about a business idea,

but that can wait.' Molly tilted her head towards the gate. 'Go on,' she said. 'Don't worry about this. There's more important stuff to sort out.'

Gabe mouthed, 'Thank you,' to Molly then looked towards Jinny before standing and holding out his hand. 'Come on.'

'What's going on? I thought we were going to chat about the business – and look at all this food.' Cam was oblivious to what was going on around him as he began to load up his plate with food.

Molly gave him a stern look and nudged her knee against his. 'We'll catch up tomorrow.'

Jinny and Gabe made their way next door.

'Molly knows who are you, doesn't she?'

'Yes, of course. She and Cam are my friends. The whole community are my friends and we all look out for each other.'

'Do you have a wife and a son?' Jinny's heart was hammering, waiting for the answer.

'Yes, I have a son, but no, no wife.' Gabe slipped his hand into hers. 'I was going to tell you about my son the other night but when your father turned up it brought everything back to me and I've had a difficult few days.'

'I don't understand.'

'You will. But it might be something you don't want to hear.'

Jinny raised her eyebrows. 'I don't like the sound of that. Would it have something to do with my father?' She braced herself for the answer.

'Yes,' confirmed Gabe. 'But first I need to know something from you.'

'Anything.'

'Why did you lie about who you were?'

Jinny opened the front door wide and they stepped into the hallway of Bumblebee Cottage. There was a long list of questions that she wanted the answers to but she also knew she had some explaining to do herself.

'Because I didn't want anyone to judge me on my father's reputation or standards. Let me explain.'

Chapter Twenty-Three

After making a pot of tea, Jinny sat down next to Gabe on the settee.

'Gabe, you have to believe me when I say I'm not here to investigate anyone. I came to Heartcross because I couldn't stand working for my father any longer and I'm deeply ashamed it's taken me this long to walk away. Yes, I didn't tell anyone that he was my father but that's because everyone knows who he is, and I usually get judged just for the simple fact that I'm his daughter. I'm not here to write a story, I can promise you that. I'm here to get away from that life and stand on my own two feet. I've opened up to you what he's like and how I feel and I told you that because I feel safe with you and I thought we were building some sort of trust here. I'm sorry if you think otherwise but honestly, it's not the case.'

Gabe nodded. 'Okay. I have to admit it was a shock to see him here and I'm sorry too that I over-reacted, but the past few days have been difficult for me and the last person I expected to see was him.'

Jinny nodded and rested her hand on his knee. 'I promise that you can trust me. I'm not going to do anything to spoil my fresh start here.'

Gabe took a sip of his tea. 'This was what I was going to tell you that night on the balcony. Yes, I am Galliard, and Margo's grandson, and yes, *Gabe* is a name Dixie and I picked out from the graveyard.'

'Why would you do that?'

'Because I needed a fresh start too, without any press intrusion.'

'Why would you have press intrusion?'

'Because a situation occurred that I never in a million years could have prepared myself for. I was never in the limelight – I chose not to be – but just being Margo's grandson brought its own challenges.' Gabe looked visibly upset. 'And for the past three days I've been thinking about how much and how little to share with you.'

'I promise whatever you say is between us,' Jinny reassured him.

Gabe took both of her hands in his. 'Jinny, my life changed ten years ago...'

She could tell by the look on his face that she needed to strap herself in. Whatever Gabe was about to tell her was going to have more twists and turns than a broken sat nav. He cleared his throat and took a breath, looking visibly stressed. She had no clue what he was about to say, but the sadness in his eyes was already telling her that he was going to find this story difficult to share.

He let go of her hands and breathed out slowly. Staring straight at Jinny, he rubbed one hand up and down his upper arm, clearly uncomfortable with the situation.

'My grandmother was a wonderful woman – kind-hearted, loving, warm, genuine, and would give anyone her last penny. As you know, the family home is Château de Laurent – not your usual gaff, I appreciate. My grandmother rented out part of the château as a holiday let and loved nothing more than playing host and chatting with guests, and that's how she became friends with Dixie and George.' Gabe smiled. 'My grandmother used to tease Dixie because of her Scottish accent, and often said she needed an interpreter to understand her. I loved hearing the stories of her guests at the château, including the story of a bright-green Volkswagen Beetle covered in flowers and bees called Donovan.'

He took a breath. 'My own mum wasn't interested in fame; she was of the opinion it left you wide open for anyone to delve into your private life and she was a very private person. As a child, she was passed from pillar to post with nannies and even went to boarding school for a while, while my grandmother was working on a film over in America. My mother vowed that when she had children, she would be the one to look after them, and she kept her word.'

'Julia is your mum?'

Gabe nodded. 'Yes, she was a single mum. I do know

who my father is but we never had much contact and over the years that relationship completely dwindled.'

'I'm sorry to hear that,' said Jinny warmly.

'Despite my grandmother being one of the most photographed women in the world, she had a close network of friends and managed to get the balance of her private life just right – until she met a man called William Goddard who was staying at the château.'

Jinny's heart felt like it missed a beat. 'William is my godfather and my father's right-hand man at the newspaper.'

'I'll come back to him.'

Jinny could see by the look on Gabe's face that whatever he was going to say about William wasn't going to be good.

'One summer, a young girl and her mum visited my grandmother's holiday let. Vivian Bamford was sixteen at the time and wanted to be an actress. It was her birthday and my grandmother, who was working on a film, took Vivian and her mother to the set as a surprise. When they arrived, they discovered one of the young actresses had fallen sick and my grandmother suggested Vivian step in. This was her chance to shine and that's exactly what she did, proving she had star quality. Vivian lit up the screen and everyone agreed she was going to be the next big thing. From that moment on, Vivian's career took off and as she stayed at the château more and more, we became inseparable.'

'Inseparable…'

'Best friends. We went everywhere together when she

was in town and when she wasn't we would talk on the telephone all the time. I was the friend she could rely on, the one she could just be herself with, out of the limelight.' Gabe swallowed and raked his hand through his hair. 'I believe she would still be alive to this day if my grandmother hadn't met William Goddard.'

Jinny placed a supportive hand on his knee. 'Take your time,' she said softly.

As Gabe lifted his head and exhaled, Jinny noticed his body language change. He was tense, his eyes darkened. 'Despite the age difference, my grandmother and William started a relationship. She introduced him to lots of influential people and global superstars, and over time I began to realise that more and more stories about her good friends were appearing in the newspaper – specifically *The Daily News*.'

This didn't surprise Jinny at all. 'If they had a relationship, Margo would have trusted William, confiding in him or sharing general chitchat like couples do, and he was using that information to sell newspapers.'

Gabe nodded. 'Exactly that. William Goddard was becoming famous in his own right. His journalism career was rocketing to new levels. He knew what restaurants the celebs were eating at, he outed affairs between co-stars... But the entertainment industry is just like any other – people talk. My grandmother's friends started to cancel their engagements with her. They didn't attend her premieres and stopped frequenting the château because William was her partner. But my grandmother didn't want to believe William had traded on their connection to dig up stories about her friends and colleagues. She maintained that he was just really good at his job and found the information on his own. She was in love and of course couldn't see the bigger picture. Unfortunately, by that point I had already confided in her about the biggest secret ever.'

Gabe put his hands to his chest and blew out a breath as his face paled.

Jinny remained silent. She could tell Gabe was suffering.

'I promised I wouldn't tell anyone but I did and in doing so I let Vivian down.'

'Gabe, I think I know the secret,' admitted Jinny. 'Vivian was gay.'

Gabe's eyes widened. 'How would you know that?'

'Because when I saw your reaction to Vivian's photograph on the front page of the newspaper, I went digging in the archives,' she admitted. 'The day she died the story about her sexuality was going to be plastered all over the front pages. *The Daily News* had the exclusive.'

Gabe breathed out shakily. 'That was exactly what she was afraid of. People weren't as accepting back then and it could have resulted in a huge loss of earnings.'

'Do you know what really happened the night she died?'

'I do. *The Daily News* were hounding Vivian. Everywhere she turned up, there they were, snapping photographs of her. She was becoming more and more anxious about leaving the house, which had become like a military operation.'

'This sounds very much like my dad's style.'

'Vivian and Eliza had been together for over just over two years.'

Jinny gasped internally. Eliza was the person who had been calling Gabe on the night of the BBQ.

'That night I had spoken to my grandmother... and I believe, because of that conversation, that my actions may have caused Vivian's crash.'

'How is that possible?' asked Jinny, noticing fresh tears spring to Gabe's eyes.

Gabe took a deep breath. 'I'd phoned my grandmother for a catch-up and mentioned Vivian was in town and we'd organised for her to be smuggled into a restaurant for a night out with Eliza, who arrived at a separate time in order not to raise any awareness that they were there together.'

'Margo mentioned it to William, didn't she?' asked Jinny, thinking aloud.

Gabe nodded. 'The newspaper wanted a picture, and...' Gabe's voice cracked.

Jinny swiftly took his hand. 'I promise, I'm here for you.'

'The photographer must have lain in wait as they left the restaurant. Vivian was driving and they hadn't clocked that they were being followed until Vivian pulled up at the traffic lights and as they shared a kiss, a camera flashed behind them. As soon as the lights changed, Vivian raced off, the car behind giving chase. The stupid thing about this situation is that they already had their photo but they pursued Vivian and Eliza because they selfishly wanted more. Taking the road out of town they were still being followed. Now in a remote area Vivian put her foot on the accelerator and began navigating the country roads but lost control of the vehicle on a bend. The car careered off the road and the driver's side collided with a tree. It killed her instantly.'

Reliving the past had left Gabe looking exhausted, the grief of that night still evident in every part of his body. He looked up at Jinny, his stare piercing through her. Her body began to tremble.

'Jinny, the paparazzo that was chasing their car was your father.'

Immediately, Jinny went numb. She was shocked to the core as it all finally began to add up. That's the reason he had been so agitated that night. He had caused the crash.

'Gabe, do you have evidence of this?'

Gabe nodded. 'Eliza survived the crash and managed to crawl out of the car. She saw that the car that had been following them had stopped on the bend and the photographer had got out. She looked him dead in the eye and has no doubts. That man was your father.'

'Did he help her?'

Gabe shook his head. 'No, he got straight back in his car and drove off.'

Jinny was struggling to process it all. She sat in silence, her head whirling. The circumstances were more extreme than anything she'd imagined. The hardest part was understanding why any human in that situation wouldn't help.

'Gabe, I don't know what to say. I'm lost for words.' Jinny looked back towards him. 'I'm so sorry.' Her voice cracked. If what Gabe was telling her was truth, her father had stooped to a whole new level. She knew it would only take her a moment to delve into the archives and see the accreditation for that photograph. That would tell her exactly who was at the scene. 'Did you go to the police?'

Gabe shook his head.

'Why not?' asked Jinny. 'He needs to reap what he has sown.' Anger was rising inside her. She was utterly ashamed of her father's and William's involvement and how they'd conducted themselves. 'We need to tell someone. An innocent woman lost her life. We can't let them get away with this. If my father wasn't chasing them, this wouldn't have happened.'

'I've turned over that thought numerous times.'

'There will be evidence. The photo he took, for one. You said Eliza recognised him. How did she know my father?' Her voice was unsteady.

'Vivian had pointed him out to her in the past. He'd often followed them. They just hadn't spotted him that night when they left the restaurant.'

'This is exactly the reason I left the newspaper. My father and William haven't learned anything from what they did.' Jinny's emotions were all over the place and the more she thought about it the angrier she felt. 'They need to be held responsible for this.'

'They've already got away with it. Vivian is gone and we can't bring her back. Believe me, I've discussed this at great length with Eliza. I would like nothing better than to see them both be held accountable for their actions, but my guess is they've covered their tracks. Besides, we also had someone else to protect.'

'What do you mean? Who?'

'When I heard the news, I was at home in my London apartment... looking after the baby.'

'Baby?' questioned Jinny, confused.

'When these words leave my mouth, I want you to keep an open mind. I'm trusting you with this information.'

'You can trust me,' confirmed Jinny, slowly. Her heart began to race again, not knowing what Gabe was going to say. How could there possibly be more to this story?

Gabe placed a hand on her knee. She could feel him shaking. 'My baby.'

Jinny's mind was racing.

The boy who opened the door that morning she went to the house had called Gabe *Dad*.

'Who's the mother?'

Gabe didn't break eye contact. 'Vivian.'

That was an answer Jinny had never anticipated.

Chapter Twenty-Four

Bewildered, Jinny was still staring at Gabe. 'But I don't understand, you said Vivian was gay and that you didn't have a relationship with her. The boy who opened the door at your house… is that your son?'

'Yes, that's Harry.'

'And the woman he called *Mum* that I thought was your wife, who was that?'

'Eliza. Vivian's partner who survived the crash.'

'I'm so confused,' admitted Jinny.

'Vivian and Eliza were my best friends. There's no other way to say this than exactly how it is. They wanted a child and spent a year researching sperm donors. They were desperate for a child but because of Vivian's fame they were apprehensive when it came to meeting with donors. They were convinced the story would be sold.'

'And no doubt it would have.'

'Eliza was aware that she could possibly have a few

complications with pregnancy so between them they decided Vivian was to carry the child.'

Jinny was quickly joining up the dots. 'Did they ask you or did you offer?'

'They asked me. At first I thought they were joking and I was initially hesitant, but these were my best friends and I realised how happy it would make them both. Plus, they knew they could trust me never to reveal who the father was, which took away a lot of anxiety for them both.'

'I have to admit, I wasn't expecting that,' said Jinny.

'How do you feel about it?'

Jinny looked Gabe straight in the eye. 'I think it was a selfless, wonderful thing to do for your friends.'

'Thank you,' he replied, looking relieved. 'Vivian and Eliza moved in and stayed with me at my apartment in London during the pregnancy. I was there on a twelve-month contract with work and between us all we managed to keep it from the press. The last few weeks have been a difficult time for us as a family, with the tenth anniversary of Vivian's death approaching.'

Jinny placed her hand on Gabe's knee and gave it a squeeze. 'I can't even imagine.'

'After Vivian died, my grandmother finally saw William for the man he was and cut him out of her life. She knew she needed to protect me and the baby, and the only other people who ever knew the whole truth were my mum, Dixie and now you.'

Jinny felt emotional. She'd been trusted with

confidential information and she wasn't going to let Gabe down. 'Thank you. That means a lot.'

'As I said, I was looking after Harry the night Vivian was killed and was cradling the gorgeous bundle of joy when I heard the news. He was oblivious to the fact that his mum had died. That moment changed me and shaped me into who I am today as a father. I never signed up to be a full-time dad but I wanted him to grow up feeling safe and protected. He was Vivian's son and I didn't want the press hounding him like they did her. At Dixie's invitation, I set up home as Gabe Warner and moved here to bring Harry up out from harm's reach. Dixie needed help with the bees and other odd jobs around the cottage.

'Dixie was also the one who helped us find the house. Eliza moved in for a while but now we split custody fifty-fifty. She is his mum and a huge part of his life. We haven't hidden from Harry how he was conceived and he knows that Vivian was tragically killed.'

'Gabe, you've certainly been through the mill. I'm sorry about everything.'

'You haven't got anything to be sorry for. Over the past few days, I've spoken to Eliza about you and she knows I'm telling you the whole story tonight.'

Jinny placed her hand on his knee. 'Thank you for trusting me. It means a lot, but my father and William should not be allowed to get away with this.'

'They know what they've done and they have to live with it. Harry is my first priority, and I just want him to live life as normally as possible, out of the public eye, until he's old enough to make his own decisions. Harry lives with me in the week and goes to school over in the town – that's why I try to finish here by three p.m. – and he's with Eliza at her place at the weekend. In the school holidays we work it out between us.'

'And what does the community know?' asked Jinny, remembering the look between Gabe and Molly.

'That I'm a single father. Molly and Cam only recently discovered that my grandmother was Margo. Just before Dixie passed away, we told them, but they didn't need to know the whole story about Harry and Vivian.'

'It's no one's business.'

Jinny was emotionally drained. She stood up and walked towards the dresser. Dixie's decanter was still there, filled to the brim with sherry. 'It's not my usual tipple,' she said, pouring the liquid into glasses, 'but I think we both need a drink.'

'I can't argue with that.'

'Can I ask . . . Outside the pub, you were arguing on the phone. You said you didn't want that life.'

'Your French is very good.' Gabe sounded impressed.

'Google Translate,' admitted Jinny, laughing as she handed him a glass.

'I've been away from the château for ten years and have made my life here, but my mother misses me and thinks it's time I went back. I understand that she feels a lot of pain in this situation. She loves Harry to bits but both Eliza and I thought that if we stayed at the château with Harry then it wouldn't be long before the paparazzi would come sniffing and wonder about him.'

'I think you've both made the right decision.'

'Harry likes living here and so do I. According to Dixie, Heartcross is the place that mends everything and everyone. She predicted that one day someone would cross my path here and she was right.'

They held each other's gaze, neither looking away. 'I think we should have a toast,' declared Jinny. She held up her glass. 'To Dixie. She saved your life and she saved mine without knowing it. And to Bumblebee Cottage, chutney and honey,' she said, laughing.

'Can I add to that?' Gabe's glass was in mid-air.

'Of course.'

'I know in the last' – he glanced towards the clock – 'hour I've done a fair bit of explaining and no doubt it was a huge shock to you, but I would like to toast Vivian, a trusted friend, a superb actress and someone who would no doubt have made a wonderful mother. A toast also to Eliza, who lost her life partner. We were thrown together bringing up a small human but out of a devastating situation we became the best of friends and Harry is turning into a wonderful boy. And to Dixie and Margo, whose chance meeting all those years ago gave us all opportunities that meant our paths would cross.' Gabe was getting emotional as he clinked his glass against Jinny's. He took a breath. 'Eliza and Harry have just gone away on holiday for three weeks but maybe when they get back…would you like to come for dinner?'

'Thank you. I would love to meet both of them.'

Jinny took a swig of her drink. 'Urghh! I don't even like sherry. How could Dixie drink this stuff? I think there's a bottle of wine in the fridge if you fancy it, or do you have to get home?' She was hoping that Gabe would be able to stay a little longer.

'I can stay as long as you like. Is there anything else you'd like to ask? I do appreciate this is a lot to take in.'

'I would like to ask how you knew that peonies are my favourite flowers? They're beautiful.' She gestured towards the vase.

'Just a hunch,' he replied. 'And how are you feeling about your father?'

'It's difficult to put into words. I'm ashamed, disappointed, angry. I have no idea who he is. I'm glad I've walked away from the business. I know you've given the reasons why you and Eliza have let it lie and I respect that, but I will be walking away from him for good. Breaking an exclusive story was so important to him that it resulted in a woman's death. Harry lost his mum, Eliza lost her partner, and you lost your friend. I'm so sorry, Gabe, I really am.' Jinny reached forward to take both of Gabe's hands in hers but he stretched out his arms and pulled her in for a hug instead. Lost in their own thoughts for a moment, they held each other tightly.

Jinny broke the silence. 'Dare I ask, are we okay? When I didn't hear from you for the last few days...'

Gabe squeezed Jinny harder. 'I'm sorry. I needed to get

everything straight in my head. And of course we are, as long as you're okay?'

Jinny tilted her face upwards towards him. 'I am,' she replied, holding his gaze. Willing Gabe to kiss her, she was rewarded when he dipped his head, brushing his lips against hers. Every nerve in her body tingled. His lips were soft, his kiss perfect, and an overwhelming feeling of happiness gushed through her body. As the kiss ended, he cradled her face in his hands. 'You are gorgeous, Jinny Birdwhistle.'

Without saying another word, Jinny kissed him softly again.

For the past few days her world had been full of unanswered questions, but now Gabe had been honest and open and she knew the truth. All she needed to do now was face her father, which wasn't a thought she relished, but that could wait until tomorrow.

'Did you say you didn't need to rush back?'

'I did.'

'That's good to know,' she replied softly, because she couldn't wait another moment to be wrapped in his arms.

Chapter Twenty-Five

J inny didn't mind waking up to an empty bed when she rolled over to see a handwritten note leaning against a cup of tea, now lukewarm. She smiled as she read it.

Best night ever, thank you! Breakfast is served...

Her heart gave a leap and, throwing back the duvet, she pulled her faithful sloppy sweater over her head and padded downstairs. Jinny knew Gabe had to be up and out for an appointment at the Clover Cottage Estate.

The previous evening he had explained why Molly and Cam had invited them round. Apparently, they had been looking over the sales figures and profits for the last few years and had been toying with the idea of expanding Bees' Knees. Up at the Clover Cottage Estate a spare unit had come up for rent with substantial land where they could potentially house more bees and increase chutney production by investing in new technology and machinery. It wasn't definite but Jinny was excited to be part of the business through any new stages of development.

The kitchen door was open and Jinny saw the table was set for one. There was a glass of fresh orange juice, a selection of bread and pastries from The Old Bakehouse, eggs, a cold meat platter and a dish of fresh fruit. Gabe had thought of everything.

'I could get used to this,' she murmured, noticing a bunch of freshly cut flowers from the garden in the middle of the table. She took in the aroma before flinging open the back door and embracing the warmth of the new day. Leaning against the door frame, Jinny knew she would never tire of this view. Bumblebee Cottage was the only place she wanted to be in the world. Since her arrival it had been full of ups and downs and this morning was going to be no different. After breakfast she was going to delve into the archives to confirm who took the photo of Vivian the night she died, and then she was going to go and face her father for the last time.

Hearing her phone ping she picked it up and saw it was a message from Jay.

What's going on in the life of Jinny Birdwhistle?

She grinned and quickly punched in a text.

You couldn't write it.

Huh?

I'll ring you later!

After enjoying her surprise breakfast, Jinny took a quick shower and then confirmed once and for all that everything that Gabe had told her was the truth. The photo had been taken by her father. Her opinion of him couldn't get any lower. Walking in the sunshine towards Starcross Manor, Jinny rehearsed the conversation with her father in her mind. She sauntered past the gatehouse and approached the tree-lined driveway leading to the impressive, elegant manor house. The hotel was set in a hundred acres of lush green grass, formal gardens, a deer park, woodlands and a wildflower meadow. The driveway leading to the entrance was grand, sweeping into a wide circle with an ornate fountain in the centre. Huge stone steps led to the large double oak doors within a broad porch of stone pillars, and ivy clung to the walls of the building. Molly had been right. Starcross Manor was the perfect place for a wedding – it was beautiful.

Climbing the steps, Jinny began to feel anxious. The conversation she had rehearsed over and over in her head had now been completely forgotten as the anger inside her began to rise again. The foyer was grand and she took in her surroundings. A huge chandelier hung overhead and the marble floor stretched for miles. The place was dotted with people going about their day, as along with the tourists there were large groups of business people wandering through the lobby, chatting on their phones, while others had taken advantage of the large chesterfields and had already set up their office for the day. As she stood waiting for the receptionist to end her call, Jinny noticed a free-standing fountain, the water cascading into a small pool below. This place had everything.

'Can I help you?' The receptionist's voice was bright and cheery.

'I'm looking for my father; he's staying here.'

'And that would be…'

'Ralph Birdwhistle,' replied Jinny.

'And your name?'

'Jinny.'

The receptionist tapped away on the computer in front of her. 'There's a note on the computer to say that's he is expecting you,' she said with a smile. 'You can go straight up.'

At those very words Jinny's heckles rose. He'd just assumed that she would arrive at some point, no doubt with her tail between her legs.

'He's in room 222, second floor. The lift is through those double doors to the right.' The receptionist resembled an air hostess as she pointed in the right direction.

'Thank you,' replied Jinny and headed towards the lift. As it rose to the second floor, she felt her chest tighten, her heart hammering so hard against her ribcage that she thought it was going to burst out of her chest at any moment. She usually didn't like any sort of confrontation but she had her piece to say and she wasn't going to hold back. She believed in owning your own actions and standing up for what you believed in.

Words couldn't describe how she was feeling about her father right now. Standing outside room 222 Jinny could hear his voice on the phone. Beginning to feel fretful, she knocked on the door and waited. She heard the click of the handle and as the door opened, Ralph lifted a single eyebrow.

'You're here, finally.'

He opened the door wide and Jinny stepped inside. The room was a magnificent size but now resembled his office. There were papers strewn all over the double bed and his laptop was up and running on the desk in the corner. Jinny wondered if it was the thrill of the chase that kept her father working.

'Sit down,' her father insisted, gathering a bunch of papers together and clearing a space for her to sit.

Feeling apprehensive, she sat and looked around the room. It was nothing like your average hotel room. It was like a mini apartment, with a living area and double doors that led to its own private outdoor terrace with a small garden. The atmosphere felt tense. Her father offered her a drink but she politely refused. She knew she was staring at him but couldn't help it. He might be her father, but she had realised something important. She knew nothing about him or his personal life. She had no clue what his real motivation for anything was. They had merely existed in the same house, like strangers.

'Have you got it out of your system yet?'

Jinny couldn't quite believe what she was hearing. He was still under the illusion that this was all just a lark.

'I'm not coming back to London.' Her tone was clear.

'Jinny, this is just silly now. You want for nothing and have a multi-million-pound company waiting for you.'

'And if I don't want it?'

Her father scoffed. 'Why wouldn't you want it? It's been in our family—'

'I'm not interested.' Jinny stood her ground. 'You're not listening to me.'

Ralph threw his hands up in the air. 'Okay, give me three good reasons why you wouldn't want it.'

Even though Jinny could feel herself trembling inside, she knew this was her chance and she didn't hold back.

'One, you drove Vivian Bamford to her death in pursuit of an exclusive. Two, you only pulled the story exposing her because doing so protected *you*. And three, you and your newspaper have no morals.' It was the first time she had ever seen her father speechless.

Jinny knew she needed to keep hold of her temper because she'd promised Gabe that her father wouldn't get a whiff of the fact that Vivian had a son who was alive and well and living in this village.

'I know everything. What I don't know is how you live with yourself.'

All of a sudden, Ralph looked frail, exhausted.

'You should be in prison. You chased a young woman to her death, watched her wrap her car around a tree and drove off without helping or even calling the emergency services. What sort of monster are you?' Jinny would never have dared to speak to her father in this way before but she'd already made the decision that she no longer had a father. 'I've seen the protected file, the photograph you took that night, and I know you lied in the story you published, claiming her death was in the South of France because you were scared of being traced to the scene. You absolutely disgust me.'

Ralph sat down and leaned back in the chair.

'And you want me to aspire to be just like you? No thank you. You and William are as bad as each other, and don't think I don't know what part he played in all this. He was the one pretending to have a relationship with Margo Laurent just to get the stories of the rich and famous when she was clearly in love with him. It's shameful.'

'How have you found all this out?'

'That doesn't even matter. Secrets don't stay secrets for ever. The truth always comes out.'

Ralph was now staring out of the window in a trance-like state. He looked pained but Jinny didn't have one ounce of sympathy for him.

'You can't even say you're sorry. Mum would be disgusted to see what you've become.'

Ralph slowly walked to the decanter on the small sideboard. Jinny watched him pour a drink and immediately swig it back.

'What are you going to do with this information?' He turned around and looked directly into her eyes.

Jinny wanted the world to know what he had done. She wanted him to take responsibility for Vivian's death, but she couldn't have that because it would have a huge impact on Gabe, Harry and Eliza, and they'd suffered through enough already.

'I'm not going to do anything because, unlike you, I care about the people that could be hurt by yet another scandalous news story. You are a coward and no father of mine. I don't ever want to speak to you again.' Her words were clear and concise. She held his gaze before turning around and shutting the door behind her.

Walking down the steps of Starcross Manor, Jinny trembled. She exhaled, knowing that that was probably the last time in her life that she would set eyes on her father. The only thing she wanted right now was to be enveloped in the biggest hug by a decent man – Gabe.

Chapter Twenty-Six

Two weeks later

I t was set to be another glorious day and the perfect weather for the Summer Fair. Jinny was up with the lark, excited to reveal the brand-new product from the Bees' Knees empire, and had every intention of claiming the prize. She wanted her product in the supermarket.

It was now approaching eleven o'clock, and with only an hour to go before the Fair opened, she wandered into the kitchen to make a pot of tea. Switching on the radio she hummed along.

As the kettle began to boil, she threw open the back door and inhaled the fresh air. Could life actually get any better than this? Hearing one of her favourite songs on the radio, she turned up the volume and jigged around the kitchen table, posing and singing her heart out. Jinny couldn't remember the last time she'd felt so free and relaxed. Finally rid of her father's expectations, she promised herself to live every day like it was the last and enjoy every second of it. And that started right now. She hopped up onto a kitchen chair and played air guitar before leaping off. When her feet were on the ground, she spun around to find an amused-looking Gabe leaning against the door frame. Bringing her hand up to her beating heart she blew out a breath then grinned.

'Good morning!' she sang. Her mouth dropped open. 'Woah, you've no beard! You look so—'

'Different?' interrupted Gabe.

'I was going to say young.'

'Do you like? I fancied a change.'

And there it was again, that tingle, the flutters in her stomach, that she felt every time she was in his presence.

'And can I ask what were you just doing?' Gabe grinned.

'You can't beat a bit of air guitar first thing in the morning.'

'I quite agree,' he replied with a twinkle in his eye, handing her a T-shirt with the Bees' Knees logo, which matched the navy-blue one he sported. 'For today, your new uniform.'

'Aw, matching T-shirts. That's cute.' Jinny walked over to him and pressed a swift kiss on his lips, noting the aroma of his divine, spicy, masculine aftershave and the smoothness of his chin. 'Thank you.' She peered behind him. 'Is Claude with you?'

'He's wolfed down his sausage roll and is now guarding

his bone outside The Honey Pot in the shade. And how are you feeling?'

'Excited! I can't wait to get the show on the road and take the trophy.'

'I love your confidence but you have to remember these villagers will not go down without a fight.'

'We'll see! At least we don't have far to walk to get to the green. It already looks brilliant out there. I took a quick look out of the window.'

The whole community had pulled together in the last forty-eight hours to prepare the green for the Summer Fair. There had been excitement growing all week in the village with everyone keeping their entries very close to their chest.

'And who will be judging the competition?' asked Jinny.

'Apparently it's being kept under wraps until this morning.'

Jinny suddenly became aware of a whirling noise above the cottage and hurried to the middle of the patio. She was amazed to witness a royal-blue helicopter hovering above the orchards.

'That's getting lower,' exclaimed Jinny, taking a step outside. 'Oh my gosh, it's going to land.'

The helicopter was now hovering over The Old Bakehouse and Gabe and Jinny hurried around to the front of the cottage to see Isla, Felicity and Allie standing outside the bakery, along with Molly, Cam, Rory, Drew and Fergus. Jinny waved and headed in their direction. Gabe was still looking up at the helicopter.

'It's definitely going to land,' he shouted after her. 'Who's in that? It must be someone important.'

'Come on, spill the beans.' Jinny looked at the gang standing on the pavement. 'Who is it? What are you not telling me?'

Felicity flapped her hand in front of her. 'Nobody whatsoever...' The smile stretched across her face. 'You'll never guess!'

All heads turned towards the landing helicopter on the far edge of the green. Jinny had her eyes peeled, waiting to see who was stepping out.

She took in a deep breath. 'Zach Hudson!'

'Back by popular demand!' added Rory, striding towards him and giving him a quick man hug.

'Rory is great friends with Zach as they worked together in Africa and filmed a TV documentary together. And since he judged the dog show a few years back he's been an honorary villager. Welcome back!' Allie said to Zach as she flung her arms around him.

'Wow, this competition was going to be brilliant!' exclaimed Jinny.

'Let me introduce you to Jinny,' said Molly, nudging Zach's arm. 'She's moved into Bumblebee Cottage and taken over Dixie's business.'

'I was sorry to hear about Dixie,' he said, passing on his regards to Cam before turning back to Jinny. 'And hello to you! It's great to be back and to meet you.'

'And I assume you already know Gabe?' added Jinny.

'Good to see you again, mate,' Zach said, slapping his back.

'And you. And good luck judging this competition – these villagers are very competitive.'

'I know! Last time we had an alpaca being passed off as a dog and these lot convinced me it was a new breed called a pacapoo! I'm not falling for that again.'

Gabe laughed. 'We're going to be in for a fun day.'

'The Summer Fair will be declared open soon. Let's get you some refreshments, Zach,' suggested Cam, walking back towards the bakery with Molly.

Knowing Jay was a huge fan of Zach's, Jinny was bursting to tell her friend about Zach's arrival but that would have to wait. They needed to get their stall set up and transport the chutney and honey across the green.

All through the village of Heartcross, colourful bunting was woven between the lamp posts and flapping gaily in the light breeze. The weather was perfect – not too hot, the sun was shining and only a few clouds dotted the sky.

With boxes of chutneys and honey in their hands, Jinny and Gabe followed the makeshift cardboard signs hammered into the grass verges that pointed to the entrance of the fair. The village green was unrecognisable from forty-eight hours earlier. Zach Hudson's helicopter was parked on the edge, which was an attraction in itself for all the children. Small coloured tepees lined the edges, alongside trestle tables selling local products. Rona and Meredith were standing at the entrance angling buckets for charity donations. The mood was jovial. Throwing a handful of coins into the bucket, Gabe stepped onto the green and noticed Jinny looked pensive.

'Are you okay?' he asked.

'I just want to make Molly and Cam proud today and thank them for giving me this chance.'

'You will. I know you will.' Gabe placed his tray of chutneys down on the trestle table then took Jinny's tray from her and stacked it on top. He reached out and took her hands. Pulling her in close he wrapped his arms around her and kissed her softly on the lips. 'Today is going to be a good day. I have a feeling.'

'Me too.'

'It's a shame Eliza and Harry aren't here but I got a message this morning wishing us luck and saying that they're having the best time on holiday.'

'That's lovely. I can't wait to meet them both again when they're home.'

As Jinny began to set out their stall, she handed a bunch of keys to Gabe. 'If you want to leave Claude in the kitchen, it might be cooler in there for him.'

'I will. I did think about entering him in the shaggiest dog contest but I think he'll prefer the kitchen's tiled floor and shade. I'll bring back a few more jars with me.'

Jinny watched Gabe wander back over to the cottage then continued setting up the stall. The green was alive with activity. There were jugglers, stilt-walkers, balloon sellers and a bouncy castle. Children were queuing up to ride on a Shetland pony and Jinny had to smile when she saw that Isla had a baby alpaca munching away on grass at the side of her stall. She'd already guessed that Isla would be entering an item in the competition made out of the alpaca's fur. Drew had the stall right next to Isla, which looked wonderful stocked with cheeses and meats from the farm. Felicity and Rona's stall was stacked with the most delicious-looking pastries and cakes and already had a queue that seemed a mile long. Jinny waved over at Felicity. Fergus and Rory were a little further on, manning the hog roast, and Martha had a multicoloured tepee with a bead-fringed curtain and a makeshift sign outside that read: 'Have your fortune told by Mystic Martha'.

Gabe was walking back towards her holding another tray. Jinny pointed to Martha's tent and asked, 'Do you fancy it?'

'What? Having my fortune told? I can already predict the future. It's one of simplicity: mountain air and a gorgeous woman to boot.'

Jinny's heart swelled with happiness at his words. 'Pinch me,' she said, holding out her arm.

Gabe raised his eyebrows and went to give her a tiny pinch.

'No, don't, because if I am dreaming, I never want to wake up! I know it's such a short time but I feel like I've known you for ever. Everything is just easy with you around.'

'I feel exactly the same,' he replied, giving her the most gorgeous smile. 'Shall we grab a quick bite to eat from the hog roast before the competition starts?'

'Sounds like a perfect plan.'

Hand in hand they walked the short distance to Fergus. Jinny noticed a crowd gathered up ahead. A group of giggling girls were swamping Zach Hudson and Jinny knew Gabe must have witnessed something similar with Vivian at one time.

'I've come up with an idea,' shared Gabe. 'One I think you'll like.'

'Go on...'

'How about we take a trip to Château de Laurent? We can surprise my mother and you can see for yourself where Bees' Knees first began. Maybe we could do a blog about it.'

Jinny's eyed widened. 'Are you suggesting you want to dabble in social media? What's brought this on?'

'I can see that there's an opportunity to promote Bees' Knees. I want to make this business a success for both of us, and if social media is used in the right way, then who am I to object?'

'I would love to visit your mum.' Jinny bumped her shoulder lightly against his. 'But if we're going to take over the world, let's start with winning this competition.'

Fergus lightly slapped Gabe on the back as he approached the hog roast and Rory held out two beers.

'What can I get you?' asked Fergus.

'Two of those please,' said Jinny, pointing at the hog roast bun, dripping with applesauce made by herself. 'Look how busy this place is,' she added, taking a look around.

'It's one of the best days in Heartcross. Everyone comes together,' Rory said, checking his watch. 'It's thirty minutes to the dog show, then straight after is the best local product competition. Are you ready?'

'Ready to win!' replied Jinny with confidence.

'I love your spirit,' replied Drew, walking past, overhearing the conversation. 'But prepare for disappointment,' he teased.

'Yeah, yeah,' mused Jinny, clinking her beer bottle against Drew's. 'May the best woman win!' she added with a glint in her eye.

***

For the next hour, Jinny and Gabe had a long line of people queuing up to browse their stall, and the jars of honey and chutneys flew off the red gingham tablecloth. Jinny was having the time of her life; she was chatting to the villagers and tourists and soon her money belt was bursting at the seams.

'We barely have any jars left,' Jinny said, smiling. 'We've made a small fortune!'

Gabe didn't have time to answer, as they both stood to attention at the sound of a loud high-pitched squeal and Hamish's voice over the crackling Tannoy announcing that all competitors for the village's local product competition should make their way to the white tent at the far end of the green. Jinny grabbed Gabe's arm. 'This is it! Fingers crossed!' She caught Drew looking over in her direction and gave him a thumbs-up.

Gabe put a sign up in the middle of the table telling any

potential customers they would be back within the hour, then Jinny grabbed a cardboard box from under the table, which housed the potential winning product.

Walking across to the tent they saw activity everywhere. The poultry show had just finished and Jinny laughed as Fergus chased a rooster that had escaped from its pen. Over towards the edge of the green, there was a band playing, and tourists had the opportunity to dress up in gaudy clothes and dance to the beat of the drums, merrily weaving, skipping and laughing. They walked past various stalls including Bree's chocolate stall, with a bright-red gazebo boldly lettered 'Layers Treats' sheltering the chocolate and sweets from the sun. She was swamped with children anxious to swap their money for a bag of penny chews. There was great excitement all around them.

'I'm beginning to feel a little nervous,' Jinny whispered to Gabe as they approached the tent and she spotted Rona holding a tray of beautifully decorated cupcakes that dripped with frosted icing.

'How am I going to beat those? They look delicious,' Jinny said.

'Keep the faith. Zach Hudson hasn't tasted your honey cider chutney yet.'

Rona was chatting to Drew and as the competitors began to follow the spectators into the tent she turned back to look at the tray of cupcakes she was holding, realising one was missing. 'Who's pinched one of my cupcakes?'

Everyone looked at each other, then Felicity nudged her mum and pointed to Fergus. Guilt flickered in his eyes.

'It wasn't me, honest!' he declared.

Rona wagged her finger at him. 'You might nearly be my son-in-law and I would love to believe you but I think that white coating of icing around your lips gives you away!'

'Busted!' exclaimed Felicity.

Everyone laughed and as Jinny looked towards Gabe, then around at all of her new friends, she realised she finally felt like she was in a place where she belonged.

The jovial atmosphere was suddenly interrupted by Hamish's voice booming out again over the crackling Tannoy. 'The best local product competition is about to begin. Please make your way to the show tent. The judging will commence in exactly five minutes.'

Molly and Cam appeared next to Jinny, Cam holding a freshly baked loaf that smelled divine and was clearly fresh out of the oven only moments before. Bree was at their side carrying the hugest slab of chocolate that Jinny had ever set eyes on.

'And what's in your box?' Molly attempted to peep in the box that Jinny was holding.

Jinny smiled, moving it out of the way so Molly couldn't look inside. 'All will be revealed very soon!'

All the exhibitors were invited to sit on the rows of wooden church pews laid out in front of the judge's table, which was covered in a crisp white tablecloth and had a chair in the middle.

Drew was already sitting on the front pew, eagerly waiting, while others were huddled together chatting excitedly. Jinny and Gabe perched on the pew next to Drew, leaving a space for Isla. Hamish walked onto the stage with his natty tweed jacket, flat cap and green Wellington boots, while the spectators sat down on hay bales that were dotted about the tent, and the local reporter, Aidy Redfern, stood poised and ready with his camera.

Hamish tapped on the table with a small wooden gavel to attract everyone's attention and Jinny's excitement began to grow as several shushes could be heard all around them. Hamish took to the microphone. 'Welcome, welcome, welcome to the very first Heartcross Summer Fair show where we are inviting all our local suppliers to showcase their best product. The winner will receive a place on the shelf of Whittaker's Supermarkets in Scotland, and James Whittaker, owner of those supermarkets, is here with us today. Please put your hands together and give him a hearty Heartcross welcome.'

The crowd burst into rapturous applause as Hamish gestured towards the side of the stage where James Whittaker stood up and smiled at the crowd before he sat down again.

Once the crowd had quietened down, Hamish brought the microphone up to his mouth once again. 'We have one judge today. He is an honorary member of this village and is welcome here anytime. Please put your hands together for the world-famous Zach Hudson.'

Zach walked onto the stage to loud cheers and clapping. The beam on his face was wide and he waved to everyone in the tent as he took the microphone form Hamish after shaking his hand.

'This is getting real now. I want this so much,' whispered Jinny to Gabe. 'Can you imagine seeing my product on supermarket shelves?'

'I can. It will be great for business.' Gabe pressed a swift kiss to her cheek before they both looked back towards Zach.

'Thank you for having me back. The products entered today must be produced in the village of Heartcross and must be your own product. You will be called up to the stage in turn, where you have the opportunity to present the product and tell us all about your backstory. Once all products have been showcased, I will make a decision. It's as easy as that! What I love about this village is the community spirit and I know all the competitors will be cheering each other on. Good luck, everyone!'

The tent erupted into applause once again while Zach took his place behind the judge's table.

Jinny caught Drew's eye and he winked at her smugly.

'Don't count your chickens,' she mouthed, enjoying the banter between them.

Gabe leaned in towards her. 'Don't let him wind you up. You'll be fine.'

Jinny hoped so. She wanted to do Molly and Cam proud for giving her a chance, and of course Dixie.

Zach sat down behind the table and the tent fell into complete silence. Jinny's heart was beating in double time.

'First up to the judges table is Isla Allaway!' Zach announced as Isla quickly hustled towards an opening in the side of the tent and reappeared with the cutest baby alpaca that anyone had ever seen. As she walked onto the stage accompanied by oohs and ahhs from the audience, Zach grinned. 'Don't tell me it's another pacapoo!'

Isla laughed, and took the microphone from Zach. 'Let me introduce you to Gertie! Last time Zach was here, Foxglove Farm had a brand-new addition, a baby alpaca called Mop, and this is Mop's daughter! Twelve weeks old and enjoying life at Foxglove Farm. It's been a few years now since we've been breeding alpacas at the farm and each year when the fleeces are sheared I keep some back and hand-knit these fabulous pure alpaca gloves. Alpaca clothing is lighter and warmer than wool and these are just what you need to keep your hands, wrists and fingers warm and toasty during the cold months here in Heartcross.' Isla handed the gloves to Zach who tried them on and immediately wiggled his fingers.

Isla left the stage, leading Gertie away to a round of applause while Zach placed the gloves on the exhibitors' table next to the judging table.

'Next, we are keeping it in the family, with Drew Allaway.'

'He's not got anything with him,' Jinny said as Drew took the stage. Hearing a drumroll, the audience watched as a small cooking stove was wheeled onto the stage in front of Drew. 'Welcome to the world of Foxglove Farm sausages! Would you like onions with your hotdog?' Drew turned towards Zach who nodded. Throwing onions into the pan and turning over the sizzling sausage, Drew began to talk about the history of Foxglove Farm, explaining how it had been in his family for generations and how he'd worked alongside his father as a child learning how to farm from an early age.

'This is a quality sausage made with the best quality pork and stilton made at the farm – a winning flavour combination which offers a smooth and creamy taste with a distinctive tangy bite of blue cheese. You will taste no other organic sausage like it.'

As soon as Drew's speech was finished, he cut open a bun, dished up the sausages and onions and offered Zach some ketchup before handing the hot dog over to him. Everyone applauded while Zach took a bite. 'Oh my, this is absolutely delicious. In fact, this' – Zach took another bite – 'is the best sausage I've ever tasted.'

Drew looked happy as he left the stage and sat back down.

For the next few minutes, Rona talked about the history of Bonnie's Teashop, Cam talked about The Old Bakehouse and Bree presented her chocolate creation.

'I have to say, judging this competition is no good for the waistline!' Zach gave a chuckle.

Next up was Eleni, Julia's right-hand woman at the B&B, who shared her latest artwork that was on display up at Starcross Manor. Then Meredith presented a new beer brewed at The Grouse and Haggis and Flynn produced a brand-new wetsuit range that had been designed at The Boat House.

Jinny was up next and feeling excited.

As soon as Zach took the microphone, Jinny looked

straight at Gabe and he gave her a look of reassurance. 'Go get 'em,' he said, as she nervously stood up.

She walked onto the stage. All eyes were on her. On her instruction, Hamish had arranged goat's cheese, crackers and pickles on a plate, which was set in front of Zach. She then placed the box next to it and took the microphone. She steadied her hand, feeling it shaking lightly. Gabe was giving her an encouraging smile.

'It's my absolute pleasure to be with you all today. My name is Jinny and I'm a very welcomed newcomer to the village. How did I end up here in the village of Heartcross, you might ask?' She took a breath. This wasn't about bad-mouthing her father; this was about sharing her story and how she'd ended up here. 'My mother passed away when I was a young girl.' Already Jinny's voice had faltered but she was determined to keep going. 'And my relationship with my father was a difficult one. After I left school, my expectations and my father's of my career path were totally different. My father owned a global empire and I was expected to follow in his footsteps, and it took me many years doing a job I didn't like to find the strength to walk away, aware that my relationship with my father would suffer even more. Not knowing what to do next, I stumbled across an advert online for a job that came with the most beautiful cottage I had ever set eyes on. I took the plunge and rang the telephone number, which took me straight through to Molly.' Jinny gestured towards Molly sitting in the second row behind Gabe. 'That business was Bees' Knees and my job was to make chutney and collect the honey, with guidance from Gabe.' She smiled at him. 'My first few days on the job were eventful, to say the least, and resulted in my first trip to the doctors' surgery, where Dr Ben Sanders had to pull a bee sting out of my backside... Sorry about that.' She smiled at the doctor who was sitting at the back of the tent grinning.

As the whole crowd laughed, Jinny realised her nerves had completely disappeared and she hit her stride. 'Bees' Knees was founded by Dixie and George Bird. Dixie made the chutneys and George looked after the bees and the honey. They were a huge part of this community for many years and without them even knowing it, they have given me the chance I was looking for, and I'm truly grateful for the opportunity to continue to grow their legacy. That's why in honour of Dixie and George...' Jinny paused and placed her hands on her heart. 'Do forgive me, I've come over all emotional.' There wasn't a single sound in the tent to be heard. Everyone was hanging on Jinny's words. 'I have combined their two products so there is still a little bit of Dixie and George out in the world together... I present to you, Bees' Knees' new honey cider chutney.'

As soon as it was over, she briefly closed her eyes and took a deep breath. Her lips were quivering slightly with the emotion running through her. All the spectators in the tent were clapping. Molly and Cam were up on their feet and as Jinny handed over the jar of chutney to Zach so he could sample it, she noticed Molly wiping a tear from her eye. Jinny took a small bow before hurrying back to Gabe, who was beaming proudly. Daring to take a quick look in

Drew's direction she saw that he too was clapping enthusiastically.

Jinny was proud of herself. She'd stood up in front of everyone with a story that was extremely personal to her. She wanted to win, but even if she didn't, she knew she was a winner because she was now living the life she wanted and being true to herself.

Molly grabbed a hug as Jinny passed her. 'That was perfect, and what a brilliant idea.'

'Thank you. I just hope I've done enough.' They looked across towards Zach and James Whittaker, who were looking over the products together.

'You are a superstar.' Gabe engulfed her in the biggest hug. 'That was amazing! There's only one clear winner in my eyes,' he said pressing a kiss to her lips.

Suddenly they heard a shout from Rona. 'Stop that alpaca!'

Both Jinny and Gabe burst out laughing to see that Gertie, the baby alpaca, was loose and had found her way towards the rest of Rona's cupcakes and devoured them in seconds.

The tent erupted in laughter and Drew was up on his feet chasing Gertie, who was soon back under control.

'There's never a dull moment in Heartcross,' said Isla.

Gabe pointed to Hamish who had walked back onto the stage. Zach and James Whittaker were looking over all the products and though Jinny was watching them closely she couldn't read their expressions. Zach eventually handed three envelopes to Hamish, who hammered on the table to get the crowd's attention.

'This is it!' Gabe squeezed Jinny's hand as they all sat back down. Waiting for the results to be revealed, the tent was now in complete silence. Jinny felt her heart beating in double time. 'Good luck, everyone,' she whispered down the line.

'This is it. A decision has been made! In my hand I'm holding the winner and two runners-up.' Drew was shuffling in his seat and Rona was still looking a little annoyed that Gertie had wolfed down the rest of the cupcakes.

Scrunching her eyes closed, Jinny waited for the first result.

'In third place, chosen by Mr Zach Hudson, is…' Hamish opened up the first envelope.

'Bree! From Layers Treats Chocolate Shop with her amazing Ferrero Rocher Sharing Slab! Over 500g of solid creamy Belgian milk chocolate topped with Ferrero Rocher pieces and crushed hazelnuts. The perfect treat to share or to keep all to yourself. I'm not sure I'd be sharing this though – looks amazing,' admitted Hamish. 'Huge congratulations, Bree! Can we all give her a round of applause.'

Rapturous applause could be heard all around and Bree stood up and bowed to the audience before sitting down again.

'Now, for second place.'

Everyone in the tent fell silent. Hamish began to open in

the second envelope and Jinny grabbed on to Gabe's knee. 'He's looking over here,' she whispered in Gabe's ear.

'I can reveal in second place is Drew Allaway with his pork and stilton sausages!'

Drew punched the air, stood up and bowed at the spectators.

Jinny was still in with a chance. She crossed her fingers and squeezed her eyes shut, waiting for Hamish to open the envelope.

'And the winner of Heartcross's best local product and a space on Whittaker's Supermarket shelves goes to...' A drum roll sounded out from the back of the tent. 'The newcomer in the village, Jinny, and her honey cider chutney!'

Gabe sprang to his feet, cheering and whooping. Jinny opened her eyes. 'Did he really just say my name?'

'You'd better believe it!' Gabe pulled her to her feet. 'You've only gone and won!' Jinny's smile lit up her face as Gabe picked her up and spun her round before putting her safely back on the ground and giving her a rib-crushing hug.

Molly was emotional as she hugged Jinny. 'Thank you. This means so much to me and Cam. Dixie and George live on.'

'You don't need to thank me. It's me that needs to thank you for giving me a job and a home.'

Jinny felt a pat on her back – Drew was standing behind her. 'Well done, you. I can't believe I've been beaten by a novice,' he said, laughing.

Hamish took to the microphone again. 'Can we all welcome our winner Jinny onto the stage?'

'Congratulations. Enjoy every second of it.' Gabe gave her a gentle push in the direction of the stage. Wide-eyed in amazement, Jinny made her way up to the front of the tent to the sound of clapping.

She was greeted by Hamish, Zach and James with a handshake. Feeling overwhelmed, Jinny couldn't quite believe it as the local reporter began taking photographs of them.

'Speech, speech, speech!' the crowd was chanting and Hamish passed the microphone towards Jinny who could feel herself shaking.

'I can't quite believe this! Thank you, Zach Hudson, for picking the new Bees' Knees product and James for putting the product onto the supermarket shelves. It's so surreal.' Jinny could feel her voice wobbling as she wiped a proud tear from her eye. 'I hope I've done Dixie and George proud.'

She noticed that Gabe was mouthing something at her, then he hotfooted it out of the back of the tent. Jinny didn't have a clue what he was up to. Hamish invited everyone who had entered to join Jinny on the stage and each one said thank you before James and Zach stood either side of Jinny and photos were taken of the whole group.

Then James took the microphone. 'On behalf of Whittaker's Supermarket, I would like to invite you to come and watch your product get stocked on our supermarket shelves.'

Jinny gasped. 'I would love that, thank you.'

'And could I possibly keep the cheese, chutney and biscuits?' added Zach.

'Of course!'

'Is there anything else you wish to say?' asked Hamish.

'I would like to thank Molly and Cam again for giving trusting me with this business and to the community for welcoming me with open arms.' Jinny took another look towards the back of the tent but Gabe hadn't reappeared. Where was he? 'I'd also like to thank Gabe who has been very patient with me, teaching me how to look after my new extended family of bees and teaching me the—'

Jinny stopped dead in her tracks. There was some sort of commotion going on at the back of the tent as all the people towards the back began to stand up and move out of the way. She looked towards Hamish for guidance. 'I think you may have forgotten to thank someone else,' he said.

Jinny followed his gaze and heard the beep of a horn. She gasped. 'Oh my!'

As Gabe slowly drove Donovan towards the stage, cheers erupted and Jinny was swamped with happiness. Bringing the microphone up towards her mouth, Jinny swung her free arm out towards Donovan. 'Dixie and George may no longer be with us but Donovan was right there with them at the beginning of the Bees' Knees journey. Please do join us outside where we think Donovan deserves a lap of honour around the green!'

Gabe tooted the horn again and gestured for Jinny to come and join him. He opened the driver's side door while he slid across into the passenger seat. Jinny quickly handed the microphone back to Hamish and made her way towards Gabe and Donovan.

After sliding into the seat, she beamed across at Gabe. 'What a brilliant idea to bring Donovan!'

Aidy Redfern, the local reporter, popped his head into the open window of the car. 'If I could just have a photograph of you and Gabe in the car?' he said, holding up the camera.

Jinny looked worriedly across at Gabe but he squeezed her knee reassuringly. 'It's absolutely fine. This is your moment and it's an honour to share it with you.'

After posing for the photograph, Jinny backed the car out towards the road, everyone patting the roof as they drove past.

'How're you feeling?' asked Gabe.

'Pretty damn good. How about you?'

'I'm just counting my blessings that you applied for the job and here we are.'

Jinny leaned across and kissed him straight on the lips.

'Listen, can you hear that?' Gabe put his hand on her knee.

A bunch of musicians had moved to the edge of the green and began to play 'Honey, Honey'.

Gabe's eyes were locked on hers, his eyes glistening with love. 'Thank you for coming into my life.' He looked like he was about to say something else and Jinny's heart thumped with excitement.

Drew popped his head into the window. 'The road is clear. Enjoy your lap of honour!'

'Here goes! I feel like royalty,' said Jinny, waving out of the window before she put Donovan in gear and began to drive. A small crowd had lined the pavements, waving flags and cheering as they passed.

'I think we have a lot to thank Dixie for,' said Gabe, waving out of his window.

'Absolutely we do,' she replied, giving Gabe a look of love. 'Here's to the future.'

The applause and cheers never stopped as they drove Donovan around the green.

Gabe's phoned pinged. 'It's Harry. He's asking if we won!'

Holding his phone up in the air, Gabe angled it so both he and Jinny were on the screen. 'I've come a long way in the last few weeks. Smile. This is my first ever selfie!'

Jinny leaned in towards Gabe and he took the photo and immediately pinged it back to Harry with a text.

We are in Bees-ness! The new chutney will be on the supermarket shelves before we know it.

That's great, Dad. Can't wait to see you and meet Jinny too!

After feeling lost in her career and unhappy at home for so many years, Jinny felt alive again and so happy to finally have a job she loved. She'd arrived in the village on a whim, but now she knew this was exactly where she wanted to stay.

Feeling proud to be part of this wonderful community, she said to Gabe, 'It's true, once you arrive in Heartcross you never want to leave.' Jinny turned the words over in her mind and stole a sideward glance towards Gabe. She was falling in love with him hook, line and sinker and knew this was just the beginning for them. She couldn't wait to see what the future held.

Gabe looked across at her. 'I'm having just the best day.'

'I second that,' she replied, her heart swelling with happiness.

Acknowledgments

My seventeenth book is published and what a way to end 2022! Tomorrow, (New Year's Day) is my 50th birthday and if everything goes to plan, I will be amongst the endless moss-covered lava fields on the Reykjanes Peninsula, in the southwest corner of Iceland where I will be sipping champagne whilst I bathe in the waters of the Blue Lagoon. I can't quite believe I am fifty and what a journey it's been. As a child I never in a million years would have ever imagined I would be an author. I simply do have the best job in the world!

This book as ever is a team effort. My immense thanks to Charlotte Ledger who turns my stories into books and to the rest of the team at One More Chapter, HarperCollins for their ongoing support. I have enjoyed working with all of you on the latest book of the Love Heart Lane series.

A massive thank you to my children, Emily, Jack, Ruby and Tilly. I'm blooming proud of you all!

Big love to Woody (my mad Cocker Spaniel) and Nellie (My bonkers Labradoodle) who are the best writing partners in crime, especially when they are asleep!

Much love to Anita Redfern, for always being there for me. Everyone should have a best friend like you in their life.

A big thank you to Julie Wetherill. In such a short space of time we have been on so many crazy adventures together and here's to many more!

Thanks to my writing chum Bella Osborne, who is always there to cheer me on when my deadline is looming and I'm having a writing wobble. You are the best!

This book was inspired by a fellow author Clare Swatman who attended a writing retreat at my ramshackle cottage in Staffordshire. A conversation took place about journalists and the idea behind *The Hidden Secrets of Bumblebee Cottage* was sparked.

And finally thank you to my wonderful readers for buying my books. I wouldn't be able to do my job without you!

I have without a doubt enjoyed writing this latest instalment in the Love Heart Lane series and I really hope you enjoy *The Hidden Secrets of Bumblebee Cottage*. Do let me know!

Warm wishes,
    Christie x

Don't miss *A Summer Surprise at the Little Blue Boathouse*

The next heartwarming instalment in the Love Heart Lane series by Christie Barlow!

Where friends are there for you no matter what...